A POISON TREE

A DCI Will Blake Novel

J.E.Mayhew

OBOLUS BOOKS

ISBN- 978-1-9998407-4-7

Cover design by: Meg Cowley Epic Fantasy Covers

For Tommy, Barry, The Collective and The Lair.

I was angry with my friend;
I told my wrath; my wrath did end.
I was angry with my foe:
I told it not, my wrath did grow.

A Poison Tree (William Blake)

Tuesday October 22nd

CHAPTER 1

Six boxes. Plain. Brown. Gerald Rees could tell they were shoe boxes from their size and the fold-down lids. They looked old in a way that only a certain type of brown card can look old. It would be hard to say what it was that made them betray their age; they weren't ripped or scuffed or dirty. Decades of sitting in a closed cupboard had dulled them and given them an airless, musty scent. Each one had a number carefully written on the corner of the lid 1, 2, 3, 4, 5, and 6.

It was eight in the morning; an hour before St Joseph's Hospice charity shop opened and the good people of Bromborough came to rifle the shelves for bargains. Gerald was alone in the sorting room. He could see Natalie Murphy, the store manager in the back office, her face illuminated by a computer screen, but she was deep in thought. The cluttered sorting room leaned in towards Gerald as he toyed with the lid of the box. Wire cages filled with old clothes pressed silently against stacks of boxes full of dog-eared books. A few mannequins peered over his shoulder, their eyes blank and expressionless. Most of the stuff that came into the shop was run-of-the-mill; paperbacks, DVDs, old suits and dresses, chests of drawers. But every now and then, something came in that was different. Something curious. Something interesting.

Gerald opened the first, relishing the scrape of cardboard on cardboard. He loved the way these boxes fitted together. If only life were like that. Inside lay a gleaming pair of stilettos; poppy red, egg-shell finish with only a few small scratches on the tip of the pointed heel. They looked almost new but the brand lettering in the insole and the plastic sheen of the toes dated them. A name had been written carefully in thick black letters inside them: Carly Simmonds. Gerald felt a twinge of unease twist in his gut and he caught his breath; he knew that name. He'd buried it under a lifetime of grey, boring office work, pub quizzes and hours of TV soaps. But the name always surfaced when he least expected it. Just like the others. Gerald glanced over his shoulder then shook himself. It wasn't that unusual a name, there must be hundreds, if not thousands of people called Carly Simmonds. He gave a nervous chuckle. "Idiot," he muttered to himself.

The second box contained a well-worn pair of old slippers, wrapped in tissue paper. What colour would you call that? Gerald thought, stroking the soft, furry fabric with his forefinger. Mauve? The tiniest spot of something brown matted in the creamy fur around the ankle. Not much but enough to make them unsaleable. Gerald hadn't worked in the charity shop long but he was learning to distinguish between what was rubbish and what might make a sale. He knew that a mark like that on the slippers wouldn't go down well. Hope it's just brown sauce, he thought dropping them back into their rustling tissue nest. It was then that he spied the name in the insole, written in the same thick, black capitals: Josie Lock. He swallowed hard. "No," he hissed, pushing the box away. "It can't be." Again, he glanced around. Was this some kind of macabre trick? Were there cameras hidden in amongst all the tat that surrounded him? He looked up at the office, but Natalie sat hunched over her desk, oblivious. The third box awaited his attention. He didn't want to open it. What might he find in there? But some dark compulsion pulled him towards it, and, with trembling hands, he lifted the lid.

An old-fashioned pair of children's sandals with natural rubber soles and a flower stencil cut out of the dull red leather lay nestled in the tissue. Gerald closed his eyes and exhaled. He knew the name without even looking. Tears blurred his eyes. What sadist had engineered this situation? It couldn't just be coincidence that he, of all people, was exhuming these relics from a past that should stay buried?

He stared down at the fourth box, his stomach plummeting. "Go on then," he muttered. "Do your worst." These shoes looked well-used. The flat plastic sole had worn at the heel and wispy filaments of silky material poked out at all angles. Almost not daring to look, he squinted at the name in the court shoes: Fiona James. He gave a squeak of surprise and glanced back at the sandals still sitting innocently in their own box. "It's not fair," he hissed and slammed the shoes down, knuckling his moist eyes. That's what you get for coming back to your roots, Gerald, for raking up old memories. For picking at old scabs. Well. Bring it on! He dragged the next box across the table and tore the lid open.

The fifth pair stopped his breath.

Rust red, the colour of dried blood. Baseball boots was what they used to call them back in the seventies. They'd become trendy again, recently. Converse was the trademark, now. He'd seen adverts for them a few years back and it had made him feel nauseous, even after all this time. What he was looking at now made the bile rise to the back of his throat. They were short ankle boots with rubber soles and a circular rubber patch at the side. The star symbol on the patch had worn away and someone had drawn a smiley face in its place. The white laces had been striped with a red felt tip. The stripes had faded over the years, but they were still visible. Silver eyelets; third one on the left boot missing.

Gerald felt as though he was falling down a

dark well. He dropped the shoes and staggered backwards from the table, crashing into a trolley full of unwanted DVDs behind him. His heart punched against his ribs. The world closed in. It spun around the boots, which crouched on the sorting table staring up at him, malevolently. He couldn't breathe. How could they be here? Now?

Natalie Murphy appeared from the back room, concern etched across her face as she hurried across the cluttered sorting area to where Gerald stood at the table, staring, ashen faced.

"Are you alright, love? You look like you've seen a ghost," she said, laying a hand on Gerald's arm.

"Those boots," he whispered. "These b-boxes..."

"What about them?"

Gerald felt his breath return but he gripped the trolley behind him tightly, not trusting his legs. "Where did they come from?"

Natalie shrugged. "They were dropped off last thing yesterday. House clearance I think..."

Gerald's eyes widened. "Which house? Where?"

"I dunno, love," she said. "You look like you're in shock. Come to the back office and have a cup of tea."

Gerald let himself be led away from the hideous things on the table and into the back room. Natalie sat him down amid the clutter of coats and papers, tables and coffee mugs. She busied herself with the kettle and the teabags. A moment later he cradled a mug of steaming, sugary tea in trembling hands. "Thank you," he said and looked up at her.

"Not a problem, dearie," she said. "Look, if you want to take yourself off home, that's fine. Better still, see a doctor. You look like you've had a funny turn."

Gerald nodded and sipped at the tea. The sweetness invaded his mouth and he winced a little. He'd not had sugar in tea since he was a teenager and he wasn't sure he liked it now. "I-I'm sorry if I alarmed you," he said. Natalie was about ten years younger than him, late forties, a thin woman in every sense. Her thin, brown hair was cut into a bob that framed her pinched face. Her thin lips were always pursed in a look of frustrated disapproval that was accentuated by a long, thin nose. Her dark green dress hung off her bony shoulders. Jamie, Gerald's coworker on the first day had said, 'she needs a few pies in her," and given him a rather annoying elbow in the ribs.

Natalie gave a tight smile. "I thought you were having a heart attack."

"No. No, I'm fine. It was just seeing... those

boots..." Gerald said and glanced at the woman. He couldn't tell her. She'd think he was a nutcase. Or worse. "They... they reminded me of something... someone... a long time ago... Just took me back." He felt his face reddening. "Y'know. School days. Bad memories some of them."

"I know what you mean." Natalie looked distantly over Gerald's head. "Never too keen on school myself..."

Gerald stared into his mug. "Our teens were meant to be one big adventure. But, somehow, it all went sour."

"Yeah," Natalie muttered. "Didn't it just." An awkward silence filled the room.

Gerald set the mug down on the table, making the milk bottle, assorted spoons and all the other mugs clink. "I'll get off, if you don't mind. I do feel a bit shaken, to be honest. Sounds silly, I know but..." He glanced out of the office window onto the sorting floor where the boxes sat on the table.

Natalie leaned forward and he felt her hand on his knee. "Doesn't sound silly at all," she said. "You get off home." She nodded towards the sorting room. "Jamie's on in half an hour. I'll be fine until then."

Spluttering thanks and excuses, Gerald jumped up and hurried back across the room. He had to pass the table to get to the door that led into the main shop and out into the street. The top of the boots glowered over the edge of the box and it was all Gerald could do not to press himself against the pile of cardboard boxes that lined the wall. He gave one backward glance to the office and saw Natalie's dark outline standing at the office window, watching him. With a faltering grin and half a wave, he banged open the double doors into the shop and almost ran out.

Wednesday October 23rd

CHAPTER 2

The girl staggered down the shadowy path, panting for breath. Darkness filled the whole wood around her, but her eyes had become accustomed to it. Tree trunks stood in mute rows, their branches casting long, twisting shadows across the path. She stopped for a minute, bending over to kill the stitch that stabbed in her side.

The weirdo had chased her along Allport Road but he was slow. She was pretty sure he was still behind somewhere. As her breath settled into a more regular pattern and her nerves jangled a little less, she became aware of a cold damp feeling around her calves. Looking down, she swore. Her new boots were soaking and her jeans were wet. They were clean on today. She must have run through a puddle. Mum would go mad. Nothing new there.

She put her hand into her jacket pocket. "Shit." Her phone had gone. It must have fallen out when she was running away from that old pervert. "Shit. Shit. Shit" She couldn't go back. Her heart thumping, she peered into the blackness that filled the gaps between the trees like a solid wall. Had something moved? A twig snapped behind her, making her turn and run.

She veered off the path, brambles dragging at her jeans and jacket; thin branches whipping her face. She could hear the old perv behind her, blundering through the undergrowth too. Then she burst out onto a clearing, recognising the railings of the old bear pit; a relic of an older time when this wood was a pleasure garden.

A black shape rose up, making her yelp. But the noise ended abruptly as cold fingers clamped around her neck, forcing her throat against the cold metal railings. She clawed at the arms behind her, trying desperately to break free, but the fingers tightened, crushing the scream from her lips. A bony knee pressed into her back, sending a sharp pain through her and increasing the force. The blood boiled around her temples, pulsing and thudding as she kicked and bucked to escape. The hands held fast, the metal crushing her windpipe. She felt as if her head would explode and the branches above her blurred. The taste of blood flooded her mouth and the strength ebbed from her limbs. Slowly the red faded to blackness and oblivion.

This wasn't the first time Detective Chief Inspector Blake had sat in his 1988 Opel Manta outside the Wirral RSPCA centre; he'd driven to the Wallasey site several times after work. It was late and dark. He wondered if he should just go home to bed. His phone told him that the place closed at three. To the public at least. But Blake wasn't 'the public.' Sometimes a warrant card got you into places even when they were closed. Although the lights were out in the main office, the gates of the Animal Centre were still open and a bulb gleamed in what Blake took to be the main cattery.

He dragged his huge frame out of his car. The hiss of the traffic on the M53 filled the air, punctuated by the occasional explosion of early fireworks. This was buffer land between the sprawling housing estates of Wallasey and the main road artery that ran the length of the Wirral and on, under the River Mersey, to Liverpool. Warehouses and a building wholesaler rubbed shoulders with a fleet hire storage yard and the local rugby club. He paused for a moment, turning back to the car, then changed his mind, striding into the carpark and across to the dark building. He had to do something. He couldn't carry on like this.

A woman answered his knock. She was tall and slim with black spiky hair. Her green eyes struck him as cat-like which seemed kind of funny under the circumstances. "I'm sorry, love, we closed at three. I'm just here to look after the cats."

Blake flashed his warrant card and she looked surprised. "I know you're closed but I couldn't get here sooner," Blake felt his throat close up and his cheeks blaze. "I-I just wondered if... you see... it's my mother... her cat... she can't look after it anymore and..." He ran his fingers through his greying blond hair.

The woman frowned slightly and then said. "Just hang on a second. I'll get you a form to fill in and a card. You'll have to bring the cat tomorrow. We can't accept it today..." She disappeared into the back of the room. Blake could hear the plaintive meows from inside the building and immediately felt ashamed.

The woman returned and handed him a sheaf of forms.

"I'm sorry," Blake said. "I wouldn't normally. I can't look after her myself. The job... I would but..."

The woman gave him a brief smile. "Don't worry," she said. "It sounds like you're struggling." She frowned. "You look kind of familiar... Do I know you?"

Blake felt himself reddening even more. "Not unless you've had dealings with the police." That usually shut them up. Few people wanted to admit to that.

It worked and she broke eye contact with him. "No, no. I just thought I recognised you, that's all."

Blake didn't answer at first. Some people recognised him but often, it was lost so deep in their memories that they never found the answer for themselves. He took the brief silence that descended to pull her back on track. "The cats... if they don't find an owner... do you...?" He left the fate of the unwanted cats hanging in the air between them.

She shook her head fiercely. "Oh no," she said. "We always find a home. Just takes time, that's all, and there might be other options. What kind of cat is she?"

"A grey one," Blake said, then felt ridiculous. "Persian. Orange eyes."

"A cat like that won't be here for long. They're very popular, valuable too..."

"She does have... issues... seems to have a pathological hatred of me, for a start."

The woman laughed. "Well if we rehome her, you won't be there to hate, will you?"

"And she's always getting stuck up trees..."

"Fill the forms in and come back tomorrow," she said, frowning at Blake in a kindly, puzzled way. "It'll be fine..."

"She craps everywhere too. Won't use the litter tray... do you think that might put people off?"

"Are you sure you want us to take her?"

Blake nodded his head. "Yes. I just... I don't know. She belongs to my mother and I'd hate for her to get rejected or something..."

Leaning against the door frame, the woman looked him up and down. "You could always get an animal psychologist in."

"Animal psychologist? Are there such people?" Blake muttered. "What do they do?"

"They deal with problem behaviour, making a mess indoors, aggression towards people, that sort of thing. Hang on." She vanished again for a few seconds and then appeared with a scrap of paper. "Ring this number. I'm sure she'd have a look at your cat for you."

Blake stared down at the scribbled note:

'PAWS FOR THOUGHT'

Laura Vexley: Behaviour Saviour.

"Behaviour Saviour," he said with a grin. "Sounds a bit kinky."

She raised her eyebrows. "Really?"

"No..." Blake stammered. He really needed to remember that he didn't have to say everything that passed through his head. "I meant... I was just trying to be funny... Erm, thanks for this. I'll have a think and get back to you." He stuffed the paper in his pocket and, as he hurried away back to his car, Blake thought that catching thieves and murderers was easier than this.

The coffee cup shook violently in her hands but it was from exhilaration rather than fear. She'd never felt like this before. In all her life of regret, recrimination and darkness, she'd never felt so free. It was like someone had thrown a switch. She was a different person; unafraid, bold. She should have done this years ago.

She'd been following the girl for weeks, tracing her movements, getting accustomed to her routines so that, eventually, they became so predictable. The moment she saw her, she knew who she really was. Of course, the more she saw of the girl, the way she moved, spoke and treated people, the truth about her was so obvious. When the idiot boy, now an old man, had appeared in the woods, it only confirmed what she had suspected. And only made matters even more delicious. Because events had been set in motion, hadn't they? By the return of the idiot boy, the idiot man. The girl was doomed the moment that man showed his idiot face. Idiot, idiot, idiot.

She felt a certain detachment when it actually happened; as if she wasn't there at all. She was watching a play on a dimly lit stage. She'd imagined the girl's eyes bulge wide; her face redden as her neck was crushed against the railing. And when the girl finally lay cold and dead, she thought he would try and hide the body; instead, the fool took his trophies, his pathetic keepsakes and left her lying there. Scurrying off like an old beetle. Pathetic idiot man.

She sipped her coffee, letting the bitter liquid burn her mouth. Nothing could harm her. She couldn't feel a thing. Now there was work to be done.

Thursday October 24th

CHAPTER 3

DCI Will Blake stood perfectly still. This was old woodland; close to the banks of the Mersey but you could be miles away from the river right now. He knew it from his childhood. Over a century ago, this wood had been a pleasure gardens with a zoo and fountains. Daytrippers had come across the Mersey on paddle steamers to Eastham Ferry to enjoy the gardens. Nature had claimed it back for its own over the decades and the specimen trees and bushes had overgrown the walls, bear pit and boating lake. Even though it was maintained by the local council, it still had a lost, forlorn feel to it. Especially now under these circumstances. The world was waking up. In a couple of hours dog walkers would be strolling along these paths. It was a popular spot. The area needed to be made secure. He knew he'd need to have a word with the park rangers but that would come later.

Blue police tape fluttered in the cold breeze, strung between branches and hedges like some macabre tinsel. Blake shivered in the feeble grey light of dawn and blinked at the flashing torches that raked across the leaf mould of Eastham Woods. The old bear pit was a circular hole, lined with large sandstone blocks. Steps led down below ground level and through a low gateway. The bear must have had a miserable existence, Blake thought, sitting at the bottom, being stared down on by Victorian tourists from Liverpool. The white incident tent crouched in the bottom of the pit, like a giant, pale fungus. Crime Scene Investigators scanned the ground around the railings above, picking up and bagging anything of interest.

Eastham was on the edge of Merseyside Police's remit; at one time, it was part of Cheshire. The suburban sprawl was dotted with open spaces and trees. Eastham Country Park, as it was known, was accessible from just about every angle; a business park to the north, playing fields and the A41 to the west and Eastham Village to the south. The trees and bushes offered any number of hiding places for would-be assailants. He'd been trying to keep his mind off what was to come next. Blake hated it when bodies turned up. Especially kids.

It didn't have to be a murder. The young girl in question might easily have come-a-cropper in the dark and landed awkwardly against a branch and somehow fallen into the pit. Accidents did happen and keeping an open mind was paramount. But, in his heart, Blake knew this was the beginning of something bad.

He ducked under another tape, flashing his ID to the constable on guard and signing into the crime scene. A figure in white coveralls approached him, waving a rubber-gloved hand. "Got here half an hour ago, sir," Detective Constable Kinnear said, the hood of the coveralls framing his long, pointed face. Kinnear always seemed to have a faint smile that made him look as if he wasn't taking things seriously enough. "Thought I'd have a peek."

Blake shook his head. "Have a peek?" He pulled on a pair of coveralls. "Give me strength. We're police officers, soft lad. We don't 'have a peek' okay?"

Kinnear squinted at Blake in the dull twilight. "Are you alright, sir? Only you've got..." The young DC traced a finger across his forehead. Unconsciously, Blake touched the long red lines that his cat, Serafina had carved. Thankfully, his thick thatch of greying, blond hair covered the rest of her handiwork. He wasn't going to explain how he had spent the first half hour of this early morning trying to get the stupid cat down out of a tree. He wasn't sure why he'd bothered; he didn't even like cats.

Mum did, though.

"Cat trouble Kinnear," Blake said, brusquely as if it was something everyone encountered on a daily basis. "The others here yet?"

"Everyone's here, sir," Kinnear said and Blake could hear the implied criticism. *Except you.*

"Who found her?"

Kinnear rummaged for his notebook. "A Mr Chowdry," he said. "Walking his dog, blah, blah, blah…"

"Blah, blah, blah?" Blake said. "Is that what he actually said? Blah, blah, blah?"

Kinnear swallowed. "No, sir…"

"Then don't you say it," Blake snapped. "There's nothing 'blah, blah, blah,' about any of this."

"No sir, sorry sir," Kinnear said, looking down to his notes once more. "Mr Chowdry was walking his dog at about five forty-five when the dog would not come back when called. He came over to find the dog sniffing at the body and called the police on his mobile."

"Good. What kind of dog?"

Kinnear scanned his notes yet again. "A black standard poodle, sir."

"Better," Blake said. "A standard poodle. Is that the big kind?"

Kinnear shrugged.

"Why was he out so early?"

Kinnear shrugged again. "He always walks his dog at that time, I guess…"

Blake drew a long, disappointed breath. "Don't shrug, Kinnear and don't guess," he said, exhaling. "We aren't paid to guess. We're paid to find out the truth. The truth about this girl's death. I want to know the colour of that dog's collar, what it had for breakfast, how many bags Mr Chowdry normally carries for scooping up its crap and how many he used this morning. Understand?"

"Yes sir," Kinnear said. "Right away sir."

"And Kinnear!" Blake yelled.

Kinnear froze. "Yes sir?"

"I want to know if the standard poodle is the big kind or is there a bigger one, right?"

Kinnear pursed his lips. "Yes sir," he said and scurried off up the woodland path, leaving Blake to descend into the pit.

After the gloom of the woods outside, the tent seemed unsuitably bright. An electric light had been set up and it reflected off the white interior. Two Crime Scene Investigators and a female detective sergeant huddled inside. Blake looked down at the girl on the ground. *How old?* Blake thought. It was hard to tell; late teens, probably. She lay on her side, almost in the recovery position, one arm folded behind her, the other under her head as if cushioning it from the muddy ground. Her blue eyes stared off into the distance. She looked cold, her skin had a greyish tinge to it. For a moment, Blake wanted to pull her up and wrap her in a blanket. Poor kid. He swallowed down the emotion. Detached himself.

"Mallachy," he said, nodding to the Crime Scene Manager. He smiled at the policewoman. "Vikki, good to see you."

"Sir," the detective said, returning the smile. Blake liked Vikki Chinn. There was no side to her. She'd worked hard to get where she was and got there on merit alone. He knew she'd put up with a lot on the way, be it comments about her height or her Chinese heritage. She frowned at him, making a subtle gesture towards her face.

"Cat trouble," Blake murmured. The confused frown that lingered on Chinn's face betrayed her nod of understanding.

"This is Callum, new CSI," Mallachy said, flicking a thumb towards the other person in the tent. Callum gave a half wave, clearly uncertain how to greet Blake under the circumstances.

"Any ideas?" Blake said, after a brief nod to Callum. "Do we know who she is yet?"

Mallachy shrugged. "No ID."

"We've had two girls reported missing in this area in the last twenty-four hours, sir," Chinn said. "So we've sent officers to the houses for photographs, just in case."

Blake grunted and gave a nod. "Good."

Malachy pointed to the displaced mud around

the girl's body. "Looks like she fell down here. Quite an impact, too." Her socks were brilliant white against the black leaves and brown dirt. "There's been a scuffle up at the railings. You can see the leaves and mud churned up there. See the bruising around the neck? Could be strangulation but we won't be sure without a post-mortem."

Blake frowned. "Where are her shoes?"

Mallachy shrugged again. "Don't know but there are no traces of mud on her socks as far as I can see. They're clean..."

"Someone took her shoes off after she was dead?" Blake said.

"That would be the most logical explanation. Perhaps they were valuable. Kids these days go mad for expensive gear."

"Perhaps," Blake muttered. "Want to hazard a guess on time of death?"

Blake wished Mallachy didn't shrug so much. It underlined the uncertainty of the whole procedure and reminded him of Kinnear. At this point, he always felt like he was stumbling around in the dark without a clue. "I'm not a pathologist but can't be very long ago, no obvious decomposition" Mallachy said. "But it was a cold night. Body's still stiff..."

"Last night then?" Mallachy's shoulders rose

up and down yet again. Blake ground his teeth and then looked up at Sergeant Chinn. "We need to get the body away; this place will be swarming with dog walkers soon. I don't think the pathologist needs to view her here. What do you think Mallachy?" Blake regretted the question the moment he said it and was rewarded with a shrug. "We'll need to get any park rangers interviewed."

"Yes sir, I'll get that sorted," Chinn replied and headed out of the tent.

Blake knelt down next to the body. "Fully clothed. Have you checked her pockets?"

"A bit of loose change. Front door key. No phone," Callum said. "It hasn't turned up out there."

"If there is one," Blake said.

"All kids carry phones on them," Callum said, blinking at Blake as if he'd just said the Earth was flat.

"Unless they forget to charge them or lose them down the back of the sofa or have them stolen or break them," Blake said, wondering if he preferred Mallachy's non-committal shrugs. "I hope a phone does turn up. It'll give us something else to work on." He leaned forward and eased a strand of damp hair back away from the girl's neck. "Nasty bruises."

“Murder?” Callum said.

Blake winced. It was like breaking a spell. Jinxing the whole investigation. “Not necessarily.” It sounded feeble, standing next to the broken body of the girl. How did she end up down here if she wasn’t thrown? How did she get those bruises on her neck?

Chinn returned with the news that a couple of constables were being assigned to interview rangers when they turned up for work and that a photograph of one of the missing girls had come through.

“One of the young ladies turned up at home a bit worse for wear, sir,” she said, holding out her phone so that Blake could view the picture. “The other missing girl looks a bit like the young lady here. Of course, I hope not but…”

Blake nodded. He looked at the image of the girl on the phone: flowing blonde hair, mascara and those weird pouts that kids seemed to do these days. He glanced down at the glassy-eyed corpse at his feet. “Yeah it’s her. We’ll need to get next of kin to identify her formally, though,” he said and sighed. “It doesn’t get any easier, this, does it?”

“No, sir,” Chinn said. “Not nice.”

Blake nodded and slapped a hand on Mallachy’s shoulder before he could shrug. Callum gave a vague nod then continued taking photographs. “Do we have a name?” he said to Chinn.

“Rebecca Thompson. Aged sixteen. Local girl. Lived in the estate right next to these woods. That’s all I’ve got so far.”

“Right,” Blake said. “Focus on the body, Malachy. Get everything you need and then get the poor girl down to the pathologist. We’ll get a family Liaison Officer to the house and then get her formally identified before the postmortem. We can see what we’re dealing with after that.”

“Will do,” Malachy said, crouching down beside the body.

“You and I, Detective Sergeant Chinn are going to make sure this place is as tight as a duck’s proverbial.”

“Sir?”

Blake looked at Chinn. “We need to secure the area. Nothing ever happens in these parts and we’re slap-bang in the middle of a wood. The Press’ll have a field day. In an hour or so, it’s going to be a bloody circus round here.”

CHAPTER 4

It was still early and Blake didn't really expect anyone to be in the visitors' centre but he thought it might be worth checking. If he could forewarn the rangers that the woods had become a crime scene, then it might save a lot of grief later on. He walked down the well-trodden sandstone path, memories of his childhood springing out from every bush. He'd lived just up the road as a child and this had been his playground. Soon, he found himself looking out across a carpark and beyond that, the River Mersey. A tarmac road led alongside the carpark where his trusty old Manta sat waiting patiently, down towards the river and the Ferry Hotel. On the right was a walled yard which housed the visitors' centre and other buildings.

A toilet block made up one side of the yard and a reconstruction of a smithy flanked the entrance. Everything was made of the red sandstone so common to older structures on the Wirral. To Blake's right, a large young man in green overalls was unlocking the information centre.

"Can I help you, mate?" he said. Blake figured that the man worked-out, judging by his broad shoulders and narrow waist. He seemed about to burst out of his work clothes.

"And you are?"

"I'm one of the rangers here," he said. "Do you need the gents or something?"

Blake frowned and then shook his head. "No," he said, pulling his ID from his pocket. "DCI Blake. I'm investigating a serious incident that occurred last night in the woods.""What, here?" the ranger said, blinking at Blake. "What kind of incident?"

"We've found a body down in the bear pit. We'll need to cordon off the area."

The man looked stunned. "Wow, right," he muttered. "I'd better tell my boss."

"If he needs to get in touch with me," Blake said, handing the man a card. The man reached for it but Blake held on. "Sorry, I didn't catch your name."

"Eric," the ranger said. "Eric Stafford."

"And you work here full time?"

"Yeah, Monday to Friday."

"And last night," Blake said. "What time did you finish? Did you notice anything out of the ordinary?"

The big man thought for a moment. "I knock off around five. I don't live far away. I'd say about five. I locked up this place and went. I didn't hear nothing. Didn't see nothing. Wouldn't do if the body was found in the bear pit, would I?"

Blake nodded. "Possibly not," he said. He'd taken his notebook out while Stafford had been talking and jotted the main points down. "And is there an address we can get you at if we need to ask any more questions?"

"Sure," Stafford said but there was an edge to his voice as if he didn't like the idea. "But, like I said, I wasn't here after five and I didn't hear nothing. I live at four Spital Cottages, just down by the train station. Is the death suspicious?"

Blake scribbled quickly. "I can't really tell you at the moment, I'm afraid, Mr Stafford but thanks for your help. If you could pass that card on to your manager, I'd be very grateful. We'll make your superiors at the local authority aware. Officers will be searching the area and parts of the woods will be no-go, for the public, I'm afraid." He turned and walked down the path, the ranger's eyes boring a hole in the back of his head all the way.

Kinnear hurried from the perimeter of the crime scene when he spotted Blake marching towards him. "Standard's the biggest size, sir," Kinnear said. "Although the British Kennel club recognises three breeds of poodle and the World Canine Organisation, four, the dispute seems to be over standard and medium."

"Really?" Blake said, frowning. "What about giant poodles? I thought you could get giant poodles."

"Not in this country, sir," Kinnear said. "Just Standard, Toy and Miniature. Mr Chowdry has a standard called Genoa. She's black, has a red collar and enjoys Chappie meat chunks with a scoop of kibble for breakfast. He normally carries a large number of dog poo bags on a roll and used one this morning. He walks the dog that way every morning at that time because there aren't many other dog walkers around then. Genoa is a bit frisky and jumps up at people." Kinnear looked down at the muddy streak on his trousers as if to illustrate the fact. "Sir."

"That's more like it," Blake said, suppressing a grin. "Now. Get uniform to do a door-to-door on the houses along Ferry Road. People will be waking up and getting ready for work. Somebody must have seen or heard something last night, surely. Check if any of these houses have CCTV. It's a slim hope but they may have picked up somebody going past."

Blake watched Kinnear hurry off. He was a good detective, but Blake couldn't shake the feeling that the young man lacked commitment.

It was probably unfair; Kinnear hadn't let him down on other cases and was unlikely to on this one, but thoroughness was essential. Miss something now and the whole case might remain a mystery for decades. Spot something seemingly trivial at this early stage and it might be easy to get to the bottom of this case, like dominoes tumbling into each other. Kinnear was eager for promotion; he made all the right noises but somehow didn't inspire confidence just yet.

Kicking a tussock of grass, Blake hissed through his teeth. They'd done well to identify the girl so quickly, even if it hadn't been confirmed yet. But he felt restless, eager to push the investigation on. It was frustrating and borne out of a wish to find out the truth of this situation. But there was a process to follow and it had to be painstaking, which also felt slow. Shortly a Family Liaison Officer would take the girl's parents to identify the body and, as soon as respectfully possible, Blake could begin asking questions. Until then, he had to wait. Not that there weren't a hundred other things he had to attend to.

The light began to grow as morning became more definite. A few birds began to sing, a wood pigeon cooed. Officers searching the undergrowth nearby still had their torches switched on but they flashed more feebly, now it was daylight.

A uniformed officer approached him from the barrier tape. "Excuse me, sir," he said. "But Aiden Davis, the Head Ranger is here and wants a word." Blake gave the officer a nod and followed him over.

Aiden Davis was a small-framed man with short, spiky brown hair and a pair of horn-rimmed glasses that made him look constantly irritated with the world. He wore the same green uniform as Eric Stafford but failed to fill it as impressively. Blake shook his hand, "DCI William Blake."

Davis nodded and gave a mischievous grin. "Tyger, tyger, eh?"

Blake looked blankly at him, pretending not to understand. "I'm sorry, sir?"

"The poem... Tyger tyger, burning bright. It's by William Blake. You must get that all the time..." Davis blushed realising what a hole he was digging for himself.

"Not really, sir. A few English teachers mentioned it when I was a kid," Blake said and fixed Davis with a stare. "Nobody does now though."

Davis stared at his boots for a moment. "Sorry... I just thought... Can you tell me what's going on?" he said, glancing over Blake's shoulder to the white tent that covered the crime scene.

"We've found a body," Blake said. "That's all I can tell you at the moment, Mr Davis. We'll need to interview your staff and any others who may have been in or around the woods last night."

Davis cursed under his breath and pulled his mobile out of his pocket. "Awful," he muttered. "What do you want us to do?"

"We'll need to keep any members of the public away from the immediate crime scene. If you can help with that, I'd be grateful. We'll narrow the cordon as quickly as possible once we've concluded the search..."

Aiden Davis frowned. "What are you looking for?"

"Anything that may be of interest, sir. We're trying to remove the body as quickly as possible before more dog walkers arrive but I can't guarantee it."

"I'll try and contact the Parks and Countryside Service but I doubt my manager is in yet."

"Just before you go, sir," Blake said. "Could you tell me what time you left here last night?"

Davis licked his lips. "Me? I-I..." he stammered. "About six thirty, maybe. I always like to make sure everything is locked and secure before I go. Why?"

"Just wondering if you saw or heard anything suspicious or unusual as you left, that's all,"

Blake said. “I’ve already spoken to Mr Stafford, the other ranger.”

“Eric? I see,” Davis said, looking puzzled for a moment. “No, I didn’t notice anything odd. I got in my car and drove home.”

“Nothing at all?”

Davis scratched his head. “No. I don’t remember hearing anything out of the ordinary. Now, if you’ll forgive me, I have to go and phone my manager.”

“Very good, sir,” Blake muttered. He nodded and watched the ranger scurry away, glancing over his shoulder as he went.

CHAPTER 5

The Major Incident Room seemed like a million miles away from the crime scene; traffic rumbled by and seagulls bickered and squawked just outside the window. To the outsider, the office would be a jumbled maze of desks covered in paper and boxes. Every now and then, a computer monitor peeped over this organised chaos. It was early afternoon and Blake's stomach grumbled at its neglect. A large team had been allocated to the investigation; Blake recognised a few people, but many were new faces to him.

DI Kath Cryer, a big, round-faced woman with dyed, blonde hair sat directly in front of him, doodling in a pad. Blake had worked with her several times; a marmite person; voice like nails on a chalkboard and a personality to match, but on the ball. Next to her sat DC Alex Manikas, tall and dark; a quiet, solid, safe pair of hands. Kinnear sat next to him, full of twitching, nervous energy. DS Vikki Chinn was another calming presence, Blake thought. A mixture of detective constables and some uniformed officers sat chatting or looking at their phones.

Blake tapped the desk with his mug. "Okay, I'm going to make this brief so that we can all get on and because it's early days and we don't have a mountain of information yet. Rebecca Thompson, aged sixteen, died around six thirty last night in Eastham Country Park. Possibly strangled. There's no evidence of sexual assault, however, her shoes were taken after her death and have not been found."

Blake pressed a key on the keyboard next to him and images of the crime scene were projected onto the wall.

"We already have a number of people who said they were walking dogs in the area and HOLMES has given a list of 'possibles' who need to be interviewed. We're awaiting DNA but the pathologist says that Rebecca put up a fight and the attacker left a lot of evidence under her fingernails. Her mobile phone is missing."

DI Cryer put her hand up. "Any boyfriends, sir?"

"Not that we know of, Kath," Blake said. "The FLO is working closely with Mum and Dad. We might discover more in due course."

"Have we been able to get into her social media accounts, sir?" Cryer asked. Blake shook his head.

"Not yet. But if you could look into that? Maybe look at any online searches she's made recently."

"Will do, guv," Cryer said, scribbling into her notebook.

Blake clapped his hands, suddenly feeling ridiculous for doing it. "Okay people. Check any actions allocated to you and let's get going."

Superintendent Martin sat at his desk, frowning over some papers when Blake knocked and stood at the threshold of his office. He was a rangy-looking man with a mane of silver-grey hair and a stubbly beard to match. His pale blue eyes always seemed narrowed in a laugh but Blake knew better than to think Martin was a soft touch. Blake had felt the sharp edge of Martin's withering scorn before now. It wasn't a pleasant experience.

Martin looked up. "Come in, Blake," he said. "I trust we're all over this case already? Nasty one. Tragic."

Blake nodded. "Well, we've got a very quick ID which bodes well, sir. FLO is with the family now. So I'm optimistic."

"Good," Martin said, lowering the papers completely and staring hard at Blake. "And you're okay? That scratch looks nasty."

Blake reddened. "Cat trouble, sir. I'm getting it sorted."

"Didn't have you down as a cat person, Blake."

"It's my mother's, sir," Blake replied, keeping his face as expressionless as possible.

"Ah. Right," Martin said, clearing his throat. "Everything alright in that department? Things sorted?"

"Not quite, sir. Bit of a ticklish family matter. I'm still talking with my brother and sister about it. Might take time."

Martin nodded. "At least you're still talking. That's a blessing. Well. I'm counting on a quick resolution to this Blake. The papers are sniffing around already. A young girl found dead in a dark wood. You can imagine."

"I'll do my best, sir."

Becky Thompson's parents lived in a recently built estate of prestige three-storey houses that bordered the Eastham Country Park. Blake reckoned the poor girl died less than half a mile from her front door. He drove past the turning for the Thompson's road, making Vikki Chinn look questioningly at him. He could have parked outside their house but he wanted to walk a little and get his head straight before stepping into the inevitable trauma and grief of two bereaved parents. He parked a little further down the road outside the Ferry Hotel; a high-fronted Victorian public house with a raised patio at its front. From here, Blake could see the river and the small stone jetty where paddle steamers from Liverpool once docked.

They climbed out of the car. Overhead, planes traced white tracks across the sky as they lifted from John Lennon Airport. Blake looked across the Mersey. "I grew up round here, you know, Chinn."

"Really Sir? I didn't know you were a wool," she said. 'Wool' was the scouse term for anyone who came from a place on the outskirts of Liverpool.

"I am, Vikki, and proud of it. Nothing against Liverpool, but it only really got going about three hundred years ago. The Wirral is ancient. It's mentioned in Arthurian legend; a marshy wilderness populated by godless people."

"Not much has changed there, then, sir," Vikki said, with a smile.

"The Welsh believed the Wirral to be a magical land; the home of the Ouzel, the oldest and wisest of birds," Blake gave Chinn a sidelong glance. "The Vikings had a parliament here. Seriously, Wirral is a weird place; caught between two rivers, staring out on the sea. It's ancient and strange. You must have noticed."

"I have, sir," Chinn said, the grin not fading

from her face. "Weird and strange."

"It's not Liverpool, Vikki, it has its own identity."

"No, sir," Chinn said, still grinning. "I mean yes, sir."

"Anyway," he said. "Let's go and see the Thompsons. You ready, Vikki?"

Mr and Mrs Thompson propped each other up on the beige sofa in their bland, oatmeal lounge. They clung to each other as if letting go would mean one or both of them being swept off into a maelstrom of horror. For years, the real world had circled them, waiting to pounce as they went about their mundane business; shopping, gardening, celebrating birthdays and Christmases as the time rolled on. Last night, they were just worried; convinced that whatever the reason for their daughter's absence, she would return. This morning the real world had leapt upon them red in tooth and claw. Now they sat huddled together, trying to blot out the images and memories of identifying her cold body on a mortuary trolley.

Blake judged Mr Thompson to be late forties, greying at the temples, clearly hitting the road every night to run off the middle-aged spread that threatened to appear any time now. His expensive fleece top spoke of a love of the outdoors. Blake had looked at the same top himself and wondered who would spend £125 on such a garment. Now he knew.

Mrs Thompson carried more weight than her husband and, even though her face was blotchy with tears, she'd refreshed her makeup. Blake might be doing her a disservice but he couldn't see her hiking up a mountain with her husband. She repeatedly ran her fingers across the back of Rebecca's school photograph that lay face down in her lap as if trying to smooth it out.

DC Tasha Cook, the Family Liaison Officer had accompanied the couple to identify the body. She would be working closely with the Thompsons. Blake never ceased to marvel at anyone who could weather that storm of grief and not get sucked down into an ocean of despair. He caught her eye and then cleared his throat.

"I know this will be very difficult but we need to ask you some questions if we are to establish what happened," he said, keeping his voice low.

"We understand Inspector," Mr Thompson said. He drew a long rattling breath and then paused, frowning at Blake. "You're him, aren't you?"

"Sorry?" Blake said but he knew straight away what Mr Thompson meant.

Mr Thompson sounded distant as if he was

dredging up a memory from more innocent times. "The fella off that Searchlight programme on the telly. You used to do all the CCTV footage and the like."

"Yes," Blake said, clearing his throat. "Yes. That was me. A good few years ago, now. I'm just a regular policeman again now." Thank God! He thought. Blake's short sojourn on TV when he was younger had been fun at first. It had turned sour quickly and had become a stick to beat him with, or a reason for subordinates to smirk and whisper behind his back. There were other, darker reasons he didn't like being reminded of that time too. Even now, thirteen years on, it surfaced with monotonous regularity.

"I used to like that programme," Mr Thompson muttered and stared at the wall behind Blake. "You always felt so distant from it all. So removed. "What was it the presenter used to say at the end?"

"It was 'Sleep tight, stay safe' or something like that, wasn't it, love?" Mrs Thompson said, in the same distant, hypnotised voice.

Blake cleared his throat again. "So... erm...forgive me but...when did you last see Rebecca?"

"Yesterday lunchtime, around twelve thirty," Mr Thompson said. "We both work from home, my wife and I, web design, online marketing and suchlike..."

Blake nodded and glanced over at Chinn whose mouth twitched. She knew he didn't have a clue what that meant.

Thompson continued. "She popped home from school with Gavin and Rory..."

"Who are...?"

"Friends from school," Mrs Thompson cut in. "Nice lads. A bit peculiar, I suppose. They have special needs, according to Becky. She's a bit of a tomboy, is Becky..." Mrs Thompson's face crumpled and her husband hugged her close, rubbing her arm. Blake waited. He could feel the tension building in him. Sometimes, he was great at soft-footing on eggshells but right now, he felt on edge. There was little they could do until the results of the post-mortem came through but Rebecca's death was suspicious and he wanted to get to the truth. Mrs Thompson composed herself.

"Gavin and Rory are like brothers to her," Mrs Thompson continued. "They go everywhere together."

"Rather eccentric brothers," Mr Thompson said, frowning. "But they've been friends since primary school."

"Do they live nearby?" Blake asked. "We'd like to talk to them."

"They might have more information about

Rebecca's movements after she left here yesterday," Tasha Cook added, smoothly before Mr or Mrs Thompson could jump to any conclusions. Blake silently thanked her.

"Gavin lives in Willaston and Rory over in Bromborough," Mrs Thompson said. "I can give you their addresses."

Blake leaned back. "Presumably, they went back to school after their dinner?"

"No," Mr Thompson said. "The school was closed in the afternoon. Preparing for a parents' evening or something. I'm not sure. The older they get, the less information trickles through. They said they were going into Bromborough. Not that there's much to do there..."

Blake nodded. "Do you think they might have been going somewhere else? I know kids sometimes make stuff up. Especially if they're doing something you might not approve of... "

"What like?"

Inwardly, Blake winced, wishing he'd phrased his question better. "Oh, I don't know," he said. "drinking or..."

"Becky has her moments, Inspector," Mr Thompson said, his voice rising. "But she's a good girl. She always tells... told us where she was going and what she was doing."

"But she didn't come home for her tea," DS

Chinn said, lowering her notepad. "Was that typical?" Normally, Blake wouldn't have appreciated the interruption, but she had drawn the woman's fire and, once again, he was grateful.

Mrs Thompson frowned. "No. She usually texts if she's going to be late."

"She sent a Whatsapp message about three pm," Mr Thompson said, pulling his phone out and scrolling his finger across the screen. "A picture. Here." He held up the screen so that Blake could see it.

Blake glanced over to Chinn and then back to Mr Thompson. "Could I possibly have a copy of that?"

CHAPTER 6

They were red boots. Converse, Hi-tops, or so Vikki Chinn told Blake. He had seen people wearing them but his taste in footwear was more thick-soled and supportive. He frowned at the image on the phone. "So, at three pm, Becky Thompson sends a picture of the boots to her father. They appear old but her parents don't recall her owning a pair. She didn't send any message with the picture other than 'Like them?' Clearly, she had recently acquired them from somewhere."

Vikki nodded. "We need to find out where the shoes came from and what value they might have," she said. "Might be a motive?"

"Yeah," Blake muttered, looking at the time. It was getting late in the day. "Two more visits? Let's see what Becky's friends can tell us about these boots."

Rory Evans' house was a small end terrace on a row in Bromborough, a couple of miles or so from the woods. Piles of bricks and hardened bags of cement peaked through the grass of the tiny, overgrown front lawn. The paint on the window frames peeled and Blake noticed that the glass in the front door had been broken at the bottom; a neat hole kicked in it and hastily covered over with a sheet of hardboard. It didn't look like a recent repair, though. The whole house throbbed with the bass notes of muffled rock music coming from inside.

"Not what you'd call house proud, sir," Vikki Chinn had muttered as they knocked on the door. Blake replied with a flick of his eyebrows and a brief smile.

A surly man wearing a denim shirt and a Motorhead T-shirt that stretched across his huge chest and stomach answered the door. Over the pulsing noise that spilled out of the house, he acknowledged with a nod of his shaggy head that he was Mr Evans, Rory's father. A livid bruise spread across his jaw and up to his eye as if he'd been punched hard in the head.

Evans pointed to his face. "Go easy on 'im. He's had one meltdown already. I got this for my troubles."

Blake looked puzzled. "I'm sorry?"

"He freaked out. I had to restrain him. Not very nice."

"Right," Blake said, still not really following.

"In 'ere," Evans said and turned round. Blake raised an eyebrow at the 'Live Fast, Die Young' motto embroidered on the back of the man's shirt. He wondered if Mr Evans ever pondered the advice and then looked around himself, realising that he had done neither.

Inside the house wasn't much better than out. Evans led them from a narrow hall, littered with old newspapers and half-blocked by a bicycle, into a square, sour-smelling living room filled by a huge lazyboy armchair, a sofa and a wall of sound. Two speakers blared out something heavy that Blake didn't recognise and was, to be frank, getting on his nerves. A panel show on the television added to the cacophony and a cockatiel bounced between two perches in a cage crammed in the corner, screeching every two seconds.

A boy rocked back and forth on the sofa; a slightly smaller version of his dad; curly black hair, a round, shapeless body, black jeans with silver metal studs poking through them. Bands and bracelets rattled on Rory's arms as he moved.

"Can we..." Blake shouted over the noise.

"What?" Mr Evans shouted.

Chinn leaned over and switched the music off, halving the noise instantly. "Can we have the telly off too, please?" Blake said. Mr Evans, shut the TV up and peace settled on the room. The cockatiel gave one last shriek and stopped leaping around its cage. Blake sat down next to Rory, who stopped rocking. “Hi, I’m Detective Chief Inspector Blake, this is Detective Sergeant Chinn. We’d like to ask you some questions, if that’s all right.”

Rory nodded.

“We’re trying to piece together Rebecca’s movements yesterday, Rory,” Blake said. “Could you tell us when you last saw her?”

“Yesterday at 4:23pm,” Rory said. His voice sounded quite high-pitched and nasal. And he emphasised the ‘p’ and the ‘m.’ For a second, Blake thought the boy was trying to be funny. “We went to the shops. Then we went to Rubens for a coffee. I had a skinny macchiato, Gavin had a flat white and Rebecca had a latte. Then we splitted up to go home.”

“Rory was in before five,” Mr Evans said, tugging at the long sleeves of his denim shirt. “It’s been a rough day for him.”

Blake nodded but held Mr Evan’s gaze for long enough to make it clear he wanted Rory to talk. “And how did Rebecca seem when you left her?” Blake said.

“What do you mean,” Rory said, staring at his shoes.

“What kind of mood was she in?” Blake said. “Happy? Sad?”

"Just normal," Rory said.

Blake pursed his lips. "What about the boots, Rory? Was she happy with her new red Converse boots?"

Rory looked up as if Blake had thrown a bucket of cold water over him. "I dunno," he said and started rocking again. "I dunno."

Blake frowned and looked over at Chinn. "The red boots, Rory? She sent a photo of them to her parents about three pm. Where did she get them from?"

"I dunno."

"Please..." Evans began.

"Do you know of anyone who might have wanted the boots, Rory?"

"I dunno. I dunno."

"Rory, if you're hiding something from us, you can get into a lot of trouble. It's better to just tell us what you know."

"I don't know nothing! I dunno. I dunno. I dunno!" Rory rocked back and forth, making the whole sofa creak. The cockatiel rattled around the cage and resumed its screeching.

"You're upsetting him," Mr Evans snapped. "He's lost his best friend, for fuck's sake..."

Blake nodded. "I know, Mr Evans, and I want to get to the bottom of what happened." He turned again to Rory. "Look, son, just tell me about the boots..."

Blake had never heard such a blood-chilling scream as Rory threw himself from the sofa and onto the floor. He kicked and thumped the ground, banging his head on the carpet. "It's not safe! It's not safe! Clocky'll come! It's not safe!"

Mr Evans leapt to his feet. "Can you leave my house," he said. "Now. I told you, he's had one meltdown already. It'll take him fuckin' hours to come down from this."

Blake nodded. "Fair enough, Mr Evans, but we'll need to speak to him sooner or later."

"Just go."

Sitting in the Manta, Blake blew out a long breath. "Well, that went well," he said. Chinn gave a tortured grin.

"I think somebody should have warned us he was on the autistic spectrum, sir," she said. "It wasn't your fault."

"He was fine until I mentioned the red boots. And what was all that 'Clocky'll come' business?"

Chinn shrugged. "Beats me, sir."

Blake's phone rang. 'Pathologist," he said, putting the mobile to his ear. "Hi. Yeah, Blake."

"Hi Will, it's Kenning. D'you want me to read

the full report out loud over the phone or do you want the headlines?" Blake had worked with Dr Jack Kenning before many times and recognised a feeble attempt at a joke. Kenning fancied himself as one of those pathologists you see on TV shows, full of gallows humour and eccentricity. In reality, Kenning was about as dull as a man could be, despite the loud bowties he wore and constantly fiddled with to draw attention.

"Headlines, please, Jack. If you read the whole report, we'll be here all day."

"I know," Kenning said, sounding a little crestfallen. "It was a joke."

"Yeah, right. The main points, please," Blake said, rolling his eyes at Chinn.

"Rebecca Thompson died of strangulation. It looks like her throat was crushed against the railings around the pit she was found in. Bruising on her neck and the internal damage is extensive. I would say she was dead when she was flipped over the railings into the pit. There's damage compatible with the fall, or rather the impact. A lot of blood and skin under her fingernails. Whoever attacked her was quite badly scratched, probably about the arms and hands. We'll be able to get DNA from there. No evidence of any sexual assault. In my opinion she died about six thirty last night, trying to fend off her attacker. I'll file the full report for you to look at in more detail."

Blake heaved a sigh. "Thanks Jack." He clicked off the phone and turned to Chinn. "Let's hope we can get a bit more out of the other lad."

CHAPTER 7

Gerald sat, trembling and twisting a mug of coffee around in his hands at his kitchen table. It was almost evening again but he hadn't opened the curtains all day. The red boots sat on the table, accusing him. It had all gone horribly, horribly wrong and now he didn't know what to do.

On the day he'd opened the boxes and found the shoes, he'd taken himself home. He felt delirious with the shock. A thousand unwelcome memories assaulted him. Even the taste of the sweet tea that he'd had from Natalie had thrown him back to his teenage years. Small details, snippets of conversation, things long buried, all came back to snap at his heels as he rushed home, ignoring the curious looks from shoppers and the blare of horns as he ran out in front of traffic.

For the rest of the day he lay on the sofa and let a couple of sleeping tablets do the work. But he still ended up slipping in and out of nightmares that took him through the whole sorry history of his teenage years. Sometime in the middle of the night, he'd augmented the tablets with a few deep glasses of Jameson's and he'd awoken some time mid-morning the next day with a throbbing head and the sketch of an idea.

It didn't matter where the shoes had come from. Whoever had sent them just wanted to lose them. Nobody knew their history. All he had to do was go back to the charity shop, buy them, and get rid. In a short while, there'd be nothing left to show for all those years of heart-ache and that would be absolutely fine.

Gerald wished he hadn't made such a fuss when he'd first seen them but he could make up some cock and bull story about how they reminded him of an old flame who had died in a car crash. That was true, in a sense, the car crash was metaphorical but she had died all the same. Nobody would interrogate him about it and if he got funny looks afterwards, he could always leave and volunteer somewhere else.

As he walked down the road into town towards the charity shop in Bromborough on Wednesday morning, he'd wondered once again what the hell brought him back to the Wirral. He'd left for college in Worcester in the September of his eighteenth year and rarely come back; Christmas, or when his mum or dad had a milestone birthday. On leaving college, he took up a job as a clerical officer in a local benefits office and lived quite comfortably on his own. Never having married, he'd holidayed with his parents every year and kept in touch by phone. He encouraged them to come down to see him as much as possible so he didn't have to travel up there.

When his mum died, his dad didn't cope well and Gerald found himself visiting more often but he was so busy shopping, tidying and taking his dad to appointments that the memories didn't have chance to surface. The place had changed so much, too. Old shops being replaced with cafes and charity shops. But, physically, it was the same place. Gerald began looking around at his childhood home more fondly. When dad finally passed away and Gerald inherited the house, he decided to sell his property down south, invest the proceeds and retire early. At fifty-five, he found himself as a man of leisure and he'd relished lying in and wasting days watching trashy daytime TV. But eventually, he felt he needed some kind of human contact and so he volunteered at the charity shop.

Now he wished he hadn't.

Still, he'd thought. By this evening, the whole episode would just be a dim, unpleasant memory and he could move on.

By the time Gerald had reached the shop, Jamie was getting ready to lock up. He looked a little non-plussed at first, when Gerald asked about the boxes and the shoes. Then his eyes lit up. "Ooh, yeah," Jamie said. "Well, to be honest, I threw the slippers and the court shoes in the recycling. I think the sandals and the stilettos went to the Heswall shop. They'll sell better there, won't they?" Jamie said, lowering his voice as if the people of Bromborough were listening. "No sense of style round here."

Gerald felt as if he was falling again. "Wh-what about the baseball boots... the con... con..." he struggled to find the word.

"Oh the Converse thingies. Yeah. A young girl came in and bought them. Seemed made up with them." He shrugged. "No accounting for taste, is there?"

Gerald didn't mean to, but he grabbed Jamie by the jumper. "What girl? When? Where is she?"

"Oy, d'you mind? That's an angora, cashmere mix. M&S. Not cheap," Jamie said, staggering back and smoothing out his jumper. "I dunno. She was with a couple of lads. They went over to Rubens, I think. I was watching them because the two lads looked a bit, well, you know, odd. Then they came out and went down towards the Co-op."

Gerald didn't even apologise to Jamie. He'd hurried across the road to the coffee shop and peered through the front window into the dimly lit cavern of a shop. A couple of mums were sipping their drinks and frowning at him while their kids kicked their feet in their buggies but otherwise, the shop was empty.

He'd spent the next hour looking in every

shop and supermarket, even the pubs, just hoping to see the girl in the red baseball boots. He even stopped at a cashpoint and drew out £100. If push came to shove, he'd offer her all of the money for them. But the girl had vanished. Finally admitting defeat, Gerald stomped home, a swarm of thoughts battering against each other in his head. It would be fine. Nobody would know.

The girl would probably get bored of them and throw them away. They were pretty worn out anyway, it wouldn't take long and they'd be binned. But what if she decided to sell them on? What if someone had recognised them like he had and then put two and two together and came up with Gerald Rees? Gerald ground his teeth as he tried to calm himself.

And then he saw the girl. Walking straight towards him. Blonde, late teens. Tight black jeans and a black leather jacket. He blinked for a second, ashamed at the sudden sexual thrill that had coursed through his body. It could almost be her, he thought and then realised he had caught her eye and she was scowling at him. He'd had to act. It was his only chance. He'd pulled out the money but it looked all wrong. The way she stared at him in disgust. The stupid way he'd tried to explain, pointing at her boots and stammering like he had some weird foot fetish. She'd run and he'd chased her.

Now he sat in his kitchen, staring at the shoes. The girl was dead and it was his fault.

CHAPTER 8

The Hooton Road took Blake and Vikki Chinn off the busy A41 and the hedgerows closed in around them. The houses grew larger with a little more land around them. Then they were into the leafy tidiness of Willaston Village.

"Would you ever think of living here?" Blake said as they slowed down to allow a green Range Rover to pass.

Vikki pulled a face. "I'd love to have the money to be able to, sir," she said. "But I like being in town, close to the shops and all the life."

"I know what you mean," Blake replied. "Great for country walks, though." They came out of the village and pulled into a short drive on the right. The Manta's tyres scrunched noisily and Blake took note of the CCTV and alarm warning signs.

Gavin Waters' house couldn't have been more different to his friend, Rory's. The Waters' house stood detached from any neighbours, hemmed in by a high yew hedge. A sea of gravel spread in front of the house and double garage. The curtains were drawn. Trailing flowers spilled out of antique chimney pots that stood guard at the studded oak front door.

As they walked up to the door, a curtain in an upstairs bedroom twitched and a pale, ghostly face peered out at them. Blake wasn't sure if it was a boy or a girl but as quickly as it had appeared, the face vanished.

Raising his eyebrows at Chinn, Blake pressed the brass doorbell. Somewhere deep inside the house, a melodic bell tinkled.

"A bit more peaceful than the previous place," Vikki said, with a smirk.

"That isn't hard, really, Vikki," Blake said. The door swung open and another pale child stared at them. It could have been the same one that had stared at them from above, but Blake wasn't sure. This one looked smaller and paler, if that was possible. Their small frame was wrapped in a black and white striped dressing gown. For a moment, Blake thought of 'The Children of the Damned,' a film about a group of creepy, alien kids who took over a village with their telepathic powers.

"Are you the policeman?" the child said.

"I'm DCI Blake, this is DS Chinn," Blake said, forcing a smile. "Are your mother or father in?"

"Are you from Singapore?" the child asked.

Chinn smiled. "No. I'm from Liverpool. But I have an uncle who lives in Singapore."

"My father has a client called Chinn. He lives in

Singapore," the child said. "It might be the same one."

"Your mother or father?" Blake said again. "Can we speak to them?"

A tall, willowy, blonde woman in tight jeans and a baggy sweater appeared behind the child. "Anastasia, I hope you aren't bothering the police officers," she said. She flashed a pearly-white smile at them. "I'm so sorry. Do come in. I'm Martha Waters, Gavin's mother. My husband and Gavin are in the drawing room." Blake glanced at Vikki, none the wiser as to which room to go in. Chinn shrugged but fortunately, Martha Waters led the way.

If Blake had still been a gambling man, he would have bet that the inside of the house would have been oak panels, thick carpets and sonorous grandfather clocks. Not for the first time, Blake was glad he no longer liked a flutter. The house was a minimalist's dream and a sentimentalist's nightmare. Every surface was stark white, bare apart from a single silver globe lamp on a glass table. A couple of white tubular steel sofas looked lost and uncomfortable in the huge white room. There were no toys or ornaments anywhere. Blake felt like he should be wearing his white forensic suit just to blend in.

Mr Waters sat on the sofa. He was as pale and skeletal as his daughter and wore a strange cream suit that had no collars or lapels. His hair was platinum blond and cut in what could only be described as a sixties pageboy style. A pair of silver rimmed pince-nez perched on the end of his long nose.

His son sat next to him, dressed, it seemed, to complement the décor in white tracksuit bottoms and a white sweatshirt. His shock of red hair was the only colourful thing in the room. He sat scowling at the floor, looking more like a sulky twelve-year-old than a sixth form student.

"Ah, DCI Blake, do come in," Mr Waters said. "Gavin and I have just been discussing the events, getting our facts straight and making sure we don't waste your time."

Blake blinked. "Right, sir. Yes. This is DS Chinn. We just want a few words with Gavin. He's not in any trouble and he doesn't have to speak to us now, if it's going to upset him." Blake thought of the chaos they'd left at the last house and hoped this interview would go a little better.

"That's quite all right, Inspector Blake, we're ready," Mr Waters said. "Obviously, Gavin has had trouble processing the terrible news, so he may find it difficult."

"No problem, sir," Blake said, giving a fleeting smile. "I'll take it steady. Is it okay to sit down?"

"Forgive me! What am I like?" Waters said, with a brittle laugh. "Please do." He gestured to the other sofa. Blake settled himself on it, feeling the whole frame give as it took their weight. "So, Gavin. Could you tell us what time you last saw Rebecca Thompson?"

Gavin kept his eyes fixed on the floor. "Yes."

An awkward pause filled the room. Finally, Mr Waters cut in, "Gavin parted company with poor Rebecca about five forty-five. He then got the bus home, arriving here about an hour later. The Reverend Smythe said hello to him halfway home around six fifteen or thereabouts. That right Gavin?"

Gavin nodded.

Blake pursed his lips and Chinn scribbled notes down. "Right. And what would you say Rebecca's mood was when you left her? Was she happy enough?"

"Happy enough for what?" Gavin muttered.

Mr Waters smiled. "Gavin didn't notice any change in her demeanour when he left her. She was quite cheerful, I think you said, didn't you Gavin?"

"Yeah," Gavin said, not looking up. "Kind of."

"So you left Rory about an hour and twenty minutes before that," Blake said. "I thought you three were as thick as thieves. That's what Rebecca's mum said. How come he went home?"

Gavin shrugged. "Didn't want to hang with

us."

"I think Rory usually has to be in by five at the latest or his dad gets worried, doesn't he, Gavin?" Waters said, he lowered his voice and leaned towards Blake. "Rory has social and communication difficulties. He gets into trouble sometimes."

Blake gave Waters a hard stare. "Where did you and Rebecca go, Gavin?"

"Home. The long way."

"They went down the Rake and wandered the streets," Waters said. "I think you said that you spent some time on the Common, didn't you, Gavin? It's a plot of land, with trees and benches, apparently."

"Mr Waters, it would help enormously if Gavin answered for himself," Blake said. He turned back to Gavin. "And what did you do there?"

Gavin shrugged. "Just talked and stuff."

"Stuff?" Blake could feel his nerves shredding as Waters gave another grin and opened his mouth to interpret but Blake interrupted him. "Is it muddy down on the Common?"

Gavin looked up at him, frowning. "A bit. Why?"

"I just wondered if Rebecca was worried about getting her new boots dirty or wet, that's all,"

Blake said. "Rory seemed really upset about the new boots..."

Waters flinched a little as he saw the conversation spiraling out of his control. "I don't think we talked about any footwear, Gavin, did we? Maybe we should stop there or get back to your movements."

Blake silenced Water with one look. "Why was Rory so upset about the boots, Gavin?"

"Cos he's a fuckin' moron, that's why," Gavin yelled, cutting his father dead. "All this bollocks about Clocky coming to get her and how we were all cursed and we'd better watch out. He's off his fuckin' head that lad. Fuckin' retard. Fuckin' wet his fuckin' pants over it."

"Gavin, I don't think that's appropriate lang..."

"Who's Clocky, Gavin?"

Gavin sneered at Blake. "Everyone knows about Clocky. It's one of them urban legends, isn't it? One of them stories that gets told at sleepovers. He was a paedo who lived round here years ago. Big time child killer and everything. He used to rape and kill kids on the stroke of midnight. Well he was caught by some teenagers from Bromborough and committed suicide in prison. But before he died, he put a curse on all the kids in the town, saying he'd come back as a ghost and get his revenge. People tell the story at

Hallowe'en and stuff. It's bollocks."

Mr Waters flinched. "Gavin..."

"Right," Blake said, trying to take in the story he'd just been told. Chinn scribbled furiously to keep up with the tirade. "And what does this have to do with the boots?"

Gavin rolled his eyes as if Blake was an idiot. "Becky bought them from the charity shop, didn't she? The Hospice shop in Bromborough. She said they looked cool. They were, like, forty years old, right? Vintage."

"And?"

"They had Clocky's name inside them see? Cameron Lock written in huge black letters on the insole thingy. That was his proper name. Cameron Lock. He committed all them murders forty years ago. They were his shoes. Rory thought so, anyhow. Fuckin' wetting himself. Fuckin' wanker."

"I think Gavin needs to go and have some time to calm down," Mr Waters said, standing up and clasping his hands as if he were begging.

Blake didn't stand. "Do you know anyone who might have wanted to harm Rebecca or might have wanted the Converses, Gavin?"

Gavin looked at Blake. "Has someone hurt her? Dad said she'd just had an accident. Is it actually a murder?"

“We are treating the death as suspicious, yes,” Blake said, not wanting to agitate the boy any further.

“And the boots have gone missing?” Gavin said, his eyes widening.

Blake groaned inwardly for the second time that day. “Well, we haven’t found them yet. They could easily be at the scene. But do you know anyone who might want to harm Rebecca?”

“Rory’s gonna go mental when he hears this,” Gavin said, a strange light in his eye. “Awesome!”

“Gavin!” Mr Waters snapped.

“Listen son,” Blake said, leaning forward. “Your friend has been murdered. It’s not ‘awesome’ it’s horrible. She died alone and frightened. Now do you know anyone who would want to do that?”

Gavin gave a toothy grin. “God, yeah. Just about everyone at school. She was a proper bitch!”

CHAPTER 9

Rock Lodge lay quiet and dark when Blake finally reached home. He pulled into the drive and climbed out of the Manta, his feet crunching on the white gravel. From here, the River Mersey was no more than a few hundred yards away and the lights of Liverpool's suburbs twinkled on the other side. He was only two or three miles south of the Birkenhead Tunnel. Here, the A41 widened into a dual carriageway, hemming in the old Victorian villas of Rock park against the banks of the Mersey. It also cut them off from the poorer estates of New Ferry and Rock Ferry and gave it a shabby, exclusive feeling.

Compared to the mansions next door, Blake's house was small. It had once been a gate house for a bigger property that had since been demolished. It had four bedrooms and a tiny, overgrown garden. You'd easily miss it if you hurried past, so thick were the bushes around the wall. His parents moved away from their semi-detached house in Eastham, where he grew up, and bought this decaying heap to renovate and sell-on. Only they'd spent ten years fixing it up and then Dad died of a heart attack and Mum was left trapped here.

Blake let himself into the house and hung his coat up, his footsteps echoing around the high ceiling. He leaned heavily against the wall and let out a breath. Darkness filled the cold hall and a hundred memories fought with each other to weigh him down with guilt and remorse. He stepped forward to switch the light on and something soft rubbed against his shins just as he moved. With a muffled curse, Blake took two stumbling steps across the tiled floor and head-butted the wall. Serafina let out a loud screech and disappeared. "Bloody hell!".

The cat sat at the other end of the hall glowering at him. It let out a plaintive meow. Blake sighed. "Sorry, cat," he said, squatting down to stroke her. "I suppose you want fee..." With a hiss, Serafina, raked her claws across Blake's hand, making him pull away and overbalancing him so he ended up sitting on the floor. She bolted into the living room.

Blake followed, half expecting to see his mum sitting in her armchair. Serafina perched on the arm, licking the paw it had just used to assault a police officer. A musty smell filled the room and Blake narrowed his eyes. "Tell me you haven't," he muttered, scanning the carpets. It wasn't until he pulled back the armchair that he found the offending turd. Blake shook his head and looked at the cat again. "There's a bloomin' litter tray in the kitchen!" Serafina sat there, blinking at him and licking her lips as if to say, 'shut up and feed me.'

When he'd finished cleaning, the smell of disinfectant was too strong in the living room, so Blake ate his ready meal standing up in the kitchen. Serafina had rapidly consumed the meagre pile of meat that she'd been given and now rubbed around Blake's ankles whining for more. Blake looked down at the cat. Even after two years, she reminded him of one of those old paintings of pigs from the seventeen hundreds that demonstrated the joys of selective breeding; tiny head, huge body. It was ridiculous that his mother had allowed the animal to get so big. She'd fed her on demand and she was a demanding cat. Blake had cut down its rations but he suspected someone else was feeding her. He wrinkled his nose. Jeez, and it farted constantly after eating. He scraped the remnants of his meal into the pedal bin and dropped his plate on top of the others that waited patiently in the scummy water to be washed.

"Half rations for you, cat," Blake said. "Until you slim down and stop making those disgusting smells."

He took himself into the living room, where the pine freshness had managed to overcome every other smell in the room. Blake threw himself down in Mum's chair, switched on a TV programme that involved nameless, toned and tanned young people in swimsuits vying for their moment of fame, and fell asleep.

Friday October 25th

CHAPTER 10

St Joseph's Hospice Charity Shop surprised Blake. He'd expected something akin to a jumble sale; heaps of clothes and musty-smelling books all competing for space in a damp, cavern. The shop proved to be light and airy with products displayed as if they were new. Only a slight sense of clutter crept in where a couple of sofas were pushed together to fit them in. But the place had a logic to it, clothes, furniture, electrical goods, books, records and DVDs all had their own discreet section. It was a big building, having once been a showroom for fridges and washing machines.

"Killing the High Street, these places are," Kinnear muttered. Blake had assigned DS Chinn to look into the Cameron Lock story to see if there were any links. In the meantime, he had acquired Detective Constable Kinnear for the trip to the charity shop to find out about the shoes. "Everyone buys online these days."

"Or somewhere like Cheshire Oaks," Blake said, shuddering at the thought of the huge retail outlet and hordes of zombie shoppers shambling around. "Everything you never wanted at a knock-down price. Mind you. I just hate shopping, even online. So maybe I'm not the best judge."

Kinnear grinned and scanned the shop floor. "Welcome to the land of tat, sir," he said.

A few old men milled around the DVDs and a woman pushing a toddler in a pushchair held up a white blouse to the light. A cheerful man greeted him from the sales counter on his right.

"Morning gentlemen, can I help?" The young man said. His name badge told Blake that his name was Jamie.

"Morning, Jamie," he said, flashing his warrant card. "I believe a young lady purchased a pair of boots from this shop a couple of days ago. Can you tell me anything about them?" Blake held up his phone to show Jamie the picture that Becky's father had given him.

Jamie rolled his eyes. "Those bloomin' things," he said. "You know, they've caused me no end of trouble..."

"Really?" Kinnear said, flashing Blake an interested look. Blake gritted his teeth.

"Why?" Jamie said, picking up on Kinnear's tone. "What's going on? Is it that murder in the woods?" Jamie put his hand to his mouth as if he was an actor in a soap. "Oh. Em. Gee," he said. "It was her wasn't it? The girl who bought those boots. It was her."

"It's just one line of investigation," Blake said, glaring at Kinnear. "I can't discuss the details, obviously. So the girl came in and bought them? Was she alone?"

Jamie thought for a moment. "No, there were two lads with her. Funny-lookin' bunch, they were. One all big and hairy, dressed in black, the other blond, dressed quite stylishly for round here. They looked through the DVDs, then the vinyl records but it's mainly Mantovani, Perry Como, that sort of stuff. Then she caught sight of the boots and bought them."

"Did you see where they went then?"

"Over to Rubens cafe," Jamie nodded out of the open door and across the road to the coffee shop. "The big hairy one, he came stamping out after a while. Looked proper cross. The others chased after him. Lots of shouting..."

"Could you hear what they were saying?" Blake asked.

Jamie shook his head. "No. But the girl was grinning and holding the boots up by the laces. She was shaking them at him and he was trying to... like... fend her off. Like he was scared of them."

"Why do you think that was?" Kinnear said.

"I don't know, do I?" Jamie said.

"Are you taking notes, Detective?" Blake said,

barely concealing his annoyance at being interrupted.

"When we first came in, you said that the boots had been nothing but trouble to you?" Blake said. "Is there something more?"

Jamie frowned as if he was considering whether to say something. "I mean, he's a lovely man and there's probably a perfectly simple explanation for it. I don't think he could be mixed up in anything like..."

"I'm sorry, who are we talking about?" Blake said.

"Honestly, it's nothing really but, the same afternoon, just as we were closing actually. About five-ish, Gerald came running up demanding to know where the shoes had gone..."

"He was looking for the Converse boots you'd sold to the girl?" Blake said.

"Yes. He was in a proper state. I told him, I said, 'the stilettos and the kid's sandals have gone to Heswall and I threw the court shoes and the slippers in the recycling.' But when I told him about the Converse boots and the girl, he ran off. He grabbed my sweater. Angora cashmere mix this is."

Blake nearly grabbed him again. "And this Gerald? What's his surname?"

"Rees," Jamie said. "Gerald Rees. He's worked

here as a volunteer for a few weeks. Nice man, really. Wouldn't say boo to a goose. I can't imagine that he'd be..."

"Do you have an address for him?"

"No," Jamie said. "Natalie, the store manager would but she's been off for the last couple of days. Left me right in the lurch, the pair of them."

"These other shoes," Kinnear said. "Stilettos and kid's sandals, why did you mention them?"

Blake pursed his lips but let it pass because, in the excitement of the information about Gerald, he'd forgotten the other shoes.

"They all came in together," Jamie said. "In numbered boxes, all wrapped in tissue, but you'd wonder why anyone would have kept them. The court shoes and slippers were proper manky but they all had names written in them in big black letters. Like I said, I dumped the scuzzy ones and sent the nice ones to the Heswall shop. Get more money for them there." He winked as if he'd let them into a trade secret.

"Can you remember any of the names?" Blake asked.

Jamie sniffed. "Only the sandals. They had 'Stephen Bradshaw' written in them. I only remember that because the shoes reminded me of that short six-word story. You know the one –

For sale, baby shoes, never worn – we did that in school and it stuck with me. The shoes kind of reminded me of that and I wondered who Stephen Bradshaw was."

"Right," Blake said, a little non-plussed. "Could you phone the Heswall shop and ask them to hold onto the other shoes? I'll have an officer go round to pick them up right away. I'll need to know where the other things went for recycling, too. We'll also need the address and phone number of your manager, in case we have more questions."

Jamie abandoned his till and scurried off to the back of the shop to make the call. Blake turned to Kinnear intending to have a word about interrupting his questions but the lad looked grey as he stared at his phone. "What's up with you?"

Kinnear looked up. "Just did a quick Google search of Stephen Bradshaw, sir. He was a toddler back in the eighties. He went missing and turned up strangled. He was Cameron Lock's last victim."

Dead-heading. She didn't even know if you did it at this time of the year. It was pretty pointless, given that briars and weeds choked the overgrown front garden. But she'd looked out and seen the roses, shrivelled and brown but reaching up for the light. Cutting down, that's what they needed, she'd decided. So she rattled around in the old shed, ignoring the rusted tools that reminded her so much of him. He loved tinkering in here.

Her face hardened as she picked up an old tin of wax polish with a faded picture of a sports car on the front. He might have loved tinkering in here but that was when he wasn't chasing his fancy woman around. Her search for the secateurs had been longer than she anticipated but had also revealed a number of other useful implements, should she need to use them. One had already suggested a plan to her. The secateurs needed oiling and sharpening after years of neglect but she got them working again and began snipping.

She knew that the police would become involved once Becky's body had been found. Maybe if that idiot man had covered his tracks a little better, they'd still be wondering where Becky was. But no matter. They were digging up the past. Good. Let them turn over a few stones and see what crawls out. A little humiliation before the final judgement wouldn't go amiss, anyway. People needed to see just how corrupt they were and the police would do that job for her. Soon, everything would be public; all their fornicating and corruption would be out in the open. Everyone would know what kind of family they were. Not that it would matter by then. They'd all be dead.

CHAPTER 11

The Incident Room buzzed with activity. Officers making and receiving calls, discussing interview notes with each other or combing through back catalogues of Converse boots. Blake's desk sat in a small office in the corner that seemed crammed with too many desks and chairs.

Right now, Blake felt even more claustrophobic, as some of the team: Andrew Kinnear, Vikki Chinn, along with Kath Cryer and Alex Manikos, were in on the briefing too. It was so gloomy and miserable outside that the fluorescent lights were on and it felt more like midnight than midday.

Vikki had set up a whiteboard and blu-tacked a recent school photograph of Rebecca Thompson next to the shots of the crime scene. A printed picture of the shoes, Gavin Waters and Rory Evans sat to the side of them. Chinn held up a photograph of a doughy-faced young man with black stubble punctuated by spots and a tangle of greasy brown hair.

"Cameron Lock," she said. "Born 1960, died 1981. Otherwise known as Clocky. He became something of an urban legend round here but in fact, he wasn't as prolific as the stories would have you believe and there is some doubt over the safety of his conviction. Stephen Bradshaw was his only victim, if he was murdered by Lock at all."

"We used to tell stories about Clocky when we went camping at Hadlow Fields with the Guides," DI Cryer said and shivered. "We knew it was based on a true story. I suppose that's how these myths get credence."

Chinn gave a tight smile. She often wondered how Cryer had got her promotion to DI. She much preferred to work with Alex Manikas, who never wasted words. With his dark, Mediterranean looks, Alex had a lot going for him, Vikki thought. "Cameron Lock had a learning disability, possibly autism too. There were suspicions of abuse when school reported sexualised behaviour towards girls in his class but nothing seems to have come of it."

"The good old Seventies, eh, Sarge?" Kinnear said. "When kiddy-fiddlers roamed the earth."

Cryer gave him a sidelong glance. "I dunno," she muttered. "Plenty of pervs still swanning around these days."

Kinnear scowled at her. "What d'you mean by that, ma'am?"

"Just ignore her and listen to the nice sergeant, soft lad," Blake said, clicking his fingers like an impatient teacher. Kinnear folded his arms and slumped in his seat, his face reddening. Blake didn't miss the smirk on Cryer's face.

Chinn shook her head but continued. "Lock began exposing himself to young girls in the Eastham and Bromborough area in the late Seventies and early in nineteen eighty but he always wore a mask. These crimes escalated in the summer of that year when he sexually assaulted a girl riding a bike on the Wirral Way.

There was a panic on the Wirral that autumn and children were chaperoned everywhere but Lock still managed to molest an eight-year-old girl in Eastham and evade capture. Officers questioned him but his mother always gave him an alibi and there were other suspects. In the meantime, six-year-old Stephen Bradshaw went missing. He'd been playing out in front of his house on Gilbert Close, Eastham and vanished. He turned up a few days later, naked and strangled. There was no evidence of sexual assault."

"Who'd let a six-year-old play out on the street?" Kinnear said.

"Wasn't uncommon, then," Blake said. "More freedom for kids."

"More opportunity for paedos, sir," Kinnear said.

Cryer shook her head. "Honestly, Kinnear. Change the record. What is it with you?"

Kinnear's jaw clenched as he glared at Cryer but said nothing; Kath Cryer outranked him and he wasn't sure how Blake might react.

"All right, Cryer. That'll do," Blake said. "Vikki, carry on."

"A few days later, Cameron Lock was caught on the Wirral Way by two teenagers who made a citizen's arrest," Chinn said. "They found Bradshaw's clothes in Lock's backpack which had been concealed nearby."

"Give those teenagers a medal," Manikas said, breaking his silence. "They sound like they came straight out of Scooby Doo or something."

Chinn nodded in agreement. "They were local celebrities for a while. Have a go heroes. Front page news. Drucilla Hunt and Gerald Rees..."

"Gerald Rees?" Blake said, glancing at Kinnear. "That's the name of the man from the charity shop. The one who was looking for Rebecca and the shoes."

"Mightn't sit right with him, a young girl getting her kicks from wearing a child-killer's boots," Cryer muttered. "It sounds pretty sick to me."

"Perhaps," Blake said, nodding. "Did we manage to find an address and pick him up?"

Manikas reddened a little. "We found the house, sir. Curtains drawn. No sign of life," he said. "Neighbours haven't seen him come or go. He doesn't have any known haunts. Just the shop and home. Keeps himself to himself. Officers are checking regularly."

"So a girl turns up dead and a person of interest disappears. Does that sound suspicious to anyone?" Blake slumped back in his chair. "If Rebecca was murdered for those Converse boots then it could be connected with the Cameron Lock case. Keep going, Vikki."

Chinn continued. "Lock always protested his innocence as did his mother and there was a hospital appointment that put Lock out of the picture for the abduction. Except that Lock never saw the doctor. He claimed the waiting room was too busy and stressed him out, so he left before his appointment time. The evidence in the bag convicted him but he claimed the police planted it. He protested his innocence right up until the spring of 1981 when he was beaten up by other prisoners and died of internal injuries. His mother died a month or so later; stabbed to death in her back garden. It was assumed someone held her responsible for her son's crimes but the killer was never caught."

"What about this Drucilla Hunt? Is she still living locally, like Rees?" Blake said. "She might be able to shed some light on the whole episode."

"Sorry to disappoint you, sir," Chinn said. "Drucilla Hunt is dead. Murdered. Her body was found dumped far out on the Dee marshes in December 1981. A local petty criminal, Gary Archer confessed to her murder and served time for it."

"Jeez," Kinnear muttered. "Four deaths. One unexplained? Is it me, sir, or have we just opened a whole can of worms?"

Blake blew out a long breath. "Looks that way, Kinnear but we've got to make sure we aren't going down a blind alley. Cryer, I want you to check up on Gary Archer; his movements, alibi etc. Also find out about the ranger at Eastham Woods. His name is Eric Stafford."

"Suspect, boss?" Cryer asked.

Blake shrugged. "Told me he was at home on the night of the murder but he was holding something back. Could be nothing but we need to check him anyway. Did you get anywhere with Rebecca's social media or internet activity, Kath?"

"Can't break into her social media accounts without the passwords and parents didn't know them. But if we can find a friend or follower on any of the accounts, we can view some activity." Cryer picked up a sheet of paper. "She seems to have cleared a lot of browsing histories but she has visited a few sites, some not surprising for a girl her age; dieting, clean eating, make-up stuff, a couple of film trailers. A couple of Ancestry dot com searches and Oh!"

"What?" Blake liked Cryer's thoroughness but her tendency towards the dramatic drove him demented.

Kath Cryer looked up at Blake. "It didn't really register before but there's one search for Drucilla Hunt. That's a bit spooky."

"Just part of a puzzle we haven't put together yet, Cryer," Blake said.

"Do you think there's that much of a connection, sir?" Vikki Chinn said.

Blake shrugged. "Drucilla Hunt and Cameron Lock are connected, that's certain. Maybe our victim just had an unhealthy obsession with the whole Cameron Lock case. It's certainly worth looking into. Any idea who led the investigations into Drucilla Hunt's death?"

DS Chinn leafed through her notes. "DCI Leech," she said. "Is he still alive, sir?"

"Oh yes," Blake said pinching the bridge of his nose again. "He's still alive all right. Only the good die young. Isn't that what they say?"

CHAPTER 12

Kinnear stared out of the window as Blake drove. The roads became lanes and the houses hedgerows as they crossed the Wirral to more affluent parts of the peninsula. Normally, Kinnear was full of questions about the Opel Manta. His fascination for the old car quite pleased Blake; he'd inherited it from his father. Kind of. And loved it because of the love he'd seen his father lavish on it. Mind you, it seemed to require more love and attention with each year Blake drove it. Finally, as they neared their destination, Blake broke the silence. "You all right, Kinnear?"

"Yes, sir, fine."

"Only I couldn't help noticing you seemed a bit rattled by Kath Cryer."

"No, sir," Kinnear muttered, keeping his eyes fixed out of the window. Blake could see the muscles in his jaw tightening. "Didn't bother me, sir. She's the DI."

"Okay. Pay her no heed. She doesn't always think but she's a good copper and will have your back in a tight spot."

"Yes, sir."

"D'you know much about DCI Jimmy Leech, Andrew?"

"I assume he must be clocking on a bit and long retired. Otherwise, nothing."

"He's a slippery bastard," Blake said. "A reptile. He retired before you were born and when I was just a kid but our paths have crossed a few times on cold cases. You'll have stumbled across his children and grandchildren, no doubt," Blake muttered. "Those rotten apples didn't fall far from the tree."

"You mean, he's part of that family?" Kinnear said. The Leeches were a notorious criminal family on the Wirral. Between the extended lineup of cousins and uncles, brothers and sisters, they managed to cover a whole spectrum of offences from shoplifting to armed robbery.

"How do you think they were so successful? DCI Leech was their inside man although nobody ever proved it, he always managed to keep one step ahead of any internal investigations. Whether that was by sheer wiliness or by greasing a few palms, I couldn't say."

"Maybe both, sir," Kinnear said.

Blake nodded. "He's not the most savoury of characters, either. He'll try to push all your buttons but don't react. He'll be fishing for information as much as we are. So please, keep schtum. Watch and listen."

Leech lived in a nondescript cul-de-sac in Newton up at the top end of the Wirral. They pulled up and Blake wondered who thought these roads were a good idea. Obviously, someone who didn't have a very big car. The round bulb of the cul-de-sac, meant that parking was awkward. Leech's house looked well cared for; the paint bright and clean, the garden clipped and neat. Despite the wholesome respectability of the property, Blake reckoned Leech's presence in the cul-de-sac probably wouldn't go down well with the other residents at all. The man was corrupt and unpleasant, not the kind of person you dropped in on for a cuppa. They climbed out of the car, swung the green, wooden gate open and walked the scrubbed path to the front door.

"Leech clearly has people looking after him," Blake muttered. "I can't for one minute imagine him mowing the lawn or clipping the hedge."

The curtains were drawn and the only evidence of life in the house was the wire crate that held a single pint of milk. Blake lifted the door knocker but, as he did, the door swung slightly open of its own accord.

Frowning at Kinnear, Blake pushed the door open a little more. "Hello?" he called. "Jimmy? It's me DCI Will Blake. Can we come in?"

Silence.

Blake nodded to Kinnear and they edged into the hallway. The house smelled of air freshener, wood polish and cigarette smoke. Beige gave way to floral patterns and back to beige again Three doors and the stairway led off the hallway. Directly ahead, Blake could see a narrow kitchen, mugs dangling from a mug tree and a gas cooker facing him. The nearest door was shut but the door into the back room stood ajar. The drawn curtains made everything seem dark and subterranean.

"Jimmy? Are you there?" Blake said, pushing the door open wider.

Jimmy Leech sat engrossed in a magazine. Blake could tell from the skin tone that plastered the front cover what kind of magazine it was. Leech looked like a living skeleton, his skin stretched tight over his bony frame. Thin, blue veins pulsed in his temples and his glittering black eyes nestled deep in his skull. He flicked over each page with long, bony fingers. The rest of his frame was covered by an old blue shirt, protected from food debris by a brown zip-front cardigan. A pair of tartan slippers and baggy tracksuit bottoms completed the geriatric chic. He glanced up from his magazine and his face split into a crooked, brown-toothed grin. "Well now," he said. "Who do we have here? Ace Detective and TV personality of yesteryear, DCI Blake, I believe. And who's the pretty boy with you?"

"This is DC Kinnear," Blake said. "We've come to pick your brains, Jimmy."

"I'm honoured," Leech said and pointed at the sofa on the other side of the room. "Sit down, why don't you?"

Blake perched himself on the edge of the sofa, not wanting to get too comfortable and Kinnear did likewise. Display cases full of books and plates lined the edge of the room and the carpet was thick and plush. Jimmy Leech exuded a malign presence that made even this innocuous domestic setting feel threatening. A thin beam of weak light forced its way through the crack in the curtains. "Cameron Lock, Jimmy," Blake said. "What d'you remember?"

Leech looked down at the magazine and then lifted it up to show them a young woman in stripy knee-high socks, red stilettos and nothing else, lying, legs apart on a sheepskin rug. "Just look at that," Leech said. "What I wouldn't give for a piece." He grinned at Kinnear. "How about you, Detective?"

"Put it down, Jimmy," Blake said. "You wouldn't remember what to do anyway."

Jimmy lowered the magazine into his lap and narrowed his eyes. "I bet I would. It's like ridin' a bike. It'd probably kill me though, now." A phlegmy laugh bubbled up from his throat and he leaned over to pull a cigarette from one of the boxes piled on the arm of his chair.

Blake ignored him. "You want to be careful leaving your front door open like that. Anyone could walk in."

Leech's mouth tightened into a grimace. "Anyone can. I'm not afraid." He looked at Kinnear. "Has he told you he was a TV star, son?"

Kinnear suppressed a grin but said nothing.

"All right, Jimmy, that'll do..."

"What was it? Spotlight... no... Searchlight. That was you wasn't it, Blake? Standing there in your shiny uniform all fresh faced. Easy on the eye. One for the Mums. Cracking crime. Keeping Joe Public safe. How come you're not on the telly anymore?"

"Cameron Lock, Jimmy," Blake said. "What do you remember?"

"DC Kinnear, is it?" Leech said, licking his cracked lips with a nicotine tongue. "What drew you to the force, Mr Kinnear? Was it the uniform?"

Kinnear narrowed his eyes but said nothing.

Good lad, Blake thought. "Cameron Lock."

"Yeah, yeah, I heard you," Jimmy said, puffing blue smoke all over them as he lit up. He coughed violently, almost doubling up and then straightened out, wiping his mouth with his sleeve. "That's better. Cameron Lock. That fat wanker. What do you want to know? He killed a little kid and got his come-uppance in jail. Didn't lose any sleep over that nonce."

"He was guilty then?" Blake said.

Jimmy took a long drag from his cigarette and gave Blake a sly smile. "Caught bang to rights. Found that Bradshaw kid's smalls in Lock's bag."

"What about Lock's mother? Did she get her come-uppence too?"

"Can't you read the files, Blake? Is the print too small for you or something?" Jimmy said. "Couldn't get to the bottom of that one. But again, anyone who'd cover for a child killer, even if it was their own flesh and blood, deserves short shrift, if you ask me."

"Thanks for the moral guidance, Jimmy," Blake said. "I can rely on you to keep me on the straight and narrow."

Jimmy gave a hacking laugh and sucked up another lungful of smoke. "I like you Blake. You're old enough to know what proper policing was all about back in the day." He turned to Kinnear. "Has he told you about the Hilbre Island affair?"

Kinnear frowned, trying to understand the mind games Leech was playing.

Blake watched Jimmy warily. "All right,

Jimmy, that's enough."

"What was that fella's name?" Leech said, clicking his fingers as if struggling to remember. Old though the man was, he still had a cast iron memory.

"It doesn't matter," Blake said, keeping his voice level and trying to control his breath. "We aren't here to talk about him."

"No," Leech said, staring straight at Kinnear. "We never talk about Hilbre Island. Anyway, Kinnear, you just made DC? All excited? Full of vim and vigour?"

Kinnear's jaw made a slight cracking noise and Blake saw him clench his fists. Jimmy Leech could get under anyone's skin, Blake knew that more than anyone. "All right, Jimmy. You've had your fun. Back to Cameron Lock. You ever seen these boots before?"

Jimmy took the phone in his long fingers and for a second, Blake wanted to snatch it back as if the old policeman was going to scroll through his other photos and somehow contaminate them. "Where d'you find these?" Jimmy said, breathing heavily.

"You didn't answer the question, Jimmy."

The old man went quiet as if he was deep in thought. "Yeah, I've seen them before," he said at last. "Is this about the girl? The one who got strangled in the woods down in Eastham?"

"It might be," Blake said. "Where have you seen these shoes before, Jimmy?"

All Jimmy's bravado had fled. "I saw them on the feet of Drucilla Hunt. When she was alive." Jimmy's magazine crackled in his lap as he ran a hand over it. "But then she was found strangled, fully clothed but with those shoes missing," Jimmy's eyes grew wide. "We never found them. Looks like you have."

CHAPTER 13

Detective Sergeant Vikki Chinn sat in the interview room with Detective Inspector Cryer. She wished Manikas hadn't been sent off to watch the Rees house for a whole host of reasons. His economy with words, was one for a start; Cryer never seemed to shut up. Natalie Murphy sat opposite them, still wearing her coat and gloves, her arms folded, looking like she was sucking a wasp. Everything about her said: not stopping long.

"Sorry to bring you out on a Friday night, Mrs Murphy but we needed to ask you a few questions regarding a case we're investigating. Can I take your coat? I hope you understand that you're here voluntarily and..."

"Miss," Murphy said, pulling her coat more closely around her throat as if Cryer might try to snatch it.

Cryer blinked at her. "I'm sorry?"

"Miss Murphy. I'm not married."

Cryer reddened. "I do apologise, Miss Murphy, I'll amend the records..."

"Miss Murphy," Chinn said. "We understand that you were present when some shoes were delivered to the charity shop that you manage. Could you tell us about them?"

Cryer frowned at the interruption but looked towards Natalie Murphy, who shifted in her seat. "We get a lot of shoes in," she said. "Do you mean the ones that came in on Monday night?"

"Yes, specifically these red Converse trainers," Chinn said, showing Natalie a picture of the shoes.

Natalie Murphy stared intently at the picture. Vikki could see her jaw clenching. "Gerald was sorting them out. They came in plain boxes. All numbered. He became agitated as he opened them..."

"Agitated?" Vikki said. "In what way?"

"Like he'd seen a ghost," Natalie said. "There were other shoes but the red ones, the baseball boot things. He almost fainted when he saw them."

"Did he tell you why?"

Natalie shook her head. "Not really. I made him a cup of sweet tea but he just mumbled something about bad memories and said he had to go."

"And he left straight after that?"

Natalie nodded. "I told him to see a doctor. I was worried he'd had a stroke or something."

"Did you have any idea why he might have been upset?" Vikki said.

"He's only been with us a few weeks. I haven't really got to know him. He keeps himself to himself, if you know what I mean. Anyway. I didn't really have time to think about it because I had a phone call from my mother's care assistant. She'd choked on her breakfast..."

"The carer?" Cryer said.

"No. My mother," Natalie said, through gritted teeth. "I look after her in the evenings but she has a carer to come in and give her breakfast and get her ready for the day. If you call wiping her face with a damp flannel and spraying her with Impulse deodorant getting her ready."

Cryer scribbled down a few notes. "So you haven't seen Gerald since then?"

Natalie shook her head. "Mother took ill after the choking attack. I've been at home with her almost all the time. I did phone the shop and Jamie told me that he hadn't been in. That was when he told me you needed to speak to me."

"And you've no idea where Gerald Rees might be now?" Cryer asked, leaning forward.

"Isn't he at home?" Natalie said, raising her eyebrows. "I mean, I gave you his address."

"He doesn't appear to be there," Cryer said. "Any ideas?"

Natalie shrugged. "No. Like I said, I don't know him that well."

"What about the other shoes?" Vikki asked. "Did you get a look at any of them?"

"Not really. I was about to have a look when I got the call about my mother. Jamie arrived just in time to take over from me and open the shop. I left almost immediately after."

Vikki shuffled through her notes. "Is there any way of telling where those shoes had come from?"

Natalie rubbed her temples with a gloved hand. "Not really," she said. "We're a sorting centre. A lot of stuff gets delivered from other shops. Everything goes through us."

"So there's no way of tracking these items?" Cryer said, sitting back in her chair.

"Most of it just gets loaded into a van that does the rounds. The shoes could have come from our other shops or just been left by the back door for us to find. If anything is brought in in person, we try to get the donor to Gift Aid it. We can claim the tax back then. But the boxes didn't appear to have any Gift Aid barcode, so I'd guess they were just blind donations."

An awkward silence fell over the room as Chinn and Cryer checked through their notes for any details they might have missed.

"Is Gerald in any kind of trouble?" Natalie asked.

"We hope not," Vikki said. "You may have heard that a young woman was found dead in Eastham Country Park yesterday morning. We've traced her movements and she bought the trainers I showed you from your shop shortly before she died."

"And there's no sign of Gerald," Natalie said.

Vikki Chinn closed the file and stood up. "Anyway, thank you for your time, Miss Murphy. You've been very helpful. If anything else comes to mind, please don't hesitate to contact us."

"Yes, I will." Natalie Murphy rose, and Cryer showed her to the door. When she returned, Cryer pulled a face.

"Didn't like her," she said. "I think she's hiding something."

Chinn shook her head. "Really? Why's that then?"

"Dunno. Just a feeling," Cryer muttered. "She was smiling too much when she left the office and it wasn't a nice smile either."

"Well, we can't arrest her for smiling," Chinn said.

" 'Can't arrest her for smiling,' Ma'am," Cryer said, fixing her eyes on Chinn.

Chinn pursed her lips and nodded. “Yes, Ma’am,” she said. “Sorry, Ma’am.”

“Good. Carry on. Sergeant.” Kath Cryer allowed herself the slightest of smiles as she stalked out of the office.

CHAPTER 14

The dusty, smokiness of Jimmy Leech's living room and the proximity to this leering creature was giving Blake a pulsing headache. The old man seemed to have regained some of his cockiness after his initial shock at seeing the picture of the boots. Now he was back on safe ground: retelling the past. Jimmy wove stories about a time that should have left him ashamed, but it was clear he revelled in it. By his calculation, the old man had to be at least 92. Better people from his generation had passed away long ago. It didn't seem fair.

"She was a game one, that Drucilla. A proper policeman's friend, if you know what I mean, Constable Kinnear," Jimmy chuckled and winked at Kinnear.

"No. I don't," Kinnear muttered.

"Oh, I think I've hit a nerve, Blake," Jimmy said and broke down coughing again. "Not your cup of cocoa, eh, Detective?"

"Just stick to the facts, Jimmy," Blake said. "We don't want any of your shaggy dog stories now."

Jimmy recovered himself and held up his

hand. "Alright, alright," he said. "It was just a bit of banter." He gave Kinnear a sly, sidelong glance. "Nah. Drucilla proved very useful even before the Lock case. She was a proper little snitch and seemed to be able to find out all kinds of tittle tattle about people. S'pose it was no wonder she ended up dead. Eh, d'you remember that Inspector? Garbutt, I think his name was? Oh, you wouldn't. You would've been shittin' your nappy when this all happened. Anyway, this Garbutt was as queer as they come. A shirt-lifter, like." Leech gave Kinnear another glance and continued. "Drucilla tipped us off that he was picking up young lads round the public bogs in Eastham. Not too far from where your victim was found, funnily enough. We fuckin' nicked him. His feet didn't touch the ground. Should've seen his face." Leech paused and scratched his chin. "I think he topped himself. Good riddance, I say. Saved us the trouble of a trial and everything."

"Bastard!" Kinnear leapt up and Blake only just managed to throw an arm around him to stop him from landing a punch on the old man.

"Kinnear, that's enough!" Blake said. "Go and wait outside." He bundled the red-faced detective outside and returned to the room.

Leech sat back in his chair, laughter bubbling in his phlegmy throat. "I haven't had so much fun in years," he said. "I knew he was one of them."

Blake leaned in close to Leech. "Just tell me what I need to know or so help me, I'll let Kinnear back in, lock the door and leave you two to get better acquainted."

The laughter stopped, abruptly and Leech thrust his face into Blake's. Blake could smell his rancid, smoky breath. The man's eyes gleamed with a sharp cruelty. "Yeah? See how that works out for you and him. I'm not scared of you, Will Blake. My boys would fertilise the flowers on my grave with your blood and bones. Now lover boy's gone, why don't you and I have a proper chat?"

Blake sat down again, never taking his eyes off Leech. "Make it quick, Leech. I want to catch whoever killed this girl. She was innocent…"

"Nobody's ever innocent, Blake, not totally. You know that," Jimmy said, settling back down and lighting another cigarette. "Like I said. Drucilla was a snitch. I don't know how she got her information but it often proved to be top notch. Small stuff was her trademark. She was only a kid, seventeen, eighteen. I think small-time crooks, burglars, and dealers liked to brag to her. She was classy. Posh. Lived in a big old house up in Raby. Her dad was an army major or some such crap. Imagine how you'd feel if you were some toe rag from the Ford Estate and you found yourself with her on your arm! You'd tell her anything just to cop a feel."

Blake frowned. "But where did Gerald Rees come in? They were a duo, right?"

"They were but fuck knows what he brought to the party. He was a specky streak of piss without two braincells to rub together as far as I could see. She used to joke that she only kept him around so she could call him Mr Rees. Mysteries. Get it? Drucilla Hunt and *Mister* Rees. Ha!"

"Lock wasn't smalltime, though, was he?" Blake said. He'd stopped taking notes because this was one story, he'd be able to write up almost verbatim later.

"Drucilla helped us with another murder case before the Cameron Lock business," Jimmy said, his reptile persona giving way to the policeman that he used to be.

Blake wondered for a moment if he'd been a good copper in some ways.

"Carly Simmonds," Jimmy said. "A proper beauty. A Bobby Dazzler, as we used to say, though she didn't look so dapper with her brains knocked out all over the canal towpath in Chester."

"How did Drucilla fit into that one?"

"Simmonds split her time between the perfume counter in Brown's of Chester and working on her back in the Grosvenor Hotel."

"She was a prostitute?"

Jimmy looked pained. “I think she’d have preferred Escort or fancy woman. She always had a bit of class, did Carly. Anyway, she turned up dead one night and we didn’t have a clue. Drucilla brought us photographs of Carly in a fancy car with some fella called David Collins, an accountant at one of her old dad’s businesses. Seems like Drucilla had been tailing him for some time because his wages and his lifestyle didn’t match and she suspected he'd been fiddling the figures.”

“So he was suspect number one?”

“He was meant to meet her that night. We found he had a hotel room booked. Not what you’d call a perfect alibi,” Jimmy said. “He did a flit and topped himself. Hosepipe through the car window job. Exhaust fumes. A suicide note with a full confession turned up in the post a few days later. He couldn’t bear the scandal of it all. A respectable family man with a wife and kids, caught with his fingers in the till and erm… somewhere else…”

“Convenient,” Blake said, eyeing Jimmy carefully.

“Considerate, I’d call it,” Leech said, winking. “It meant we could tie the case up in a nice, neat bow. Drucilla saved my bollocks a couple of times like that. The Stephen Bradshaw case would’ve been a nightmare if we hadn’t nailed

Lock."

"But then Lock's mother gets killed," Blake said. "An innocent old woman and nobody bats an eyelid."

"I told you, Blake, nobody's innocent. The things she did to her son. You wouldn't want to know. No, we didn't look too hard, I'll be honest."

"But you looked haunted when you saw those shoes, Jimmy. Something's eaten away at you all these years. What is it?"

Jimmy heaved a huge sigh of blue smoke right from the bottom of his black heart. "Drucilla had been following some smalltime weed seller called Gary Archer when she turned up dead. He fessed up before we'd even fastened the handcuffs..."

"Nice and clean," Blake murmured. "How you liked it."

"He was a trouble-maker. I didn't care if he spent a few years behind bars," Jimmy said, his voice rising to a whine. "But something nagged at me about that one. When we interrogated him, I asked him where her shoes were. He said, 'how should I know?' I knew he didn't do it then. I could tell. Just from the way he said that."

"So why was he confessing? Covering for someone? Who? They must have been wealthy to pay him off for a life sentence."

Jimmy waved his hand in the air as if clearing a bad smell. "Life sentence, my arse," he said. "Archer had a history of psychiatric problems. Diminished responsibility was the verdict. He went to hospital for a while, secure unit for a bit longer and he came out after about thirteen years. And a few years later, I hear he's living somewhere over in Spital in a nice little cottage with a garden and everything. How the fuck does that happen?"

Blake shrugged. "It does happen, Jimmy. People turn their lives around."

"Yeah right," Jimmy said. "Not Archer. He wasn't meant to make old bones."

"Anyway, it seems a bit odd, you railing against the injustices of the world seeing as you turned a blind eye or two in your time."

Jimmy shrugged. "No comment." His face clouded over again. "It wasn't so much that as when I asked the question, something clicked. You must know it. That feeling when you realise there's a connection. That the case you're on is just part of something bigger. Most of the time, people who croaked or got put away deserved it. They were criminals of one sort or another. But kids getting killed never sat right with me."

Blake nodded. "Go on."

Jimmy stared at Blake and his voice dropped to a whisper. The room seemed to close in, as if the faded wallpaper and old cabinets were all listening. "It was the shoes, Will. Carly Simmonds' shoes were missing, no sign of them. Red Stilettos. We recovered all of Stephen Bradshaw's clothing apart from his sandals. Josie Lock was found dead in her garden in dressing gown but no slippers. They weren't in the house; we checked because it seemed so odd. Then Drucilla's feet were bare. And I remember at the time wondering if there was some maniac out there, taking them as trophies. And I've wondered ever since."

CHAPTER 15

Alex Manikas sat in the passenger seat of his car outside Gerald Rees' house in Kylemore Avenue, Bromborough. He'd been told that people ignored passengers in cars. How true this was, he wasn't sure, but he could stretch out a bit more in this seat. The house looked like all the others in the avenue; a semi-detached built in the 1930s; bay windows with rendered walls painted white. The privet hedge was clipped neatly and kept low so that Manikas could see that the curtains were still drawn. A uniformed officer had knocked on the door a couple of times but there was no answer. He was on his fortieth level of a Bubbleshoot game when a movement distracted him, losing him the level. Cursing under his breath he squinted over at the house. The upstairs curtain had been pulled back for a brief second and a pasty, round face had glimpsed outside.

A moment later, a grey-haired man in a tweed jacket and a trilby pulled down low over his eyes came out of the front door. Manikas fumbled with his mobile. It was Rees alright and he was on the move.

◆ ◆ ◆

DCI Blake threw himself into the driving seat next to Kinnear who opened his mouth to speak. "Not a word!" Blake snapped. The awkward silence grew in the car as they drove down Telegraph Road, the long, hedge-lined route that ran down the Deeside of the Wirral. On one side fields edged housing estates and school playing fields. On the other, they ran down to the river Dee and the rolling Welsh hills beyond. The skies always seemed so open and big on this side of the peninsula. Finally, when they were some distance away from Leech's house, Blake glanced at Kinnear.

"So, what the hell was that all about?"

"I'm sorry, boss," Kinnear said after clearing his throat several times. "I shouldn't have lost it with Leech back there. I should've been more professional."

"I told you, Andrew," Blake said. "Leech is a reptile. He's a relic from another time. Him and his kind are dying out. Trust me."

"Yes sir."

"Just don't... don't fly off the handle like that again. Next time, someone might make a complaint and then where would your career be?"

Kinnear reddened. "Yes, sir, sorry, sir."

Blake looked at Kinnear. "If you've got a problem with anything like that. Any kind of abuse from anyone, Andrew, you know I'll always listen. Okay?"

Kinnear looked out of the window. "Thanks, sir. I will," he said.

Blake knew his words sounded trite, anything he said would seem superficial, but he meant it. He was hopeful that things were changing but he knew that a lot of the old attitudes in the force had slipped underground; had become a sidelong glance rather than an open insult. Or embarrassing, personal questions disguised as an 'attempt to understand.' Blake related everything that Leech had told him and Kinnear listened in silence.

"If there was someone killing random people and taking their shoes for trophies, sir, they'd be pretty old now, surely. Even someone in their twenties then would be in their sixties now. Why would they start up again? From what I've read about serial killers, they aren't usually older men."

Blake nodded. "True. It could be a copycat. Or it could be that we're just allowing ourselves to be completely distracted by these shoes and there's a simpler explanation."

"Maybe someone just stole the shoes thinking the girl was blind drunk or something," Kinnear said, not even convincing himself. "There's still the chance that someone attacked her for the shoes and didn't mean to kill her. That make and design of shoe from the eighties is up on eBay for over a hundred quid."

"It's possible," Blake said. "We need to build a better picture of Rebecca, her friends and life-style. Mum and dad seem to think she's an angel but Gavin wasn't so complimentary and he's meant to be her friend."

"So, forgive me, sir, but why are we charging off to Victor Hunt's house then?"

Blake shrugged. "No stone unturned, I suppose. You never know. There was something about the haunted look in Leech's eye that convinced me that the death of Drucilla is tangled up with this one in some way."

They drove through Heswall and Blake wondered aloud how one small town could support so many cafes and coffee shops. Soon the road widened into dual carriageway and Blake found himself back in murder territory.

Victor Hunt's house stood on an easily missed lane close to Raby Mere. Last century, the mere had been an attraction for Wirral people, with a tearoom, rowing boats and swings. Even as a child, Blake could just remember some swings and people still brought their kids down to feed the ducks. It wasn't that far from Rory Evans' place in terms of distance but in every other way, it was in another world. Woodland surrounded the mere and the lanes here became narrow and twisting. Two solid stone pillars, either side of a dark path and an old wooden sign bearing the name 'The Priest House' were the only evidence of a dwelling from the road. A thick curtain of trees skirted the property and the tyres of Blake's car crunched on deep gravel as they approached the house itself.

The sandstone manor house took a little while to reveal itself as the drive twisted around several bends and the trees continued to obscure the view. Blake's first impression was of antiquity. This house had been down here for many hundreds of years, of that he was sure. It looked like a miniature castle, with gothic windows and ornate chimney stacks. He counted at least eight upper windows. His second impression was that the whole place had seen better days. The treeline gave way to a lawn that now looked mossy and unkept. There were a few slipped tiles on the roof and ivy engulfed much of the house. They drove past a tennis court, the net ripped and sagging.

"Needs a bit of TLC," Kinnear said.

Blake nodded. "Still quite impressive, all the same."

They parked their car outside the front door, a huge solid oak affair studded with black iron rivets. "The place doesn't even look lived in,"

Blake said, peering in through the grimy windows. "The floors are bare inside. No carpets or furniture at all."

At that moment, an engine roared from the road. Blake could see headlights shining through the trees and then a bottle green Range Rover burst round the corner, kicking up gravel. It headed straight for Kinnear and Blake leapt forward pushing him out of the way as the car skidded to a halt inches away from them.

The door swung open and a grim-faced man with dark hair and a khaki jacket jumped out, shotgun in hand. "What the bloody hell do you think you're doing here?"

Blake pulled his warrant card from his pocket and held it aloft. "DCI Blake, Merseyside Police. Would you mind putting that gun down before I arrest you for any number of offences including threatening behaviour, dangerous driving and assaulting a police officer?"

The man stared for a second before lowering the shotgun, breaking it and resting it in the crook of his arm. He struck Blake as a military man, someone used to giving orders rather than taking them. His black hair was cut short but not squaddie short. He was craggy-looking but handsome. A slight scar interrupted his right eyebrow but only served to enhance the tough-guy appearance. He stood straight and wasn't cowed by the fact that he and Kinnear were police officers. "What are you doing on my property, then?" the man said.

Blake raised his eyebrows. "D'you mind telling me your name, sir?"

"Marcus Hunt," he said, brusquely.

"And could you tell me what you're doing here?"

"I live here! Well, I did. I've just had the house cleared."

"I'm sorry, sir, you've lost me," Blake said. "I was under the impression that this was the residence of Victor Hunt. I take it you're his son."

Hunt frowned. "Well of course I am. My father is dying. He's in a hospice. Cancer. Won't be long now. Once the old man's gone, the house can go up for sale."

"I'm sorry to hear that, sir," Blake said. "About your father, I mean. Would he be able to answer a few questions do you think or is he too ill?"

"That wily old bastard? Still sharp as a pin, I can tell you," Hunt muttered. His frown grew deeper. "What's all this about, anyway?"

"I'm afraid I can't go into details, sir," he said. "Just wanted to ask your father about something. I'd advise you to drive more carefully in future, even on your own land. If you could pop into your local station with your gun licence in the next ten days, we can forget the whole incident. Good day, sir."

Blake climbed back into the car along with a bewildered Kinnear. "What was all that gun licence malarkey, sir?" he stammered as they drove off.

"Just making the stuck-up divvy's life a bit difficult," Blake said, smirking. "Well that was a wasted journey..."

Before Kinnear could answer, Blake's mobile trilled. "Manikas? He has? Bring him in. Arrest him if you have to but bring him in. Mr Rees has more than a few questions to answer."

Alex Manikas stepped out of the car, closing the door as silently as possible. Rees was hurrying down the road with his arm looped through a carrier bag. In the time it had taken Manikas to call Blake and get out of the car, the distance between him and the suspect had opened up. Putting his hands in his pockets, Manikas began a casual stroll in the same direction as Rees but on the other side of the road. He didn't want to spook Rees and precipitate a chase. For all he knew the man might have a heart condition or might run into traffic. Once he was closer, he could call Rees' name and reassure him.

Rees glanced over his shoulder and looked

straight at Manikas then swung his head forward and continued walking. Manikas swore under his breath and scurried forward a little in a comical half walk-half run. For a moment, he remembered a game they played at primary school called Grandmother's footsteps. One person stood in the front of the hall and the rest of the group had to sneak up on them. Manikas smiled at the memory as Rees glanced round a second time. Maybe it was the smile or maybe the Detective Constable's suit just screamed policeman but suddenly Rees was running.

"Oh well," Manikas muttered and sprinted after him.

CHAPTER 16

It was a beautiful black eye, everyone agreed. It squeezed Detective Constable Manikas' right lid shut almost completely and the halo of red, purples and blues around it reminded Blake of a thunder cloud. Cryer pouted and made sickening clucks of sympathy as she pressed a bag of ice against his eye.

"All right, Cryer," Blake said. "Take it easy. He was hit by a pair of boots not punched in the face by a street-fighter."

Vikki Chinn smirked at the rebuke but then saw that Cryer was watching her and straightened her face.

"It hurt all the same, sir," Manikas said, taking control of the ice pack. Manikas had given chase when Rees made a break for it and, in a panic, Rees had thrown the carrier bag he was carrying. The shoes inside it flew out and caught Manikas in the face. Rees had nearly escaped too but an attack of cramp brought him down before he'd run more than twenty yards. Manikas had the foresight to arrest him for assault rather than just invite him to the station to help with their enquiries.

"Where is he now, sir?" Manikas asked.

"Talking to his solicitor," Blake said. "In private."

Cryer sat down at her desk and pulled out a file. "So he's in there talking about the arrest for assault," she said. "Do you think he'll mention that we also want to talk to him about him having a murdered girl's boots in his carrier bag?"

"He'll have to," Blake said. "But to be honest, I think his solicitor is out of his depth. Rees only called him because he'd handled his parents' will."

Gareth Cornell, the solicitor, finally announced that Rees was ready to talk to them. Blake took Chinn into the room with him. A female officer might seem less threatening, but he knew Chinn could be hard as nails when required. Cryer could too but Blake preferred Chinn's quiet intensity beside him when he was questioning. Cryer might butt in and he didn't want to risk having his questioning thrown off course.

Gerald Rees looked as though he hadn't slept in days. He was pale and a healthy crop of stubble spread across his pudgy face. He wore a tweed jacket and a white shirt with a grimy collar. His grey hair hung in lank ringlets around his temples, the baldness at the top making him look like a bewildered Roman emperor.

Blake switched on the recorder and read Gerald Rees the caution. He also introduced himself and DS Chinn. Confused by the formality and strangeness of the place, Rees kept smiling and nodding. Sweat beaded his brow.

“Can you tell me, Gerald,” Blake began. “Why did you run away from DC Manikas when he approached you today?”

“I didn’t know he was a policeman, did I?” Rees said, trying to keep his voice steady. “He just started following me...”

“How do you know he was following you?”

Rees shrugged. “I don’t know. He kept looking at me.”

“Are you often worried that people are following you, Mr Rees?” Blake said, running the ‘Mister’ into his surname so it sounded like ‘mysteries.’

Gerald Rees blinked and frowned at Blake. “No. No of course not.”

DS Chinn smiled. “He is quite imposing, DC Manikas. I could see how he might make you nervous,” she said. “Where were you going?”

“To get ri...” Rees glanced over to his solicitor. “To get a bottle of wine. It’s Friday. It’s been a busy week...”

“You work at the charity shop in Bromborough,” Blake said. “A volunteer.”

"Yes, that's right..."

Blake sat back in his chair. "But you went home sick on Tuesday," he said. "So how has it been a busy week?"

Rees looked to Cornell again. "No comment."

"How come you were in possession of a pair of shoes that had been bought by Rebecca Thompson on Wednesday?"

"No comment," Rees said.

"A few hours after she bought them, Rebecca Thompson was strangled to death," Blake continued. "And those shoes went missing."

"N-no comment."

"Did you take them off her feet after you strangled her, *Mister* Rees? I thought you were a crime fighter in your youth?"

Cornell looked confused at the line of questioning.

"No Comment!"

"Did you recognise the trainers, *Mister* Rees? From your illustrious past?" Blake turned to his colleague. "Did you know, DS Chinn, this fella used to solve murders and all sorts with his girlfriend Drucilla Hunt. Was that it, Gerald? Did you see the boots and want them back?"

"Do you think he killed the girl to get the shoes back?" Chinn said, a brilliantly affected look of shock on her face. "Imagine that, guv, strangling a girl with her whole life ahead of her just for a pair of boots."

"I didn't kill her!" Gerald yelled, slamming his fist on the table.

"DCI Blake, I think you're pushing my client too hard," Cornell said. He turned to Rees. "You're not obliged to say anything. I strongly recommend that you do not comment."

"It's all right," Rees said. "I did see her that night. She had the shoes on. They used to be Drucilla's, you see. I just wanted them back. I offered her money for them but she mistook that for me making… unseemly advances to her. She ran off. So I chased after her but she was too fast for me and I lost her."

"So where did you get those boots?" Blake said.

"I kept searching for her. Then I found her in the woods. I knew she was dead but I didn't kill her. I swear I didn't. I took the boots and ran."

Chinn stared at him. "You just dragged them off a dead girl's feet and ran? You didn't call the police or an ambulance?"

Rees licked his lips and glanced over at Cornell. "No comment," he said.

"What is it about those shoes that makes them so important, Gerald?" Blake said, quietly.

"No comment."

"If they're that special, then maybe they're important enough to kill for."

"I didn't kill her," Rees said. "She was dead when I found her."

"And if they belonged to Drucilla Hunt," Chinn said, "then why do they have Cameron Lock's name written inside them?"

"I don't know," Rees said. He shook his head. "I want to go home now."

"I'm afraid we decide when you can go home, Mr Rees," Blake said, leaning across the table. "If we decide to charge you with murder, you mightn't be going home for a very long time. Can you do me a favour? Can you roll your sleeves up, please?"

"Is this strictly necessary?" Cornell said, half rising as if he was going to wrestle Blake to the ground but then sitting down again.

"Mr Rees doesn't have to do it," Blake said. "I'm asking as a favour."

Rees looked puzzled. "Very well," he said, taking his jacket off and rolling up his shirt sleeves. Blake scanned the man's pale, freckly forearms. They were smooth as alabaster. Not a mark on them. The killer would have gouges and scratch marks up and down his arms, according to forensics.

"Thank you," Blake said. He drew a long breath and then exhaled slowly as he regarded Gerald Rees. Rees was a broken man but what weighed him down was more than the toll of the last few days. "If I said I thought you were telling the truth, would you explain why you took them?"

Rees paused, some kind of inner battle playing itself out. "No comment," he said at last, his voice flat and dull.

"Very well," Blake said, sighing again. "Gerald Rees, I'm arresting you on suspicion of the murder of Rebecca Thompson. You do not have to say anything. But, it may harm your defence if you do not mention when questioned something which you later rely on in court. Anything you do say may be given in evidence."

"Wh-what are you doing? You just said that you thought I didn't kill her. You can't do this!"

"I can, Gerald and I just have. I'm afraid your Friday night glass of red will have to wait," Blake said. "Mine on the other hand, is calling to me. DS Chinn will go through the charge sheet with you and we'll organise for swabs to be taken etc. You look like you've been wearing the same clothes all week. We need to examine those too." Blake stood up and turned to leave. "I'll speak to you soon. Maybe a night of reflection in the cells will focus your mind."

◆ ◆ ◆

It was late when Blake finally got back to Rock Lodge. As he stood there in the dark hallway of his mother's home, Blake almost envied Rees his night in the cells. The cells would be busy, and people would be talking or even shouting. Drunks would be kicking at the steel doors. Guards would be yelling for them to calm down. The chaos of the custody suite would be preferable to the resentful silence of Blake's mother's house. A house he now occupied; a prodigal squatter with nowhere else to go.

It had been a similar Friday night two years ago that Blake had come home to the same darkness and emptiness. The front door had been ajar. Not wide open so that you could see down the hall, but just enough to elicit a nervous intake of breath. Just enough to tell him that all was not right. He hadn't really lived in the last two years; he hadn't really lived for a good few before that, if he was being honest. But in the last two, he'd become a ghost in his mother's house. Just waiting for something that would never happen. The cold River flowed only a few yards from his front door and it had been a high tide that night.

He sighed and flicked the light on. Serafina yowled and scurried past him out of the front door, pausing only to bat at his trousers with her paw. "Tomorrow," Blake muttered, "I'm making that call."

Entering the kitchen, Blake was halted by a memory of his mother bending down and pouring dry cat food into Serafina's bowl. Her white hair was permed into a neat candyfloss ball and the kitchen light glinted on her thick glasses. She stooped, her knees bent as she emptied the whole packet into and then over the bowl, frozen like a statue. "I think you've spilt some there, Mum," Blake had said, gently taking the box from her thin fingers. "Let me tidy up."

Blake shook his head at the memory. He wasn't the ghost. There were too many memories in this house. Too much guilt. He grabbed a half bottle of red wine from the work top and unscrewed the lid. Right now, he was going to fulfill his promise to Gerald Rees. That bugger might have the company of other people but Blake had the wine

Saturday October 26th

CHAPTER 17

St Joseph's Hospice nestled in a wooded hollow at the Northern end of the Wirral, just on the outskirts of Birkenhead; close enough for the hospital but faraway enough to be semi-rural. Fields surrounded the trees, although suburban rooftops were never out of sight. Blake noticed a gardener, pruning bushes on the well-tended grounds. There was a calm cheeriness around the complex that Blake found almost therapeutic. Working against criminals in dull offices and on grimy streets in a stressful job, he was taken aback by the wholesomeness of this place. People faced death every day here and yet a positive atmosphere pervaded.

He had been directed to a brightly lit reception area with tables and chairs and a small bookcase for those waiting. At the reception counter, an elderly lady, with short, grey hair beamed at him and asked him to sign in. Her face fell a little when he identified himself and asked to speak to whoever was caring for Victor Hunt but she rallied quickly and made a phone call, telling him that Dr Mather would be along right away.

Blake scanned the bookshelf while he waited.

A collection of books about sports blunders stood between one about Gratitude, and one entitled 'Am I Middle Class Enough Yet?' All around him, people came and went. The place was busy but not hectic.

A short, round woman in a green suit bounded up to him with her hand extended. "DCI Blake?" she said. "I'm Dr Karen Mather, I believe you're here to see Victor Hunt?"

Blake shook her hand. "I'd like to speak to him, if that's possible. I understand he's very sick and I didn't want to arrive at his bedside unannounced."

Dr Mather led Blake into a side room and shut the door. "That's very considerate of you, DCI Blake," she said. She dropped the smile. "To be honest, I wouldn't worry yourself too much about Victor Hunt's sensibilities."

"Really?" Blake said, taken aback.

"He's been through a lot, what with the pain and the unpleasantness of the treatment but he's as tough as old boots. He speaks his mind and a lot of what he says isn't always agreeable. Not what you'd call our most popular patient. I think we'll be moving him off Bluebell Ward to a private room if he carries on upsetting the other patients."

"I see," Blake said. "I'll bear that in mind."

Even after the ravages of cancer treatment and eighty or so years on the planet, Blake could tell that Victor Hunt had been a vigorous and handsome man. Dr Mather introduced Blake and Hunt looked him up and down.

"You're the policeman off the television, aren't you?"

Blake tried to conceal the wince. "Yes, sir. I was involved with the Searchlight programme a while ago, now..."

"But you're a real policeman?"

Blake gave a tight smile. "Yes, sir."

"Any relation to the real William Blake? The poet?"

A double whammy. Great. It never ended. "Not that I know of, sir, no."

"Shame. Anyway, how on earth do you think I can help you, DCI Blake?" Hunt said, smoothing the sheets of his bed with long, liver-spotted fingers.

"We have recovered a pair of red boots from a suspect in a murder enquiry," Blake said, showing Hunt the picture. "Converse boots to be precise. Do you recognise them?"

Hunt heaved a long sigh. "Yes," he said. "They belonged to my daughter, Drucilla. But then you knew that already, didn't you, Inspector? Why are you asking me?"

"The boots disappeared almost forty years ago. Your daughter was wearing them the last time she was seen alive but they were missing when her body was found. Now they've cropped up, recently, at the scene of a similar murder. I don't know if you've heard about it? A young girl was strangled in Eastham Woods."

Hunt lifted his arm, showing Blake the IV tubes and cannulas that tethered him to his bed. "I hadn't heard, no. In case it escaped your notice, Blake, I have other things to worry about." He gave a cheerless smile. "And I can assure you, I do have an alibi. I haven't moved from this bed in days."

"I'm not suggesting you were in any way involved, sir," Blake said. "The shoes appeared at the hospice charity shop earlier this week. The girl bought them and was found dead the next day. Those shoes have been lying hidden somewhere all this time. Do you have any idea where they might have been?"

This time Hunt shrugged. "How would I know? Presumably they came from the lowlife that killed my daughter. A trophy. Don't killers keep such things?"

Blake nodded. "Sometimes. What do you know about Gerald Rees?"

Before he could answer, Hunt launched into a spluttering cough and reached for a glass on the bedside cabinet. A greetings card fell to the ground, caught by his flailing fingers. Blake passed him the glass and picked up the card. It flapped open, revealing spidery writing inside: 'To Victor, Remembering good times and happy 'stolen' hours. Hope you do too. Love always. J.'

Hunt regained his composure and placed the glass back on the cabinet. "Rees? A fool. Not very bright, as far as I could see. He was very fond of Drucilla. His father was a pen-pusher of some kind, I believe. Worked for the council." The last phrase came out as a snort of contempt. "Why? Surely you don't think he killed this girl?" Blake noticed the numbers on the heart rate and blood pressure monitors go up a little.

"He's helping us with our enquiries. Protests his innocence."

"That boy couldn't swat a fly. Really, he couldn't. Look Blake, my daughter had her moments. Her mother died when she was young and, although I loved her dearly, I was probably the worst father you could imagine..."

"In my line of work, you see some fairly bad parenting, Colonel Hunt," Blake said. "I wouldn't be too hard on yourself."

"No, I confess," he said. "I failed her. She had no moral guidance and look where it led her. I'm guilty of that, not Archer. She used that boy; wrapped him around her little finger and led him on. I wasn't so naïve as to believe all that crime-fighting nonsense. I could see through it. The police used her to plant evidence. She was a friendly witness from a respectable family and an informant. Gerald Rees was nothing more than a useful idiot. I don't know what she made him do but from what I heard, she blighted his life. Dead-end job, never married. And look where he is now. In your custody, I imagine, and all because of my daughter."

Blake could see the numbers on the monitor creeping higher. "Well, thank you for your time, Colonel Hunt."

"I'd concentrate on the present," Hunt said. "Don't waste time raking up the past."

"Does your son visit?"

Hunt looked surprised at the sudden question. "You've met him?"

"Briefly," Blake said.

"Then you'll know what an arse he is, too. Bad mannered and hot tempered. Thinks the world owes him everything. He's just waiting for me to die. He might get a shock when the solicitor opens the will." Hunt glanced over to the card on the bedside cabinet. "Might find he's not the only pebble on the beach."

A nurse appeared at Blake's shoulder. "Excuse me Colonel Hunt, the doctor will be here soon as you requested."

"Very good, DCI Blake was just leaving anyway," Hunt said. "And get me a coffee, strong and black."

Back in the Manta, Blake sat, mulling over what Hunt had said. On paper, Gerald Rees looked like the killer; he admitted to chasing Rebecca shortly before she died, he had been at the crime scene but he had no scratches or marks on him. Kettering, the pathologist had said that, from the amount of skin and blood under the victim's nails, the assailant would have scratches on their arms, hands and possibly their face. Rees didn't have a mark on him. But he was hiding something. Blake looked at his watch. He should go home; God knows what that cat would be up to by the time he got back. She had behaved herself last night, as far as Blake knew. He'd settled into his mother's armchair and fallen asleep again after the first sip of the wine. It was Saturday which meant that a visit to Rebecca Thompson's school was out of the question. Maybe a quick chat with Gerald Rees to see if a night in the cells had changed his attitude would be a good idea.

CHAPTER 18

A night in the cells hadn't agreed with Gerald Rees. He'd looked rough when they brought him in, but he obviously hadn't slept much last night and worry etched his face. Gareth Cornell, his solicitor wasn't best pleased about being dragged in on a Saturday; he sat in a crumpled shirt, his tie slightly askew. Clearly, he did his ironing on a Sunday, Blake thought.

"My client has had an unpleasant night, DCI Blake," Cornell said. "Unless you have any actual evidence that he committed this crime, I'll be insisting you release him later today."

Blake raised a hand. "We're just waiting on forensic evidence, Mr Cornell," he said. "Besides, I could charge him with assaulting a police officer right now, if I wanted. Not to mention perverting the course of justice. Of course, we can clear this all up if Mr Rees cooperates with us."

"I've already told you," Rees said. "I didn't kill the girl."

"So you just took the boots. How could you see a young girl lying there and your first thought is to take the shoes off her feet? It beggars belief."

Rees pursed his lips and looked down at the table. "I'm not proud of that," he said. "But I didn't know what to do..."

"Phone the police. Call for an ambulance. Either one of those would have been an obvious place to start," Blake said. He tried a different tack. "Where do you think those shoes have been all this time?"

Gerald looked up at him. "I-I don't know. Gary Archer, perhaps? He killed Drucilla after all."

"Yes, that's one of our lines of inquiry, Gerald," Blake said. "But, to be honest, I can't see why, after all these years, Archer would pull a pair of shoes from his wardrobe and give them to a charity shop. Can you?"

Gerald stared back down at the table.

"You say these shoes were Drucilla Hunt's and yet, they had Cameron Lock's name written in large letters inside them. Why would anyone do that? Write the name of a child killer inside their shoes? It doesn't make sense."

"Does everything we do have to make sense? Drucilla was a teenager when she died. Surely you did stupid things when you were that age, detective," Gerald said.

Blake smiled. "I suppose so," he said and eased back in his seat. "Tell me about when you first met Drucilla Hunt. The very first time."

Gerald looked a little taken aback but Blake's request had clearly triggered memories. "Well... it was the summer and I was sixteen. August 1980. I was in the library searching for any Science Fiction books I hadn't read." He paused, returning to simpler times. His voice became distant. "I loved that library; the smell of plastic book covers mingled with floor polish. Everything had a place there, including me."

"You were a bit of a loner in your youth?"

"You could say that. I'd just finished my 'O' levels. 'A' Levels would start soon but I had two or three glorious weeks yet. All I wanted to do was read," Rees said. "I can remember the Sun streaming in through the huge library window. Leafing through the books, trying to decide which ones to take out."

"And this is where you met her?"

Rees nodded. "She grabbed my arm. Gave me a shock. She was startlingly beautiful. She reminded me of a blonde Diana Rigg. Hair in a perfect bob, almond-shaped face and piercing blue eyes. Do you remember the Avengers, Detective?"

"A little before my time, sir, but I am aware of the TV series, yes."

"She said, 'Does your name rhyme with 'trees' or with 'grease?' in this cut-glass accent." Gerald fell silent and stared down at the table, not seeing it. Lost in a dream of days gone by. "I said 'trees' and she smiled that funny smile of hers and replied, 'perfect.'"

"How did she know your name?" Blake said, gently, so as not to break the spell.

"It was written on my school bag. Drucilla pointed to a man and said he was 'up to no good.' She said he worked at one of her father's businesses and had far too much money for the job he did. I said that he was obviously waiting for someone because, although he held a book, he was glancing around and not reading. "

"Very astute of you," Blake said.

Rees nodded. "Drucilla said that too. Then a beautiful, tall woman walked in wearing dark sunglasses and a red, wide-brimmed sunhat. She didn't look like she was getting a book out, either. She had this short red dress on and a pair of red stilettos. I noticed how her hand brushed his and he slid the book back onto the shelf. In another moment, they walked out of the library side by side. It was like being in a movie. Drucilla was so excited, she kissed me." He paused again, half-closing his tearful eyes. "It was a long passionate kiss. I'd never touched a girl before that moment, detective. And there was I, skinny, bespectacled book worm, Gerald Rees, kissing Drucilla. Beautiful, clever talented Drucilla. I felt like a hero." He looked up. "That's how we met."

"And that man," Blake said. "That was David Collins, right? The woman was Carly Simmonds, found dead on a canal towpath in Chester."

"I didn't know he was a murderer," Rees said. "Drucilla had said all along that a man who steals from his employer and cheats on his wife is capable of anything. So when the woman's body turned up, we had the dirt on her fancy-man."

"And what was your role in this crime-fighting duo, Gerald?"

Rees paused and then looked a bit crestfallen. "I don't know, really. She used to bounce ideas off me. I'd do jobs for her. Some basic surveillance. I was still at school. Drucilla didn't seem to go to school. I think Daddy paid for a governess or tutor but Drucilla came and went as she pleased. My parents got quite cross about the amount of time I spent away from my studies but I didn't care. I just loved being with her."

"Were you lovers?"

Even though forty years had passed, Gerald reddened at the question. "No," he said, heaving a sigh. "She hugged and kissed me now and then but never like that first time and nothing more than that. But I was hooked by the mere possibility and the thrill of being known as her close friend."

"What about Cameron Lock? How did you help solve that case?"

Gerald swallowed. "Observation," he said. "Drucilla told me he'd exposed himself to her a while back. She said that it was only a matter of time before Lock killed some little kid if he hadn't done so already. So we started to follow him." Rees paused and shifted in his seat. "We'd been watching him for a while and he went onto the Wirral Way, near Willaston. He'd been following a young girl on a bike. Anyway, Drucilla told me to find a payphone and call the police while she went and caught him in the act..."

"So you weren't actually there when she caught Lock?"

"No. I was close behind but she already had him pinned to the ground and the little girl was in tears by her bike."

"Drucilla managed to pin Lock down? He was a big lad by all accounts..."

"She could handle herself," Rees said and Blake thought he saw a twinkle of admiration in the man's eyes. "She did Aikido or something. Besides, Lock might have been big but he wasn't clever."

"And where was Lock's backpack?"

"It was nearby, open with the Bradshaw boy's clothes poking out. We held him until the police came."

Blake rubbed his face with both hands. "Were

you never worried that it was all a bit too easy? Too tidy?"

"What do you mean?"

"Well, why on earth would Lock carry a cumbersome bag around when he was committing opportunist crimes that required him to escape quickly and nimbly if needs be?" Blake said. "A bag containing incriminating evidence."

Gerald blinked at Blake. "I-I don't know."

"And how did you know that Lock would be on that section of the Wirral Way at that time? If he was that predictable, then surely the police would have cottoned on to any patterns."

"Well, Drucilla said she'd been watching him..."

"There's a lot of 'Drucilla said this' and 'Drucilla said that' in your story, Gerald. Do you ever wonder if there was another version of this whole sorry tale?"

"No," Gerald said, his face hardening.

"One in which Drucilla is planting evidence, perhaps?"

"No."

"I think there's more to these stories than you're admitting. I think you went after Rebecca Thompson to retrieve those boots to stop people from opening up the past."

"No comment."

"Oh come on Gerald. You aren't just an avid collector of Drucilla memorabilia, are you? There's a very good reason you took those boots."

"I was just shocked when I saw her in them. She looked... like..."

"Like Drucilla? Oh, behave. You're expecting me to believe that Becky Thompson reminded you of Drucilla? They couldn't have been more different. Or do you mean just from the ankles down?"

"I'm telling you, she was the spitting image of her," Gerald said, close to tears. "Not in her hair or clothes but the look on her face and her mannerisms. Maybe I wasn't thinking straight but to me, it was spooky."

CHAPTER 19

Blake drove home deep in thought. Was Rebecca's death an echo of crimes committed almost forty years ago? He'd had to admit that nothing would come to light by the end of the day and had released Rees on police bail. But that still meant they could call him in at any time for questioning. Blake hadn't finished with him by any means.

The familiar stink met Blake as he let himself into the Lodge. He shook his head. "Why can't you use the bloody litter tray?" He said to the stuffy air. A trail of shattered china ornaments lay strewn across the hall floor where the cat had jumped up onto the shelf over the radiator. A picture of Blake's brother Jeffrey, lay face up, the glass splintered. It was a headshot of Jeff that had been used for one of his novel covers. Mum had said he looked so distinguished but Blake and Rosie his sister agreed their younger brother looked like he had a broom handle up his arse. Serafina was nowhere to be seen.

The landline rang and, startled, Blake snatched it up. "Blake," he said, as if he was at work, then cursed himself for sounding like such an idiot.

"Hello?" It was Jeffrey. Glass scrunched under Blake's feet and for one crazy moment he wondered if Jeffrey knew about his photograph.

"Hi Jeff," Blake said, trying to sound casual.

"Are you okay, Will? Is it a bad time?" Like when was it a good time?

"I'm fine. I've just come in. The cat's made a bit of a mess, that's all."

"Christ, have you still got that cat?" Jeff snorted. "I'd have ditched that thing months ago."

"Yeah, Jeff. I know you would." An awkward pause began to build into a suffocating silence, but Blake let it grow. He hadn't called, Jeffrey had called him, and it was his job to kill the silence between them.

"So, I was just wondering. Have you done anything? About the house?"

"I've been kind of busy, to be honest, Jeff. I haven't had chance to do anything. I'd have thought you'd be too busy to worry about the house; rushed off your feet with book tours or something..."

Blake heard Jeff clear his throat.

"Well, yeah, of course. I'm just working a few pitches up at the moment. Trying to choose a new agent. I just wondered. It's been two years, Will. You've got to let go."

"Let go and sell up, you mean? What's up, Jeff? Run out of money again? For a best-selling author, you always seem a little short of cash. I could lend you another five grand, if you want. It's not like I'm spending my hard-earned wages on wine, women and song and I'm living rent-free in the family abode, so..."

"There's no need to be like that, Will..."

"Isn't there? I never get these calls from Rosie. She seems happy doing her hippy commune shit up there in Scotland. What's the great urgency?"

"There's no urgency. But are you just going to sit there in that house like nothing happened? Is that the plan?"

Blake sighed and rubbed his eyes. "I don't have a plan, Jeff. I just happen to be here. Like I was here when Mum lost her mind. If you want to come up and sort things out, be my guest. I don't care. But don't pretend that you're concerned for my wellbeing when what you want is your share of this house." He slammed the phone down before his brother could answer. For a few seconds, he stared around the floor at the carnage he stood in and thought about his brother's words. *I'd have ditched that thing months ago.*

"Well sod you, Jeffrey," he muttered. "I'm not giving up on her that easily." He pulled the 'Behaviour Saviour' note out of his pocket and thumbed the number into the phone. "Hello?"

The voice sounded more wary than was warranted for an unfamiliar number.

"Hi, my name's Will Blake. The RSPCA at Wallasey recommended your services for my delinquent cat," Blake said, smiling at his own little joke.

"Oh! Right, yes. Great, okay. When do you want me to come and see the cat? I'm free now, if that's convenient."

Blake frowned. The woman sounded a bit too keen. Perhaps there wasn't a huge call for animal psychologists on the Wirral. "Okay," he said. He gave her his address and she told him she could be round in half an hour.

As he hung up, Serafina bolted for the door and vanished through the cat flap. Blake groaned. What were the chances that the cat would wander back in within the next thirty minutes? He was going to look like a right chump or worse, with no cat around. He hurried out into the front and glimpsed a pair of orange eyes glaring at him from the bushes. Then they vanished.

"Food," Blake muttered and hurried back in, banging cupboard doors as he dragged a tin of cat food out and scraped an overgenerous portion into Serafina's bowl. He headed out into the front again, tapping the bowl with a fork and making encouraging sounds. "Come on Sera," he called. "Food. Come on..."

Each house in Rock park was set back in its own garden, far enough from the next to be away from prying eyes but Blake still felt his face reddening. He felt such an idiot. He tapped the bowl a few more times but then caught sight of Serafina sauntering across a garden and away through the bushes into the road. Blake stopped clacking the fork against the bowl and stepped back inside the house. His heart sank as two observations struck him.

One: The place looked like it had been burgled. Shards of glass glittered amongst the headless china ladies lying on the hall carpet. Clothes lay strewn around the lounge and a Matterhorn of dishes awaited an intrepid cleaner to climb them.

Two: What would anyone in their right mind make of the Bates Motel vibe to the house? A single man in his late forties living in an old house on the banks of the river, decorated to the tastes of his eighty-seven-year-old mother. At the very least, Blake would look like a total loser. At the very worst, the woman would run screaming from the house.

With a shake of his head, he pulled out the phone and called Paws for Thought back. "Hi, I spoke to you a moment ago. Look, I've changed my mind. I'm a bit busy today. Sorry for the inconvenience..."

"How busy?" The woman said, not letting Blake finish his sentence.

"Pardon? Well it's just that the cat's made a bit of a mess..."

"I don't mind. You do want to help her, right?"

"Yes, of course."

"I've seen all kinds of mess. She'll keep making a mess until we fix the problem, won't she?"

"Erm, yeah, I suppose..."

"Then I'll be around in twenty minutes. Okay?"

"Okay... fine. See you in twenty minutes. Right." Blake hung up, frowning at the phone. That hadn't gone quite as he'd planned; he'd expected to brush the woman off. He felt like he'd been played in some way; tricked into saying 'yes' too many times until he just agreed to anything. He was a detective; not a gullible pushover but he hadn't even asked how much she charged or how long she would take. This cat was Kryptonite to Blake; reducing him to some kind of gibbering imbecile.

It didn't matter. He didn't have to take this woman's advice and, if she was a pain, he could send her packing. He'd still be left with a psychotic cat but there must be other animal behaviour people around. That's what he kept telling himself but, as he hurriedly tidied the hall and the living room, he couldn't get the impending visit out of his mind.

The doorbell finally rang, and Blake slammed the kitchen door shut on the huge pile of dishes that crammed the sink. He yanked open the front door and stared. "You're the woman from the RSPCA centre."

"Hi, yes. Erm... Laura Vexley. Paws for Thought?"

Blake shook her hand. "You're the Behaviour Saviour?"

She reddened. "I'm sorry," she said. "I don't like to mix my roles and the RSPCA might take a dim view of me touting for trade on company time. So I didn't tell you when I gave you my number. But you looked like you needed help. Can I come in?"

"Please do," Blake replied, stepping back. "I'm sorry about the décor. It's my mother's house. I'm not sure where Serafina is; she ran out before. She probably won't show up for hours..."

"Serafina," Laura said, looking around the hall. Blake blushed wondering what she thought of the peeling paint and ageing décor. "That's something to do with angels isn't it?"

He couldn't help grinning. "I think so. I don't know where my mother got the name for her. If that cat is an angel, she's a fallen one, that's all

I'm saying."

"There's a witch called Serafina in Pullman's Northern Lights books, too," Laura said. "Ever read them?"

Blake shook his head and glanced out into the hall where Jeffrey's glassless photo sat. "I'm not a great fan of books. Don't get much time to read."

"You should make time," Laura said, firmly. "With a name like yours, I thought you'd be a poet..."

Blake groaned. "My name is what probably put me off English lessons for ever. So, no."

"How long is it since your mother passed away?"

"Well, it's complicated," Blake said. "Two years, give or take."

He led Laura into the living room, feeling that same flush of embarrassment. "And you live alone here?" she asked.

"You can tell?" he said, widening his eyes in fake horror. Laura flashed a white smile at him. "Look," he said. "What's this got to do with the cat?"

"Sorry, Mr Blake. I just like to get a bit of background. There are reasons why your cat is aggressive and not using her litter tray but they don't exist in isolation. So has Serafina's behaviour changed since your mother's death or has she always experienced problems?"

Blake wasn't used to being questioned and he wasn't sure he liked it. He could see Laura's logic, though so he sat warily on the arm of his chair. "My mother didn't 'pass away.' She went missing. She had dementia and let herself out of the house one day. We never found her. You might have read about it in the papers."

"No, I missed that. I'm so sorry," she said. "Has the cat been this way ever since your mother left?"

Blake thought about it. "She was okay at first. Then a bit vocal. A bit clingy; you know, following me round everywhere but this escalation has been more recent. The last sixth months, I'd say."

"I see," Laura said, arching her eyebrows as Serafina came scurrying in and jumped onto Blake's lap. "Here she is. She's gorgeous!"

Blake looked down at the cat, waiting for her to strike. "You think so? Honestly, I don't know what she's up to but normally when I come in, there's crap everywhere and she's demanding food from me. I've cut her rations down quite a bit. She..erm... she farts like a trooper..."

Laura laughed and nodded. "When your mother was... here, would you have described yourself as her prime carer?"

"I did what I could but my job means unpredictable hours. She had quite a package from Social Services, especially towards the end. But, yes, I did look after her when I could."

Laura looked around. "And you don't think your mother could still be alive, somewhere?"

"Well, I don't think she's changed her identity and is living a secret life in Argentina, if that's what you mean," Blake said. "We haven't had her declared dead, yet. I suppose we keep putting it off. Well, I do."

"Siblings?" Laura said.

"Yes," Blake said. Serafina was like a little motor in his lap and he'd sunk back into the chair, the tension slipping away. It had been years since he'd spoken to anyone about anything so intimate. He suddenly felt a little ridiculous and sat up. Serafina stirred. "Can we get back to the cat?"

Laura fixed him with her green eyes and gave him a brief smile. "We can," she said. "How many litter trays?"

"One."

"Try two or even three. In different locations. Cats are fussy about where they go. Feeling she has to go behind the sofa may be increasing her stress levels..."

"You think the cat is stressed?"

"Could be. Maybe she hasn't let go of the idea

that her mistress may return. Nothing in this house is telling her that things have changed. There's just absence. We need to think of a way to fix that." Laura jumped up. "I need to go now. But try the litter trays and give me a call if you think of any ways you can acknowledge that your mother has passed away." She extended her hand and began to leave before Blake had finished shaking it.

"Right," he said as the front door slammed shut. He turned to the cat. "Was that about me or you?"

Serafina gave a hungry yowl and bit at Blake's ankles.

Sunday October 27th

CHAPTER 20

Blake's mobile rang as he was just putting away the last of the dishes. He hadn't even had chance to admire the clean surfaces or wonder why he had felt it was so important to clear up.

"Hi Vikki, what's the problem?" he said.

"Sorry for ringing you, sir but I thought you should know. It's Rory Evans, Rebecca Thompson's friend. There's been a disturbance at the Evans household. Rory has been arrested and his dad is in hospital. I think it might be related to the case. We brought Rory to Birkenhead station. Didn't want to take him to the custody suite."

"I'm on my way," Blake said. He plonked a bowl of cat food down in the kitchen and hurried out of the door.

Twenty-five minutes later, Blake strode into the station. A number of uniformed officers gathered at the desk, talking to DS Vikki Chinn. They looked shaken. One had a cut lip and Blake noticed scratches on their hands.

"What happened?" Blake said.

"A call from neighbours," Vikki said. "Apparently, it sounded as if Rory was murdering Phil.

Some argument about a mobile phone. By the time police got there, Phil Evans was hiding in the bedroom and Rory was banging his head against the door. It took three officers to restrain him and get him down here. The lads are pretty cut-up about manhandling him but he doled out a fair bit of punishment."

"Where is he now?"

Vikki nodded behind her. "In the voluntary interview room, calming down," she said. "Looks like Phil Evans has a broken arm and numerous lacerations. We still aren't sure what caused all the commotion but Rory keeps shouting about Clocky."

"Do we have an appropriate adult who can work with Rory? I'd like to talk with him when he's calm."

"His mother is on her way. She lives over in Liverpool but should be here soon."

"Good," Blake said. "As soon as she arrives let me know. Keep me posted on any statement from Rory's dad, too." He hurried to the room to have a look in on the boy. Rory sat hugging himself and rocking on the bench in the small room. His head was down but Blake could tell he was sobbing from the rhythmic jerk of his head. "Poor kid," he muttered.

Corrinne Todd, Rory's mother, was a tiny powerpack of a woman dressed in leather and carrying a crash helmet. Her long, white hair hung down her back in a plait and her tanned face looked as though it had been sandblasted smooth.

"Where is he?" she demanded, thumping her crash helmet on the reception desk. "Where's my son?"

"He's in an interview room, Miss Todd," Blake said. "It was the safest and quietest place we could put him. He's not in any trouble but we're trying to get to the bottom of what happened. It may be connected with the recent death of his friend, Rebecca Thompson."

Corrinne Todd looked as though Blake had just sworn at her. "That bitch? She was never his friend, mate. I thought Phil had warned her off months ago."

"I understood that they hung around together," Blake said.

Corrinne pulled that face again. "They did but they were never friends. Becky Thompson was a manipulative little cow and a bully. She messed our Rory's head up. You ever see a puppy that's been slapped and stroked and slapped and stroked, until it doesn't know what to think but runs back to its master every time? That was our Rory. To be honest, when I heard she was dead, I thought 'good riddance.'"

"Really?" Blake said, glancing over at Chinn.

"I'd like to talk with Rory about what happened but I'll be led by you. If you don't think it's wise now, that's fine, you can take him home and we'll catch up later."

Corrinne looked Blake up and down as if seeing him for the first time. "Thanks," she said. "I'll go and have a chat with him. See how he feels. You wait outside and out of view and we'll see."

Blake and Chinn stood outside the room while Rory spoke to his mother. It seemed like the anxiety attack had burnt itself out as Rory looked spent. Corrinne popped a head outside the cell and gave them a nod. "Just a couple of minutes. Then I've promised I'll take him home on the motorbike. He loves that."

"Hi Rory," Blake said, gently as he sat down on the bench next to him. "How are you feeling?"

Rory shrugged. "Not good. Three out of ten. Is Dad okay?"

"Cuts and bruises and a sore arm, apparently. He'll be fine. What happened at the house, Rory?" Blake said.

"It was Clocky on the phone," Rory whispered, his left foot starting to tap rapidly. "Clocky on the phone."

"Take a breath, son," Corrinne said, hugging him tightly round the shoulders and rocking slightly. Rory's foot slowed down.

Blake waited. "Clocky... phoned you," he said. "How did you know it was Clocky?"

Rory looked up at him, his face blotched with tears. "He used her phone. He said she was with him and soon I would be too."

"Steady, Rory. Take your time. Breathe slowly," Blake said. He waited again. "Whose phone number was it, Rory?"

"Becky's it was Becky's phone. Clocky was phoning me on her phone because he killed her and now he's coming for me." Rory sobbed and bit his lip. Blake noticed a dark stain at his crutch. The poor lad had wet himself.

"Can I borrow your phone, Rory? Just to see and make sure for myself?"

"I'm not lying," Rory said, rummaging in his jacket pocket. "I'm not."

Blake took the phone. "I'm sure you're not, Rory. There just might be another explanation for this." He looked at the phone, Rebecca's number showed up several times last night and during the day.

"Dad said it was just someone messing around but I know. I know. He kept saying to leave it! He went mad at me." Rory lowered his head. "I went mad at him."

Blake knelt down in front of Rory. "None of this is your fault, Rory. Someone did make those calls and we'll find out who because whoever has that phone is holding onto evidence from a crime scene. I swear, Rory, whoever made the calls is not Cameron Lock. He was just a boy about your age. He died almost forty years ago. I'm not even sure he killed the little boy they said he did."

Rory looked up at Blake, frowning. "He's a ghost, like Michael Myers in the films..."

Blake shook his head. "No. He was just an ordinary boy who had a sad life. That's all he was."

"Do you have a picture of him?" Rory said, hugging himself and looking at the floor.

"If Mum says it's okay, DS Chinn can show you some of the files about him. There's a picture of Cameron Lock."

"Okay," Rory said, slowly.

"Can I borrow your phone for a while? We can track the signal next time he rings," Blake said. Vikki Chinn frowned at him but said nothing.

A faint smile twitched Rory's lips. "Like you'll put a trace on the call?"

"Exactly," Blake said, nodding. "I'll give you your phone back as soon as I've traced the call. Deal?"

"Deal!" Rory said and held his hand up for a high five. Blake slapped his palm, trying not to wince at the enthusiasm with which Rory slapped back. Outside, he instructed Vikki to show Rory a few details about Lock's background and a photograph. "Just emphasise how ordinary he was."

"Right, sir. Where are you going?"

"To apprehend the little shit who has Rebecca's phone but I'll need some uniformed back-up," Blake muttered.

"Back-up, sir?"

"Yeah, if only to stop me from tearing the scrote's head off. Because I know EXACTLY who's doing this."

CHAPTER 21

There were a number of missed calls on Rory's phone, presumably during the time the poor boy was clobbering his father. The Manta had refused to play ball when Blake had turned the key in the ignition. He'd spent several frustrating minutes listening to it turn over and then die before he told one of the uniformed officers to get a car. Now he sat in the passenger seat of a marked car with one officer driving and a female officer in the back. They'd been there half an hour and the constables were getting restless.

"Are we going to knock on the door, sir?" The driver said, peering up the gravel drive at the immaculate house.

"In a moment," Blake said. "It shouldn't be long." Rory's phone rang again, flashing up Rebecca Thompson's name or rather 'Beka' as Rory had typed it in. Blake answered it and then killed the call. "That should annoy the little get. Come on."

The phone started ringing again as Blake knocked hard on the door. Ted Waters answered, his face a picture of puzzled indignation. "Detective Blake," he said. "Can I help you?"

Blake answered the call and put it on speaker

phone. "It's me, Clockeeee. Are you there Rory? I'm coming to get you," said a squeaky but recognisable voice. "Why don't you kill yourself?"

Blake hung up. "Can Gavin come out to play, please, Mr Waters?" he said.

Ted Waters' face hardened, and he stepped aside. "He's up in his room, second on the left at the top of the stairs. Be my guest."

An hour later, Gavin Waters sat in the interview room with his mother beside him. Ted Waters, it seemed had washed his hands of his son and was taking his daughter out for a meal. Rebecca's mobile phone sat on the table in front of them. Blake leaned forward and explained to Gavin that the interview was taped and that he wasn't under arrest… yet. His mother, in a slightly different-coloured sloppy jumper and tight jeans than the ones Blake remembered last time, sat opposite smiling benignly and nodding as he explained.

"So, you can start by telling us how you came by Rebecca Thompson's phone," Blake said.

"Sorry to interrupt but," Mrs Waters said, as if she was about to offer them all sandwiches, "well, does Gavin have to answer any of these questions. Legally, I mean."

"No, Mrs Waters," Blake said. "He doesn't but we may then have to charge him with taking a phone from a crime scene, perverting the course ofjustice, making

threatening phonecalls, causing a disturbance of the peace and possibly even conspiracy to murder."

Mrs Waters went pale. "I think, Gavi,'" she said. "That under the circumstances, you'd better just answer all their questions."

Gavin sat silent and as pale as his mother.

"So," Blake said. "Where did you get Rebecca's phone from?"

"I nicked it from her, didn't I? Just before she went home..." He lowered his head. "Before she was murdered."

"And why did you do that?"

Gavin pursed his lips and glanced at his mother. "Can't say."

"Look Gavin," Blake said. "Whatever you think is too dreadful to say in front of your mother just isn't, okay? We're talking about murder here. Rebecca was strangled to death. What's worse than that?"

Gavin took a breath. "We were smoking weed."

"Oh my," Mrs Waters said, her back straightening and her self-control, clearly cast-iron after years of living with Ted Waters, kicked in; she said nothing more.

"Go on," Blake said.

"She was blabbering on about how great she was, as usual; how she was getting more weed that night and how I needed to get more cash to buy my share. So I thought, 'you know what? I bet she's ripping me off. This stuff costs me a fortune and I never see the dealer. It all goes through Becky."

"So you stole the phone to get the dealer's number?"

Gavin nodded. "Yeah. I watched her for a bit and learned her PIN. I was going to see how much the dealer charged and then rat on Becky for selling it on at a higher price."

"That's not very nice," Blake said.

"She wasn't very nice," Gavin said. "Always going on about how she was better than us. Cleverer and smarter..."

"Then why did you hang around with her if she was so mean to you?"

Gavin lowered his head. "Because we had nobody else, did we? We're the freaks at school, aren't we? The 'special' kids." He looked up. "We kind of got used to it and she kept the bullies away, a bit."

Blake felt a twinge of compassion and thought about Gerald Rees being trailed along by Drucilla Hunt, pouncing on and treasuring to the tiniest nugget of affection.

“But she was proper stoned this time and wouldn’t shut up about how she was a cut above the rest of us,” Gavin said.

“A cut above?” Blake said, frowning.

Gavin waved his arms about as if he could pluck the words from the air. “Yeah, that's what she said. She said she was real posh. Like royalty. She reckoned she was adopted or some shit like that. She said her mum and dad weren’t her real parents and another family were going to claim her back. Like I said, she was out of it. Talking bollocks.” He gave his mum a sidelong glance.

"Did she say who these people were? This other family?”

“Nah,” Gavin said. “She said she was going to meet them soon.”

Blake pursed his lips and caught Mrs Waters' eye whose smooth, botoxed brow gave a faint ripple of apology. “Gavin,” Blake said. “Why didn’t you tell me this sooner?”

Gavin swallowed. “I didn’t remember properly. I was out of it too. We’d gone down to the common to smoke. Rory hadn’t come with us because his saddo of a dad told him he had to come home and he wasn’t allowed to use dope.”

“Neither are you, young man,” Mrs Waters said

and even Blake flinched a little at the waspish tone.

"So Rory's dad knew about the cannabis?" Blake said.

"Yeah. I'd had him down for a proper stoner, the way he dresses but he's mental. He threatened Becky."

Blake thought about Corrinne Todd's comment earlier about Phil Evans warning the girl off. "Threatened her when?"

"A couple of weeks ago. He said he'd kill her if she didn't stop smoking dope around Rory. Said it would do Rory's head in. I think it might have mellowed him out..."

"A bit like your helpful phonecalls did?" Blake said, slamming his hand on the table. "Mr Evans has a broken arm and Rory had to be physically restrained. Police officers were injured. I don't really want your thoughts on the therapeutic benefits of marijuana, Gavin, I just want plain facts."

"I was only winding him up," Gavin said, his voice weak. "It was a joke."

Blake ignored the comment. "This 'other family' of Rebecca's. when you said she was going to see them soon. Do you think she could have meant that night?"

"I don't know, do I?" Gavin said. "It could be.

She didn't say, like, 'I'm going to meet Big Bro' tonight' but she said she would meet him very soon."

"Big Bro?"

Gavin pointed at Rebecca's phone. "That's his name on her contacts."

It had been a simple thing to get his number, given her connections. She tucked in the sheet under the mattress and smoothed it down. Plumping the pillows, she gave a satisfied smile. The right tool for the job had been located and awaited her downstairs. It was a stroke of luck that she'd found it in the shed when she was looking for the secateurs. She considered taking the secateurs for a fleeting second but then she'd dismissed the idea. There was no need for them. A simple phone call once she had reached her destination and it would all just happen. Fast.

She frowned for a moment. It could go wrong, of course. A broad grin replaced the frown and she flapped the duvet high over the bed. It wouldn't go wrong. She felt powerful and in control. She would be in place, ready when he arrived and that would be an end of it. An end of him. One more down.

Monday October 28th

CHAPTER 22

The Incident Room was abuzz with the news of Rebecca's mobile phone turning up. Blake stood in front of the detectives and glanced behind at the board. Alongside Rebecca Thompson's photograph, and the pictures of the crime scene were some headings in block capitals and a picture of Phil Evans.

"Some new lines of enquiry have emerged," Blake said. "It seems that Rebecca was a frequent user of cannabis, so I want to track down her dealer. She had him on speed dial under the incredibly cryptic heading of 'Mr Weed.' We tried calling but he wasn't picking up." There were a few smiles around the room. "The death could be related to debt or a disagreement. I find it strange that her parents didn't know or suspect anything, so we need to talk to them again."

Kinnear raised a hand. "Wasn't Gary Archer, the fella nicked for Drucilla's murder a dealer?"

"Good point," Blake said. "Worth keeping in mind. Cryer, any news on Gary Archer?"

DI Cryer looked like she'd won the lottery. "Yep, sir," she said. "No offences after he was released from prison. Looks like he went straight. But in 2005, he had a motorbike accident on the

A540. Shunted from behind at red lights by an articulated lorry that couldn't stop in time. Due to extensive spinal injuries, he was paralysed from the waist down. He's been confined to a wheelchair ever since."

"So he couldn't have killed Rebecca," Blake said. He frowned at Cryer. "You've found something else, haven't you?"

"You asked me to check up on Eric Stafford, the ranger at the woods. He's not known to us. Clean as a whistle apart from a speeding offence a year ago. 35 in a 30 zone. BUT..."

Blake blinked at her, "But?"

Cryer beamed. "Eric Stafford and Gary Archer live at the same address."

"Really?"

"I know, strange, right? I double checked it, thinking it was a clerical error or something but sure enough, Stafford and Archer both live at Four Spital Cottages. The house is registered in Archer's name," Cryer continued, breathlessly. "So I mentioned Stafford's name to my cousin who's lived round that neck of the woods for years. She told me that Archer is Stafford's grandfather."

"Excellent work, Kath. I was kind of hoping the new leads might separate the deaths of Rebecca Thompson and Drucilla Hunt but they keep crisscrossing each other. Right. So we have a dealer, unknown as yet. Cryer, could you look into any Bromborough locals nicked recently for dealing? It strikes me that Rebecca and her little posse didn't travel much beyond Eastham or Bromborough, so they probably shopped locally. The other lead we have is Big Bro," Blake said. "Kinnear, any thoughts?"

"I'll need to look more closely but from what I can see, calls to Big Bro started six months ago. There are intermittent bursts of text and then gaps of a couple of weeks. The texts seem to be suggesting a meeting place; Rebecca saying how she can't wait to meet up, Big Bro never has another name and sounds just as eager to meet her. Calls her Lil Sis."

"Where and when was the last meet?"

"About six weeks ago. September 12th at the Compass pub in Bromborough, 2pm," Kinnear said. He looked up. "Classy."

The Compass was a well-known dive at the heart of what used to be Bromborough's council housing estate; a huge, brick-built cathedral to booze that sold cheap lager and cider all day. You only went into the Compass if you were up to no good, wanted to get very drunk very quickly or both. The kind of place where your feet stuck to the floor even after you'd stepped out of the pub. The local residents frequently raised concerns about the pub and few drank in there. Rumour had it that its days were numbered and the council were just waiting for the chance to revoke its alcohol licence.

"Could we ring him? Or text him on Rebecca's phone? Arrange a meet?" Cryer suggested.

"It's a possibility," Blake said. "But our friend Gavin didn't just send whacky phonecalls to Rory Evans over the weekend. So we can assume that Big Bro may be alerted to the fact that the phone has fallen into someone else's hands. Try a text. Just a 'hello' or something."

Kinnear texted but a few seconds later it came up as failed to send. "Looks like the phone is off. Probably destroyed, sir, but I'll keep trying."

"Okay, Vikki and Alex get down to the Compass and see if you can jog any memories of September 12th," Blake said. "Kinnear, you keep checking the phone for anything that might help."

"Will do." Kinnear settled down to his desk, thumbing and scrolling through the phone.

"Me?" Blake said to nobody. "I'll go and pay Big Phil Evans a visit."

The Manta had sputtered into life when Blake ended his shift the previous night which had made him groan; an intermittent fault played to his greatest weakness. Now he'd keep putting off getting the bonnet open and the car would keep letting him down. Maybe at the weekend he'd have a look at it but as he pulled up outside the Evans Household, he put that to the back of his mind.

Rory answered the door, looking rather sheepish but at least he was calm.

"Hi, Detective Inspector Chief Blake," he said, raising a hand. "Do you want to speak to my dad?"

"Hi, Rory, yes please," Blake said, stepping into the cluttered house. "Did you get a call from Gavin?"

"Yes," Rory said. "He said he was very sorry but I'm not going to hang around with him anymore. Mum says he's a jerkoff. I told him."

"Good for you, Rory," Blake said. "Your mum's a good judge of character."

"So is Gavin," Rory said. "He agreed with my mum that he was a jerkoff."

Big Phil Evans sat watching a TV programme about properties abroad. The big man had cushions supporting his hips and his arm which was encased in an impressive plaster.

"Dad, it's Chief Blake," Rory said, making Blake feel like somebody out of a Batman cartoon.

"Detective Blake," Evans said. "Can't get up, sorry." He nodded at the plaster.

Blake settled on the chair opposite Phil. "That's no trouble, Mr Evans," he said and looked up at Rory. "Is it alright if your father and I talk in private?"

Rory nodded but didn't move.

"Go up to your room for a bit, Rory and listen to some music on your headphones while Detective Blake and I have a chat, okay?" Phil said.

Rory nodded again, gave a little salute and vanished upstairs.

"Thanks for the other day," Phil said. "I didn't know how we were going to get him down from that one."

"No problem," Blake replied. "I realised what had happened the moment Rory mentioned the phone calls. I think Gavin Waters has learnt his lesson."

Phil Evans' face darkened. "I hope so," he muttered.

"There is something I'd like to talk about though, Mr Evans," Blake said. "When I was interviewing Gavin about why he had the phone, he told me that you'd threatened Rebecca Thompson. Could you explain that to me?"

Phil Evans shrugged his big shoulders. "I tried to put the frighteners on her, didn't I? She was smoking dope and trying to get Rory into it. Rory's got enough problems without being high as a kite, too. Plus the stuff they smoke these days, it's really strong, not like what we used as kids. I didn't want Rory getting mixed up in that sort of crap. He's obsessive and gets hooked on things easily, give him one biscuit and he'll eat the whole friggin packet." He looked down at his huge stomach and grinned. "Dunno where he gets it from."

"So you approached Rebecca and what happened?"

"I caught up with her after school a couple of weeks ago and laid down the law. Told her what would happen if Rory came home stoned or stinkin' of grass."

"And what did you say would happen, Mr Evans?"

Phil Evans reddened and cleared his throat. "I- I said I'd... kill her but I was just trying to scare the little cow. Honest, I wouldn't've done nothin'. You've got to believe me."

"Perhaps, Mr Evans, but you have to admit that it doesn't look good. You threaten a girl and she turns up dead two weeks later."

"Please. Honest. I never saw her again after that. I wouldn't harm a fly," Phil winced as he shifted in his chair.

"Whoever killed Rebecca had a fair scrap with her. She scratched them quite badly. You're covered in cuts and bruises..."

"That's from Rory. He's bloody strong when he loses it. And he can't control it. He's broken my arm in two places," Phil Evans lifted his plaster slightly and winced.

"We have a ton of DNA evidence from under Rebecca's fingernails," Blake said. "I'm trusting your word at the moment but we'll need samples from you. This is a murder investigation."

"I'll give you any kind of sample you want. I swear down; I was here with Rory. He'll tell you. I was trying to calm him down. All evening. The neighbours probably heard the racket."

Blake nodded and made a note to check. "Any ideas where Rebecca got the cannabis from?"

Evans glanced around the room as though someone might be listening. "No," he said. "I'm not a grass, Detective Blake but I really wouldn't have a clue. It's been donkey's years since I bought any round here. I think the Compass would be a good place to start but you don't need me to tell you that."

Blake stood up. "Yes," he said. "It seems like all my leads are pointing me that way."

CHAPTER 23

DI Cryer phoned Blake just as he arrived back at the station. "I've got a name, sir," she said. "Adam Sampson, he lives on the Dale Estate in Eastham. He's been arrested for possession and supplying. Currently has a suspended sentence. He looked like a weak link, if you know what I mean? A stretch inside hanging over his head. D'you want me to see if I could talk to him?"

Blake thought for no more than a second about the pile of paperwork waiting for him on his desk before answering. "Yes, in fact I'm just in the carpark. Come down and we'll go together."

The Dale Estate was built in the seventies and was a curious mixture of small rows of houses and blocks of low-rise flats. Most were well-maintained, their high fences creosoted and clean windows. Every now and then, a row would be punctuated by a shabby, broken house with an overgrown garden littered with old sofas or a broken fridge on its side. Others looked poorly maintained; rented accommodation where the boundary of responsibility for the upkeep of the place was blurred between owner and tenant. Adam Sampson occupied a small end terrace that reminded Blake of Rory Evans' place only with the dilapidation turned up to eleven. The downstairs windows were boarded over and the upstairs had sheets hanging up over them. Bottles and cans littered the path up to the peeling front door which looked like it had been kicked in a time or two.

"You knock on the front door," Blake said. "I'll go round the back."

Cryer nodded and Blake slipped around the side of the house to the passageway at the rear. The wiry skeleton of an old mattress, old wheelie bins and lengths of smashed fibre board filled the alleyway. Blake picked his way through them to the rotten timber fence that stockaded an equally overgrown and rubbish-strewn back garden.

He waited, straining his ears for the sound of Cryer's knock or any movement from the house. Blake was beginning to wonder if anyone was actually in when the sound of the back door scraping open alerted him. Stealthy footsteps hurried through the long grass. The gate in the fence rattled and a pale face peered round it.

"Hello, Eric," Blake said. "Shouldn't you be at work?"

Eric Stafford's eyes widened and he pushed the gate wide open. The fence holding it up was so rotten that the gate came off its hinges, catching Blake full in the face. Pain lanced through his forehead and he staggered back. The sound of Stafford's footsteps receding up the alley echoed in his throbbing head. Blinking and dazed, Blake started after the disappearing figure of Stafford but something snagged at his feet and suddenly the world turned upside down. The ground rose up and beat the breath out of Blake's body. Confused, he looked at his feet and realised that they were tangled in the rusted coils and springs of the old mattress. Cursing, he pulled himself free and staggered to his feet. The alleyway ahead of him was empty. Stafford had escaped.

Cryer, it appeared, had been more successful. A mournful Adam Sampson sat in the back of Blake's Manta, staring out of the window.

"What happened, sir?" Cryer said as Blake staggered back round to the front of the house. "Are you hurt?"

"Only bruised pride, Kath, that's all," Blake said, grimacing as he massaged his back. "I'm going to have a word with the local council about keeping those alleys clear." He peered into the back of the car. Adam Sampson looked about fifteen with an acne-riddled face and a mop of greasy brown hair held down by a black baseball cap. He had a chunky gold chain round his neck and a black T-Shirt with an image of a topless woman writhing across the front. Friendship bracelets and leather bands queued up at the boy's wrists.

"Where d'you find Ali G?"

"Cheeky beggar was smoking a spliff as he answered the door," Cryer said. "I arrested him on the spot. Don't know if there are any others in there. Thought it might be risky going in alone..."

"He'll do," Blake said. "Eric Stafford appeared out the back but he got away."

"Stafford? Really?"

"Interesting, yeah?" Blake said, going round the other side of the car and sliding onto the back seat next to Sampson.

"What you doin' man?" Sampson said, pressing himself against the passenger door to make as much space as possible between him and Blake.

"Just thought we'd have a little chat before we take you down to the station and call the probation service. You're going to prison, Adam."

"It was just one spliff, man," Sampson said. "I is just relaxing, innit?"

Blake winced. "And you can drop the weird accent, too, Adam. This is the Wirral, not the mean streets of Brixton."

Adam looked down at his wristbands. "Okay."

"I'm Detective Chief Inspector Blake, Adam. I want to ask you a few questions. If you tell me something I like, then I may let you get out of the car and finish your spliff in the comfort of your own home. If you keep up with that accent and don't tell me anything, then I'll take you down to the station, send you to prison and have your house raided and searched. How does that sound?"

Adam nodded. "I- I'll help if I can… but, I don't know nothin'"

"So, what was Eric Stafford doing in your house?"

"Just visiting," Sampson said. "We went to school together. We're mates, like."

"Mates," Blake said. "Right. So he pops out of work in the middle of the day, just to say hello?"

Adam looked out of the window but Cryer was staring in at him so he looked back to Blake. "Yeah, we're good mates."

"Where did you get the weed, Adam?"

"The Compass. Out the back. Some guy was there selling it."

"Who, Adam?"

Adam shrugged. "Dunno, never seen him before. He had a Manc accent. Wasn't from round here."

"You're lying to me," Blake sighed. "Guess we'll have to go down to the station after all then."

"No! Please!" Adam said almost grabbing Blake's sleeve. "I can't go back. Please. I can't."

"Tell me where you got the weed then," Blake said.

"I can't tell you," Adam said. "He'd kill me."

"Who would?"

Adam pursed his lips. "Look, Eric is a good mate of mine," Sampson said at last. "He looks after his grandad. He helps him tend his garden and everything. His grandad is dead good with plants and stuff. They've got those raised beds so he can garden from a wheelchair. That's all I'm saying."

Blake thought for a while. "So... you're saying that Eric's grandad grows lots of plants. Herbs and the like. For selling?"

Adam looked at him. "I'm not saying any more. Eric's a big lad with a temper. Very handy, too. I don't wanna get on the wrong side of him."

"Okay," Blake said. "Out you pop. I'm giving you until five this evening to clear out whatever you've got in your flat. Then I'm sending a team in. Dogs, the lot..."

"But you said..."

"If you're not happy, we can talk about it down at the station."

Adam's shoulders slumped and he climbed out of the Opel Manta. "That's a dope car, man," Adam said. "But you're not cool."

"Bugger off before I arrest you for that terrible accent, too!" Blake yelled. He shook his head and watched Sampson stamp back up to his front door then pulled out his phone. "Vikki. Can you and Manikas go over to Eric Stafford's asap and look the place over as best you can. If Stafford turns up, arrest him for assaulting me. That'll do for now but I want to get a warrant to search the place and need to know the layout.

"Okay, sir," DS Chinn said. "Are you hurt?"

"Nah," Blake said. "But my ego will make a better recovery if we pick up Stafford. Cryer and I are on our way over."

CHAPTER 24

Number Four Spital Cottages was a surprisingly large property to be called a cottage. Standing on the main road from Bromborough to Bebington, it looked as though it had once been a number of smaller houses knocked into one.

Other properties huddled beside it and tall trees grew in the front gardens, cutting them off from the outside world. A thick holly hedge made it difficult to see the house properly but the top half of the building rose above, revealing four or five bedroom windows set in red, engineering brick from the early nineteen hundreds. The roof looked at odds with the quaintness of the rest; modern tiles with smooth, opaque skylights set in them.

DS Chinn frowned up at them. "That's quite a house for an ex-con who hasn't worked for years."

DC Manikas shrugged. "Perhaps. Maybe he got some compensation from the motorcycle accident."

They parked the car in the road and tried, unsuccessfully, to peer over the hedge. "Listen," Chinn said. A constant rush of air sounded from somewhere deep in the building. "Air con?"

"Or ventilation," Manikas said. "Look at those skylights, too. The light is shining out of them, not in."

"Let's talk to the neighbours before we knock on the door," Chinn said. "Just see if our suspicions are justified."

The house on the left of number four had a beautifully tended front garden. Even though the trees had shed their leaves, the lawn was clear and cut short. The soil in the flower beds was dark and rich, not a weed in sight. An old woman with a shock of short, white hair and wearing a waxed jacket was gently pruning some roses. She greeted them with a smile. "Can I help you?"

Chinn flashed her ID. "Merseyside Police, ma'am. I'm DS Chinn, this is DC Manikas. We were wondering if you knew who lived next door?"

The woman straightened up from her plants and gave a slight grimace. "Sorry," she said. "I'm not getting any younger. Next door. Yes, Mr Archer and his grandson, Eric. Lovely boys." She frowned. "Are they alright?"

"Absolutely fine, ma'am," DS Chinn began.

"Call me Monique," the lady said. "Monique Taylor. What do you want to know? They're very quiet. I hardly see them from one week's end to the next but they're always polite and neighbourly. Eric always puts my bins out every fortnight. He's very early. Never actually see him do it. Gary can't do much, being wheelchair bound, poor man, but he always gives me a cheerful hello when we meet. We talk gardening over the fence."

"Have you noticed anything unusual about the house? Funny noises or smells?"

Monique pulled a face. "Nothing recently. Of course, there's that extractor fan always on the go day and night but apparently that's for Gary. He needs a rarified atmosphere," Monique dropped her voice, "because of his condition. You know he was hit by a lorry a while back. I think he picks up infections quite easily."

"I see," Chinn said, glancing over to Manikas. "Nothing else?"

"Not really," Monique said. "Sometimes the cleansing fluid smells a bit but I quite like it..."

"Cleansing fluid?" Manikas said, looking confused.

"Yes," Monique said. Her face reddened. "I feel a little embarrassed talking about such personal matters. Gary explained it all to me. Because of his... condition, he has to use a lot of cleaning fluids. It must be hard, you know, to get to the toilet and whatnot. So he has a tank of disposable personal items. Every couple of months, the people come to empty it and take it all away.

So there's a bit of coming and going, vans and suchlike and the smell. I feel so sorry for Gary. He's such a martyr to his injuries. He never complains."

DC Manikas rubbed his chin. "He sounds quite a trooper, Monique. You said you sometimes talk over the garden fence. Is there any chance we could come into your back garden and have a look over?"

"I don't see why not but what for?"

"We aren't allowed to say at the moment, Monique," DS Chinn said. "It would be really useful if we could see the property from the back, though."

Monique shrugged and led the way behind her house and into a much larger garden. Most things were dormant now but Chinn imagined it would be quite a place in the Spring and Summer. The blurred golden outlines of carp shimmered in the waters of a huge pond and a number of red-leaved acers drooped on its banks.

But the distinctive smell and the sound of crackling soon distracted Chinn from the landscaping. "Oh my," Monique said. "He usually warns me if he's having a bonfire."

A massive leylandii hedge ran between Monique's garden and Archer's but a small panel fence filled the gap between a garage and the start of the bushes. Chinn peered over to see a newly lit bonfire beginning to blaze. A man with pigeon-grey hair tied back in a pony-tail and sitting in a wheelchair held a cannabis plant in both hands. “Who the fuck are you?” he squeaked, then threw the plant onto the fire.

It fell in but sent another burning plant tumbling out. It rolled under Archer’s wheelchair, sending flames flickering up his cheap denim jeans. Yelling loudly, he tried to beat them down with his bare hands. Chinn leapt over the fence and dragged Archer from his chair. Tearing off her jacket, she smothered the tongues of fire that were licking their way through Archer’s clothing. Smoke filled the gardens and Chinn felt light-headed. Archer gave a yelp and passed out.

“Call an ambulance, Manikas,” Chinn said, wrapping her jacket around Archer’s legs. “Then let the boss know what’s happened.”

Blake stood beside the ambulance and watched as Archer was wheeled in. The man had regained consciousness but had kept his oxygen mask firmly pressed over his nose and mouth. His eyes were full of anger, fear and resentment at Blake and his team for disturbing what must have been many years of peaceful cannabis farming.

Vikki approached him. “Do you think we should take a look in the house?”

"I think we may need a warrant," Blake said. "After all, you leapt over into Archer's garden to save his life. The fact that he was holding a cannabis plant might not be enough."

DS Chinn nodded in agreement. "He was destroying evidence," she said. "He'd only just started. D'you think Stafford tipped him off?"

"I imagine so," Blake said. "Once I clocked Stafford coming out of the house of a known dealer, he'd realise that we'd come sniffing around here."

"Doesn't really help us with Rebecca's murder, though, sir," Manikas said.

"Let's see if we can find Eric Stafford," Blake said.

"Then maybe we can make sense of this. Adam Sampson more or less admitted that Stafford supplied all the weed round here. It makes sense that Rebecca bought her cannabis from Stafford and a lot of it. He works at the scene of the crime and Adam said he was 'handy'. It doesn't take a huge leap of the imagination to see Eric Stafford as a prime suspect."

"Talk of the devil," Chinn said, looking beyond Blake. He turned to see Eric Stafford running directly at him.

CHAPTER 25

If Eric Stafford was a source of fear for Adam Sampson, Blake struggled to see why. On the face of it, he was a big lad. He worked out, that was obvious. But when Stafford came charging towards him, Blake had stepped aside, grabbed the lads flailing arms and pinned him up against the side of the ambulance. The boy had no real strength in him. No real aggression. His angry yells sounded petulant to Blake.

"What have you done to him, you bastard?" Stafford yelled. "Where's my grandad?"

"Relax, Eric," Blake said. "He's going to be okay. If you hadn't tipped him off, he wouldn't have got injured trying to burn the evidence. I don't think he got very far though, so I'm arresting you for supplying drugs as well as assaulting me, twice. You got any cuffs, Vikki?"

Chinn cuffed Stafford and cautioned him. "Let me just see him," Stafford said, lunging forward towards the ambulance.

Blake nodded and steadied the boy as he climbed into the back of the ambulance. "Grandad, are you okay?"

"I'm sorry, son," Archer said, pulling the oxygen mask from his face. "It was all my fault. I should have waited but..."

"That'll do," Blake said, dragging Stafford back. "Now. I'm pretty certain that when we search your house we'll find quite an impressive cannabis farm in your loft space, Eric. The only question is, are you going to let my officers go in and have a look around or are you going to put me to all the trouble of getting a warrant?"

"Cannabis farm?" Stafford said. "You mental, or what? You're goin to have to get a warrant, mate."

"I'm kind of glad you said that, Eric. It means I can be very specific about what I'm looking for and I can tear the place apart," Blake brought his face close to Eric's.

"And believe me, son, I'm looking for so much more than a few pot plants."

Before sending someone to interview Stafford at the custody suite in Birkenhead, Blake called everyone together. His head throbbed after being hit by the gate earlier that day and he knew he had a shiny new black eye. He leaned on the desk at the front of the Incident Room.

"So, what do we have?" he said. "Any more on this 'Big Bro' character from Rebecca's phone?"

Manikas raised his notebook. “The landlady of the Compass knew Rebecca quite well, even though she was underage. Remembers her meeting a man much older than her on a couple of occasions. One we pinned down to around September 12th which would tally with the text Kinnear found. Described Big Bro as tall, over six foot was the best she could say, dark hair, thinning on top. He wore a dark jacket, green maybe, though, to be fair, how anyone sees anything in that dingy pub, beats me. He also wore red jeans, white shirt. She said he had a posh accent. They used to meet, have a swift drink and then go off somewhere else. She didn’t know where.”

“Okay,” Blake said. “Anything about their demeanour?”

“The landlady said Rebecca always seemed really pleased to see him. Hugs, kisses on the cheek, that kind of thing. She wondered if he was some kind of sugar daddy.”

Blake gave a faint smile. “Haven’t heard that phrase used for a while.”

“She said she tried to find out who he was but Rebecca wasn’t giving anything away,” Vikki said.

“Kinnear?” Blake turned to the Constable sat at his desk.

“Rebecca met with Big Bro nine times since April. The texts are deliberately vague, ‘great afternoon, yesterday, thanks,' or 'I'll meet you at 2pm,' that kind of thing. It's as if they've agreed to keep any written evidence of who they are a secret, which is curious. The meetings are clustered. So there will be three meetings in a week and then nothing for a month or more. It suggests that Big Bro wasn't in the area."

"They might have had other means of contact, social media maybe," Vikki said, glancing over to Cryer.

Cryer gave a grimace but kept her eyes on Blake. "Still working on that one, I'm afraid, Guv."

"She may have used social media to talk to Big Bro but I don't think so," Kinnear conceded, picking up Rebecca's phone. "It's a set pattern of calls and no small talk. The last text from Big Bro is interesting: 'Meet soon. Complications.' That was October 21st. Two days before Rebecca was killed. She didn't respond to it but it looks like they were going to meet up."

"But we can't be sure that they did," Blake muttered. "So we have a man who is 'posh' whatever that means, who has interests elsewhere, possibly but claims to be related to Rebecca. Was he grooming her?"

"Sexually, sir?" Cryer cut in. "You wouldn't claim to be her brother if that was your game, surely. Not unless you were really sick."

Manikas raised his bushy eyebrows. “Unless it’s true and he really is her long-lost brother. It’s not impossible.”

“True,” Blake said, straightening up and wincing slightly. “You and Cryer have a word with Stafford when he’s ready. I’m going to have another word with Rebecca’s mum and dad. Vikki, you can come. Kinnear can you alert Tasha Cook, the Family Liaison Officer that we’re on our way?

For a brief second, Blake wondered whether Mr and Mrs Thompson had moved since he’d last seen them. They still sat in the middle of the sofa, clinging onto each other. Mr Thompson had the beginnings of a scrappy beard and his wife seemed to have aged ten years in the last few days.

“These are really delicate questions I’m going to ask you but I do need to,” Blake said, clasping his hands together. “We’ve evidence that Rebecca was using cannabis quite a lot. Were you aware of that?”

Mr Thompson blinked at Blake as if he’d just slapped him across the cheek. “No,” Thompson said. “Rebecca wouldn’t do that. She was too smart to do drugs. Who told you that? It’s a lie.”

Blake raised his hands. “I’m sorry if these are

upsetting questions, Mr Thompson. I take no pleasure in asking them, believe me," he said. "We haven't had the toxicology reports back but she had the number of a local drug dealer and seemed to make a lot of calls to him. Plus a number of witnesses have said that she smoked cannabis quite heavily." Blake looked to Mrs Thompson.

"I knew," she said in a soft voice. "I tried to talk to her about it but she went off the deep end whenever I did. So I just... kind of... ignored it..." a tear trickled down her cheek.

"You knew?" Mr Thompson said, staring at his wife, as if seeing her for the first time. He broke away from her. "You ignored it?"

"Mr Thompson..." Blake began, trying to face down an argument between them that would slow things down. They could fight all they wanted once he'd left but right now, he needed their full attention.

"Why didn't you tell me?" Mr Thompson said, ignoring Blake.

His wife scowled at him. "And what would you have done? 'Grounded' her? She would have gone out anyway. You'd have gone wading in and driven her even further away from us."

"There were problems between you and Rebecca?" Blake said, trying to regain control of the conversation.

Mrs Thompson nodded. "Yes. She was a free spirit, was Becky. There was a wildness about her… It was in her blood."

"Spoilt by you…" her husband muttered.

"We were always so busy. Too busy. We never gave her the time and so she found her own way," Julie Thompson sighed.

Mr Thompson gave an exasperated hiss. "Let's be honest. She was off the rails. Trouble at school. Trouble with Rory and Gavin. Rebecca seemed to be at war with everyone. Whenever we tried to talk some sense into her, she'd say that we weren't her real family. That we didn't have the right to tell her what to do. I don't know where she got these notions from. She needed some kind of counselling or something." Mrs Thompson said nothing but stared at the carpet, crushing a wad of soggy tissues in her fist.

"Rebecca did have phone contact with somebody she called Big Bro. Is it possible somebody could have been feeding her these ideas?"

"Why would anyone want to do that?" Ken Thompson said.

Blake shrugged. "To manipulate her? I don't know. Mrs Thompson have you any thoughts?"

She shook her head but continued to stare at the carpet.

Blake paused and something clicked into

place. “Mrs Thompson. Do you know anybody currently at the Saint Joseph’s Hospice, by any chance? Someone ill?”

“What are you talking about, Blake?” Mr Thompson cut in.

Blake ignored him. “Julie, did you send a card recently?” he said, gently. “Just signed ‘J’?”

Julie Thompson snapped her head up and stared at Blake. “I want to speak to my husband. Alone.”

CHAPTER 26

"Why do you keep asking about Becky Thompson?" Eric Stafford whined, burying his head in his hands. "I've admitted we've got a cannabis farm in the loft space at home. Can't you just put me on bail or something?"

DI Kath Cryer leaned forward over the desk. "We're asking because you supplied Rebecca Thompson with cannabis and now she's dead. You work in the woods where her body was found. Can you answer the question, Eric? Where were you around 6:30 pm on Wednesday the 9th of this month?"

Stafford glanced over at his brief who looked back at him as if to say, 'I've told you not to say anything but you're going to anyway, aren't you?'

"I knocked off around 5pm," Stafford said. "Picked up some weed and took it to the Compass. I was there until about 8:30."

"Witnesses?" Cryer snapped.

"Kerry, the Landlady'll vouch for me. And I sold some stuff to Adam Sampson, too. He dropped me in the shit. May as well return the favour."

Manikas frowned. "How long have you been running that farm?"

"About ten years, I reckon," Stafford said. "Grandad's lump sum was running out and he didn't have any pension."

"You see," Manikas said. "A decent set-up like yours, shifting decent cash, it always attracts attention. I've known smaller cannabis farms get rolled by other growers to keep the competition down. Yet you keep on going. How come?"

Stafford glanced away. "Dunno. Lucky, I guess."

"Or is it because of your grandad's connections?" Cryer cut in.

"Haven't a clue what you're going on about," Stafford said.

"You DO know what your grandad went to prison for, right?" Manikas said. "He killed a girl. Strangled her. Doesn't that bother you? Your grandad a murderer?"

Stafford's cheeks blazed. "You don't say that about him. He was framed."

"Really? Who by?" Cryer said.

Manikas lowered his voice. "You see, we heard that he took the blame for the murder for a big payoff. That's how he got the house. Has he got connections, Eric? Is he protected? Is that why your business has never been rumbled by anyone else?"

"No," Stafford said. "Look. I admitted growing cannabis and selling it. Why don't you just charge me?"

"We will, Eric, we will," Cryer said, smiling sweetly at him. "So, going back to Rebecca Thompson. When did you last see her?"

"I don't know," Stafford said, throwing his hands up. "A week ago, maybe?"

"Did she usually come alone to buy the drugs from you?"

Stafford frowned, thinking back. "Yeah. No, wait. There was one time when she rolled up in this fancy car. I couldn't see who was in it but she wasn't driving."

"What kind of car?"

"A Range Rover. Dark colour it was, green or blue. Hard to tell. It was night time. I don't know where she got the cash from but she spent a lot of money. I remember that car because I wondered if she was giving blowjobs for cash or something and whoever was in the car was a client." A brief grin spread across his face and then it crumbled into a look of confused disgust. "Thought she might do me a favour... God, she's dead..."

"Nice," Cryer said, icily.

"This car, do you remember anything else about it?" Manikas said. "A registration or anything?"

Stafford picked at his fingernails and then looked up. "Yeah. I did actually. It was one of them personalised ones. Hard to forget."

The Thompsons had only been in the room a matter of ten minutes before Ken Thompson came staggering from the living room, blinded by tears.

He dragged his hand over his eyes. "You happy now, Blake? Now you've got to the bottom of everything?" he said and dragged open the front door, staggering off towards his car.

Blake, Vikki and Tasha Cook, the FLO, had been waiting in the hallway, listening to the increasingly agitated voices in the living room. He nodded in the direction of Ken Thompson. "Chinn, can you follow him. Make sure he doesn't do anything stupid?"

Vikki nodded and hurried after the stricken man. "Did you know?" Cook said, her arms folded. Clearly, she wasn't very happy with the way this had been handled.

Blake shook his head. "More of a hunch. I saw a card next to Victor Hunt's bed in the hospice and when Gerald Rees had said that Rebecca reminded him of Drucilla Hunt, I began to wonder if there was a connection."

"Next you have a 'hunch,' sir," Tasha Cook said in a low voice, "can you share it with me before you go charging in? I can find out with maybe a little more finesse. "

"Fair comment, Tasha. I'm sorry. Shall we go in?"

Julie sat in the same position that they'd left her, a tissue pressed to her nose. "I'm sorry," she said. "I thought he ought to know before I said anything to you. At least I owe him that."

"Do you want to talk about it?" Blake said.

"Or maybe you've had enough for one day and we can come back tomorrow," Cook said, giving Blake a sidelong glance. "You've been through a lot, Julie."

Julie Thompson shook her head. "No," she said. "If you think it'll help find out what happened, then you need to know the truth."

Blake settled on the armchair, leaning towards her, feeling anything but comfortable. "So, Ken isn't Rebecca's biological father?"

"No," Julie said. "Eighteen years ago, Ken was setting up the business. It was early days for the internet and many small businesses hadn't really cottoned on to its power for selling and advertising. Ken was struggling to make his business work. He'd made a few bob over the Millenium bug scare but that ran out soon enough. So it was up to me to make some money. I took three jobs. Bar work in the evenings, a soulless telesales post in an office in Speke and I cleaned for Victor Hunt."

Blake stayed quiet, gently noting down salient points.

Julie Thompson sniffed and wiped her eyes. "Ken was focused on getting the business up and running. Too busy meeting people, playing golf with investors and schmoozing to realise I was depressed. I was carrying the burden while he went off on his great adventure. So I was flattered when Victor Hunt paid me a compliment."

"That's only natural, Julie," Tasha Cook said.

"He was thirty years older than me. A man in his sixties but he was still good-looking in a rugged, well-kept sort of a way. And he was wealthy. Influential. I'd dusted around his office enough times to notice papers and letterheads that showed he had fingers in a lot of pies round here. I wasn't so naïve as to think a fling would last forever but I knew I could swing things in Ken's favour if I played nice with Victor Hunt."

"And it worked?" Blake said.

Julie smiled. "Yes. I had the most wonderful few months being pampered by Victor at the big house. I felt like a teenager again and Ken was so happy because suddenly, there was a rush of interest in his services. I remember him saying that it was like a tap had been turned on." Her smile faded. He told me off about how negative I'd been about all those lunches and meetings on the golf course and look how it had paid dividends. I could hardly put him straight, could I?"

She fell silent for a moment, staring into the past.

"But then you fell pregnant," Blake said, quietly.

"Yes. I knew Victor would lose interest but, you see, Ken and I had been trying for kids for so long with no success. I assumed the problem was with me. The business became Ken's child, his labour of love. And I had a baby of my own." She paused again and smiled, her eyes twinkling with tears. "I stopped my jobs and helped Ken run the business whilst bringing up Rebecca. I thought I was so clever. That I'd got it all; child, husband, business." She lowered her head. Deflating in the chair as if telling the story had taken every last bit of energy.

Tasha Cook slipped next to her on the sofa and put an arm round her shoulder.

Blake's mobile rang, jarring the silence and making him grit his teeth. "Sir?" Manikas said in an excited voice. "Stafford gave us a positive ID on a registration plate for Big Bro. It's a green range Rover HNT34. Big Bro is..."

"Marcus Hunt," Blake said, wearily.

No sooner had he ended one call than another came in. “It’s Vikki. It looks like Ken Thompson is heading into the Hospice. I think you should get over here right away.”

CHAPTER 27

Ken Thompson stood in the middle of Bluebell Ward, holding Victor Hunt by the scruff of his pyjama collar. In his other hand he held an ice pick, presumably left in the boot of his car after one of his outdoor winter adventures. Blake pushed past the uniformed officers and stood next to Chinn. Victor Hunt hung half out of bed, suspended by his pyjama jacket. He looked terrible; grey, his eyes closed tight and a line of saliva drooling from the corner of his mouth.

"I couldn't stop him, sir," Vikki Chinn said. "By the time I'd caught up with him, he'd already got the pick out of his car and run in."

"You did what you could, Vikki" Blake said.

Ken Thompson glared at them. "It's always the Hunts of this world, isn't it, Blake? They take what they want without thinking of anyone else. While we're all working hard, they sit back laughing at us."

"Mr Thompson," Blake said. "Ken. Listen to me. You're not going to accomplish anything by this."

"Have you got a daughter, Blake?"

Blake paused, then nodded. "I did have."

"You did have?" Thompson said, blinking at him, trying to understand his reply.

"She passed away, Ken. Some time ago."

For a brief second, the anger faded from Thompson's eyes as he struggled with what Blake had just said. Then the rage returned. "Well, I never had one. How would you feel if you suddenly discovered you weren't the father? My whole life is a lie. That's what I'm faced with." He tugged hard at Hunt's pyjama jacket, making the old man groan. "All because this reptile fancied my wife and used his power and influence to dazzle her..."

"So what are you going to do?" Blake said. "Kill him? He's got weeks left at most; you'd spend the rest of your life in prison for murder. And how are you going to kill him? With that?" he nodded at the ice pick. "I saw a victim who had been killed with a sharp spike, once. You couldn't imagine the blood. It requires frenzied, repeated blows. It takes a certain type of person to kill someone with a pick like that. You aren't one of those people, Ken."

Ken raised the pick. "Aren't I?"

"No," Blake said, stepping forward. "Look at him. Whatever you think of his past actions, he's a frail old man, now. Are you going to trade your business, your home, your life for a moment of blood and madness?"

Ken Thompson lowered the pick. "I was a father," he said, tears coursing down his cheeks. "A dad..."

"You'll always be those things, Ken. Always," Blake said, inching forward. "All those sleepless nights when Rebecca was a baby, nobody else was there just you and Julie, all those happy moments still happened. You were there when it really mattered. You were Becky's real dad and you always will be."

The ice pick made a loud clunk on the tiled floor as the energy drained from Ken Thompson. He loosened his grip on Hunt and looked at him vacantly. Then, without thinking, he lifted the old man up, plonked him in the centre of the bed and pulled the covers up to his chest. He scrubbed at his eyes and looked over to Blake.

"You going to arrest me now?"

"We'll take you down to the station. Make sure you're okay. Then we'll assess the situation. Do you want DS Chinn to phone Julie and tell her that you're safe? She's worried sick about you."

Ken thought for a moment and then nodded. Blake glanced over to Chinn who nodded back and led Thompson out of the building to the car. Nurses and other staff hurried to reassure the other patients and check they were alright.

Blake stood at Hunt's bedside and the old man looked groggily at him. "He knows, then?" he said and gave a faint, humourless smile.

"Looks that way, Mr Hunt," Blake said.

"She caused so much trouble," Hunt croaked. "If only I'd acted sooner. Maybe we wouldn't be in this mess..." He closed his eyes and Blake was jostled out of the way by a team of nurses.

On his way out of the hospice, Blake phoned Kinnear. "We need to find Marcus Hunt as quickly as possible. He was in the area on Friday. We met him at the house."

"I don't think he'll be there now, sir. It was gutted of furniture, remember?" Kinnear said. "I'll get a check of local hotels done. I'll try the classier ones first. Hunt didn't strike me as a man who liked slumming it. Is there any way his father can help us?"

"No," Blake said. "I don't think the nursing staff would appreciate me trying to question him right now. It turns out that Rebecca and Marcus shared the same father, Victor Hunt..."

"You're thinking that maybe Marcus killed Rebecca because of any inheritance there might be when the old man died, sir?" Kinnear said.

"It's as strong a motive as any. We know Marcus is eager to get his hands on the family fortune; he's sold the contents of the family home with indecent haste. Maybe Marcus found out about Rebecca and just lost it. He's ex-military, a trained killer and has quite a temper on him. Look at the way he threatened us with the shotgun. We need to find him, quick."

"I'll get onto it, sir. Want me to check airports too?"

"If you can, thanks." Blake pocketed his mobile. The light was fading fast. He wanted to go home, open a large bottle of red and watch a mindless film. Anything to block the memories that his conversation with Ken Thompson had unearthed. He felt drained by the encounter and he hadn't missed the curious look Vikki Chinn had given him.

He didn't talk about his past life. There were rumours, he knew that, but he clamped down hard on any speculative questions about family. It was in the past and it was nobody's business. His stomach rumbled and it dawned on him that he hadn't eaten anything all day. Hunt wasn't going to miraculously appear overnight and if he had absconded, then he'd be long gone by now. Blake started the Manta. Or at least tried to. The engine gave a grating cough and remained silent. "Bugger," Blake muttered.

A blue Hyundai sat on the side of the road outside Blake's house. As he paid the taxi driver, Laura Vexley got out and gave him a wave.

"Laura. What brings you out here?"

"I thought you said to meet today. As I left."

Blake frowned. "I don't think I did..."

"Well, I'm here now, so I may as well have a look at Serafina." Laura said, with a shrug and a grin.

Blake grunted and turned to the front door. "I haven't been in all day, so I don't know what to expect."

The air smelt clean as Blake flicked the light on. Everything was in its place, ornaments, Jeffrey's picture, still minus the glass. He'd replace it. One day. They went into the living room and Serafina sat on his mother's armchair, curled up and purring.

"She looks happy enough right now."

Blake's eyes narrowed. "Yes. It makes me suspicious, to be honest. I'm beginning to wonder what she's up to." He scanned the room but it all looked unmolested.

"Can I?" Laura said, pointing at the sofa.

Blake nodded. "Sure." Then he wondered why he always seemed to be saying, 'yes,' to this woman. "Look, I appreciate your concern about the cat but I can't help wondering how much all this is going to cost..."

"Well, that depends on how successful we

are," Laura said. Serafina jumped down from her armchair and up onto Laura's lap. "Hello, princess," Laura cooed and tickled the cat under the chin.

"She certainly trusts you," Blake said.

"Which means she's a terrible judge of character,"Laura said, with a laugh. "Is she using the litter trays?"

Blake nodded. "Yes. I only got them on Sunday. So early days yet."

"Good. And how about you?"

"No, I don't use the litter trays," Blake said, suppressing a smile. "D'you think I should? Set a good example?"

Laura tilted her head and raised an eyebrow at him. "I mean how are you? How do you feel?"

For a second, Blake froze. It had been so long since anyone had asked that question and really meant it. The Super might ask him, but that was more of a 'can you get the job done' kind of question more than a genuine enquiry as to his wellbeing. "I'm fine."

"We're all fine, Mr Blake..."

"Will, call me Will," Blake said, feeling himself blush. "No, I mean, I slept well last night. The cat still demanding food and going for me occasionally, but I feel good. Yeah. I feel more relaxed at home."

“That’s good, Will,” Laura said, gently. Blake stared deep into her green eyes for a moment, then blinked and looked away.

“Anyway,” he said. “The cat. What next?”

“I think you should spend more time with her. Be around.”

“I can’t. I’m in the middle of a serious case.” For a fleeting moment, he imagined standing in front of the Super announcing his need to spend more time with the cat.

Laura shrugged. “Quality time then? Play with her. Does she chase things? Bits of string? Stuff like that?”

Blake looked at her in horror. “Play with her?”

“You’re in a vicious cycle at the moment. You come in tired, restrict her food. She lashes out at you. You yell or whatever. Just be around her. Be calm. Be fun.” Blake noticed the quirk in her lips as she gave a faint smile. “You can do ‘fun’ can’t you?”

Blake frowned. “I don’t know,” he muttered.

“Maybe we need to work on that, too,” she said, giving him a knowing grin. “But I’ll have to go. Call me, soon.”

Tuesday October 29th

CHAPTER 28

Blake slept soundly and woke to find the cat curled up at his feet. He tried to hurry but somehow found himself lingering to watch Serafina eat. Laura Vexley hadn't stayed long at the house but she'd been in his dreams. He blushed at the memory. The kitchen units looked dated and tired. He needed to move things on. Maybe the Manta needed to go too. He'd arranged for a garage to pick it up and have a look but, for now, he was relying on taxis and other people's cars.

When he got in, the Operations Room was in full swing. There was a note to call in on Superintendent Martin. Blake heaved a long breath. Better get it over with, then.

Superintendent Martin ran his fingers through his hair and dropped his biro on the desk in front of him as Blake entered the office. "What is going on, Blake? An old man in a wheelchair hospitalised, a hostage situation in a hospice. Do you go out looking for headlines or do they just fall into your lap? Hoping to resurrect Searchlight, or something?"

"No, sir," Blake said, his heart sinking; if only he'd refused to go on that bloody programme all those years ago. "With respect, sir, we've closed down a major cannabis farm as a result of our investigations…"

"And got nowhere with the case. You're also ruffling feathers higher up the tree, Blake, with your investigation of the Hunt family."

"Really, sir? Who might that be?"

"Let's just say Victor Hunt has some very influential but concerned friends within local business and the Authority. Word has got back to them that you've been interviewing him at his bedside. It looks like harassment, Blake."

"I can't help that, sir and Victor Hunt has been fairly cooperative despite his illness," Blake said, looking over Martin's head; the less eye contact the better. "We think there may be some connection between Rebecca Thompson's death and previous cold cases. It appears that Marcus Hunt and Thompson were half siblings and were communicating with each other…"

"Is that a crime?"

"It's suspicious, sir, when Marcus Hunt is suggesting they meet clandestinely. And he may have good reason to murder another possible beneficiary of Victor Hunt's will."

Martin slumped down in his seat again, mollified.

"Very well. But don't let this descend into chaos, Blake. All the kids on the Wirral are up in arms about this 'Clocky' nonsense and the time of year doesn't help. We've had gangs of so-called trick or treaters terrorising young children and pretending to be Cameron Lock's ghost. I've lost count of the number of callouts we've had from hysterical children claiming to have been attacked by him. Fireworks are being set off right, left and centre. It's getting out of hand."

"Yes, sir. We'll get to the bottom of it."

"Do it, then. Because if you can't, I'll find someone who can."

Blake nodded and left the room, his knuckles white and his teeth cracking in his jaw. When he found Marcus Hunt, innocent or guilty, he was going to make sure the bastard realised the trouble he'd caused, one way or another.

"Kinnear struck lucky last night, sir," Manikas said, as Blake returned to the Incident Room. "Hunt is staying at the Grosvenor Hotel and as far as they know, he hasn't checked out yet. All his belongings are still in the wardrobe and his credit card is still open at Reception. He didn't have any food or drink in the hotel last night and none of the staff have seen him for a couple of days. He hasn't reported to any local station to show his gun licence either."

"Where the hell is he?"

"I phoned around the local barracks, just to see if anyone remembered him. There's a TA Captain out at Burton Point who said he'd be happy to talk to us, sir."

"Good work, Alex," Blake said. "Fancy a drive out? I know I do. I'm afraid the Manta's out of action but we can use your car..."

The TA building out on Burton Marshes looked like a small village hall. It had a carpark and inside, a large assembly area with some offices and a kitchen at one end. The similarities ended there because the hall adjoined several hundred acres of firing range. Blake could hear the distant pop of gunfire as he showed his warrant card to the guard on duty at the gate. It was a bleak place, ramps of grassed over earth formed barricades from the shooting practice but beyond that, the muted colours of the marsh faded into a distant grey. Blake could see the Welsh hills beyond and remembered that this was where Drucilla's body had been found.

Captain Harrison was a tall man, near retirement with short-cropped, grey hair and an easy manner. He wore camouflage trousers and a green jumper and leaned against his desk, sipping a steaming mug of coffee.

"Yes, I know Marcus Hunt of old," he said in answer to Blake's question. "We served in Afghanistan together. I didn't get on with him, to be honest. I always thought of him as something of a bully. Of course subsequent events proved me right…"

Blake frowned. "I'm sorry. What events, sir?"

"It's a matter of public record," Harrison said, raising his eyebrows. "A number of new recruits left training and accused Hunt of picking on them. One even accused him of making sexual advances to her. There was a full inquiry and Hunt was dismissed. It's a wonder there weren't criminal proceedings, to be honest. I think certain parties were paid off."

"I see," Blake replied.

"There was also the matter in Afghanistan. Rumours more than anything and never substantiated. There were stories about him using excessive force against prisoners, that sort of thing but, as I say, nothing ever came of it. Marcus Hunt, it seemed, was coated in Teflon."

Blake made a note. "Do you think he was capable of such violence?"

Captain Harrison shrugged. "Maybe we all are in the right circumstances, Mr Blake, but I'd say Hunt relished conflict and he was more than capable. Of course that's just my opinion."

"We're trying to get hold of him but he isn't at his hotel. Would you have any idea where we might find him?"

"I'm sorry," Harrison said. "I decided to keep away from Marcus Hunt a long time ago. I don't really know where he might be, these days."

Blake nodded and thanked the Captain for his time. He returned to the car with Manikas. "That was interesting but not unexpected," he said. "Where else might he be?"

They checked in on the hospice but Marcus hadn't visited since Saturday afternoon. Victor Hunt was sedated and so unable to help them further.

"We could check out the Hunt residence, sir," Manikas said. "You never know."

Blake nodded. "I can't think of anywhere else he might be, Alex, let's go and see, shall we?"

The skies were darkening and threatening rain by the time Blake and Manikas pulled up in front of the Priest House. The branches hung down over the narrow drive, giving the place an eerie feeling. They were less than a couple of miles from the busy centre of Bromborough and yet it was so still and silent here. Blake felt as if he was driving into another, darker world.

"That's Hunt's car," Manikas said as the house swung into view. The green Range Rover sat by the front door which hung open.

They climbed out of the car and approached the house. "The front window is broken," Blake said, keeping his voice low. His heart thumped. This didn't feel right. He pushed the door wider gently and led the way as they stepped into the hallway.

"Hello?" Blake yelled. No answer. He gripped the thick bannisters and stared up the grand staircase that had faced them as they entered. "Mr Hunt? Police! Are you there?"

Even empty of chairs and tables, the house gave off an air of opulence and grandeur as they stalked around it; oak panelled walls surrounded them, the sheen of the wood brighter where pictures had once hung. The wooden floorboards looked almost brand new, testament to the thickness and quality of the carpets that had covered and protected them over the generations. The place had a stillness to it. As if it was waiting for something to happen.

"There wouldn't be much to steal," Manikas said, his voice echoing in the cavernous living room. A huge empty fireplace stood on the inner wall of the room, its gaping mouth making the place feel somehow colder. A few packing boxes lay on their sides as if thrown around. "I bet whoever broke in was disappointed," he called as Blake stepped into the dining room.

"I don't think so," he murmured and pointed to the body that lay on the floor, face down in a pool of congealed blood. "I think they got just what they came for. Marcus Hunt."

◆ ◆ ◆

The rain that had threatened held off but the low cloud created a gloom that made the inside of Priest House so dark that the Crime Scene Investigators set up arc lights inside. Jack Kenning squatted beside the body but Blake could see the vicious entry wound in the back of Marcus Hunt's head. It made him think of Thompson's ice pick.

"Struck from behind?" Blake said. "Sharp implement?"

Kenning looked up at Blake and slid his glasses down his nose. "You should qualify, Will," he said. "You're a natural. Yes. Taken completely by surprise, I'd say, judging from the spatter pattern. He was hit and fell like a tree. Never saw it coming. The assailant followed up with a second blow. Bit of a frenzied attack; there are a number of other wounds around the shoulders and back but look where the weapon has punctured the floorboards. I'd say they were misses but made after the fatal blow. If he'd had a body blow first, he probably would have rolled over to defend himself. I'm pretty sure these body blows came after death."

"And where would the attacker have been standing?"

"First of all, over here, behind the curtains, I'd have said."

"A surprise attack from behind, then."

"He was a big lad, Blake. I don't think many people would have wanted to take him on in a fair fight."

"What kind of weapon?"

Kenning shrugged. "A small pick axe. Something with a long wooden handle and a sharp point. Old, I'd say. Rusted slightly at the tips."

"You can tell all that from the entry wound?" Blake said, screwing his face up.

"No, Will, it's over there behind the curtain, leaning up against the window ledge," Kenning said, with a brief smile. "The killer left it behind. We might be able to get something from it."

Blake knelt down by the pick. It was old, with a worn handle. If it hadn't been covered with blood and bits of Hunt's brain, Blake would have thought it quite beautiful; a symbol of labourers of the past, hewing rock and earth to tame the land. "Do you think it came from here?"

"Quite possible," Kenning said. "I'm no expert but that looks like an antique. The handle's well-used and there's no branding on it of any kind."

"Premeditated," Blake said. "Somebody must have known he was coming, possibly even lured him into the house and then killed him. Any sign of his phone?"

"Not here on the scene. Unless it's been dropped somewhere. A fingertip search of the place might find it. Bit of a bind, eh? I hear he was your main suspect."

Blake stood, hands on hips surveying the carnage. "He was, Jack, he was."

"So, back to square one, then?"

"Not quite."

Blake looked unhappy as he paced the Incident Room. Cryer, Chinn, Kinnear and Manikas all sat, their faces reflecting Blake's frustration back at him. He stopped, rubbed his face and let out a huge breath.

"We've been jumping around on this case. Getting pulled in all directions. Drugs, sibling rivalry, petty squabbles. Now we have another body on our hands. Thoughts?"

"They're both Hunt's children, sir," Cryer said. "But someone would have to know Rebecca's true parentage for that to link them."

"True," Blake murmured, thinking aloud. "And even then, why would you kill them? What would you hope to gain?"

"Not money," Vikki said. "You'd kidnap and

ransom them for that."

Blake nodded. "Rebecca and Marcus had only just started to get to know each other, so I find it hard to believe that they'd be involved in anything that might get them killed."

"Revenge, sir," Manikas said. "If you wanted to get back at Victor Hunt, you might make sure he outlived his children. It could be revenge, pure and simple."

"But revenge for what?" Cryer said.

Manikas held his hands in the air. "Victor Hunt wasn't exactly all sweetness and light, was he? He might be dying now but, by all accounts, in his prime he was a total bastard. He's bound to have made enemies."

"Enemies who want his children dead?" Chinn said. "What would he have to do to provoke that?"

"Hunt has lost all his children," Manikas said. "Don't forget Drucilla."

"All the children that we know about," Cryer said. "There might be more lurking out there."

"When Kinnear and I interviewed Detective Leech, he said he feared that a serial killer was responsible for those deaths," Blake murmured. "The collection of shoes that turned up at the charity shop might well point to that. But Gary Archer doesn't strike me as a one-man killing machine. And he was physically incapable of killing Rebecca or Marcus. We need to try and trace Marcus Hunt's final movements but I want us to delve into these past cases too. As far as I can see, this whole business kicked off when those shoes appeared. There's a connection between the killer and the shoes. We're going to find it."

People certainly looked different, she decided as she walked through Bromborough Village. They reminded her of cattle; dull-eyed and slow. She could still feel the blood spatters on her face even though she'd wiped them off long ago. It wasn't an unpleasant feeling. She felt more alive than she ever had. But her smiles and nods of the head went unacknowledged by the people she passed. They stared through her. If only they knew she was different from them. They were prey. She'd been like them once; trying to connect with others who might have the same grievances. Not realising that she was really a huntress.

She stopped and looked at the butcher's window. Chops, sausages, liver and steaks lay cold side by side. It had gone very well, better than she had imagined it would. Well, that wasn't strictly true because she'd never doubted that it would go well. He was a big man and strong with it. Full of red, red blood. And she'd known what would push his buttons; he was territorial and grasping. The mere suggestion that Priest House was being burgled would bring him charging down to the house. She knew he wouldn't call the police; he wasn't the type. He was a 'deal-with-it-myself' sort of person. All it took was a phone call to bring him hurtling down in that oversized car of his.

A police car flashed by, blue lights reflecting in the shop window and she turned to watched it. When she saw his shotgun, she'd been a little afraid then. Just a tiny bit. But she'd moved so fast, brought the pick down so hard, he really didn't know what had hit him. which was a shame really. His skull had just popped. It was a ridiculous sound, really and she had wondered if it was real or just her imagination. His gun had gone clattering across the room unused and he had fallen like a sack of spuds. Then she'd been on him, boiling with rage. She frowned at her reflection. Why couldn't she remember those few seconds, when she'd made such a mess? She'd hit him and hit him. She smiled at herself; a secret smile. Nobody knew. Nobody but her.

CHAPTER 29

Gary Archer sat up in his hospital bed, looking like a faded Country and Western star. His long, grey hair spilled down over his shoulders and a huge bushy beard hid his hawkish face. Fortunately, Chinn's fast action meant that any injury was confined to his legs and his hands when he had tried to beat out the flames himself in panic.

The hospital had called to say that he had recovered enough to answer questions, so Blake left the rest of the team bringing in stacks of files on any case that Drucilla Hunt had been involved in. They would be ploughing through old documents and, although Blake wanted to solve this case, secretly, he was relieved that he could get away from the paperwork and ask a few questions for a while. Kinnear had let him borrow his car too, which was handy.

"How are you feeling, Mr Archer?" Blake said, pulling up a chair to Archer's bedside. "You know you can have a brief here, if you want, but it's nothing formal yet. We can discuss the cannabis farm in your house later. I want to talk about Drucilla Hunt."

Gary Archer's long face grew longer. "I'd rather not talk about her. I've put that behind me. I'm not that man anymore."

"Oh, I dunno," Blake said. "I don't think you've changed one bit, Gary. I think you're the man you've always been; a smalltime weed seller, nothing more. You never were a murderer, were you?"

"I think the jury had a different opinion back in the day, Mr Blake," Archer said, with a nervous laugh. "I did it. I strangled that poor girl and I wish I hadn't every day of my life."

"Yeah, you say it with such conviction. What did you do with her shoes then, Gary?"

Archer blinked in surprise. "Her shoes? I-I don't know. I threw them in the water, maybe. There was a big pool nearby..."

"Why?"

"What? I dunno why. I just did. I wasn't well. I was a loony. You may as well ask me why I killed her. And before you do, I don't know that, neither."

Blake scratched his neck. "So, you threw them in the water and they floated out to sea or sank to the bottom of the marsh, never to be seen again?"

"Yeah, that's right. I remember now. I threw them away. They're gone. I had a whole thing about feet then." He pointed a twirling finger to his head. "I was a proper fruitloop."

“How come they turned up again, forty years later in perfect condition, then?”

Archer looked as though a freight train was bearing down on him and he was tied to the tracks. “Have they? I don’t know. It was a long time ago. I can’t remember what happened to her boots...”

“I never said they were boots, Gary. How d’you know that?”

“I-I’ve been questioned before. Look, I want a brief here. I’m not making any more comments. You’ll just tie me in knots...”

Blake raised his hands. “That’s fine,” he said. “I just want to work this all out for Eric’s sake.”

Archer glared at Blake. “What d’you mean? What’s Eric got to do with this? He’s a good lad. Didn’t know about the weed or any of that.”

“Last week, a girl was murdered right in the woods where Eric works. Found minus her boots. When we recovered them, it turns out they used to belong to Drucilla Hunt. Also, they have the name of Cameron Lock, the infamous child killer, written inside them. Eric can’t account for his whereabouts on the night of the murder.” It was a lie but Blake hoped it might give him some leverage on Archer.

“He was with me,” Archer said. “All evening.”

“No. He wasn’t. He’s tangled up in the murder

of a young girl and he's mixed up with the Cameron Lock case somehow."

"He wouldn't harm anyone. He's a good lad," Archer said.

Blake shrugged. "I dunno. Maybe he's got the same problems his old grandad had. You know, a bit too much wacky backy, a secret thing about shoes and feet... and killing young girls..."

"No. Eric's got a good job. He's a..."

"Good lad. Yeah, you keep telling me. The other scrotes inside won't see that, though, will they? To them, he'll just be a nonce. Up for grabs. I bet you know what that's like. Is that what you want for him?" Archer lowered his head, then shook it. "Then help me, Gary. What happened that day Drucilla died?"

Gary Archer paused and looked out of the hospital window as if he was weighing up his options. "Alright. I'll tell you what I know."

"In your own time, Gary."

"It was December 1981. Bloody freezing it was. D'you remember that snow and ice?"

"I was just a baby," Blake said. "It was lost on me, I'm afraid."

"Snow everywhere," Archer said. "Never seen anything like it, since. The weather must have been bad for me to even notice. I was in big trouble."

"What kind of trouble? Law?"

Archer laughed. "Worse than that," he said. "I'd been growing a bit of me own weed on the side and pocketing the takings from one of my suppliers too. Bloody stupid. They were a big outfit from over the water in Liverpool. They'd rumbled me and sent someone over to make an example of me."

"You must've been scared."

"Dead right I was. I had a wife and a little kid to think of. What use would I be if I was found face down in the Mersey or something? I was hiding anywhere I could think of, but they caught me in the Jockey."

Even though he didn't live in Neston on the other side of the Wirral, Blake had heard of the Jockey. It was a notorious pub on the edge of the town, a locals-only drug den. It had since been sold and become a classy Italian restaurant but back then, you took your life in your hands if you went into the Jockey uninvited. "They must've been an evil mob if they went in there and came out unscathed," Blake muttered.

"I'm tellin you. These blokes were hardcore. Connections all over the place. Anyway, this guy, Millington, a big rasta sat down opposite me and I thought, 'this is it. I'm gonna die.' But he asks me what I'm drinkin' and gets me a pint. 'We got a big job for you, Gary,' he said. They told me that if I confessed to the Hunt girl's murder, they'd wipe my debt and even pay me handsomely. There was no haggling. It was like money wasn't a problem. I didn't ask any questions. They told me what to say and I said it."

"Which was?"

"That this Drucilla kid was investigating me and following me around and I started to get paranoid. That I believed she was from MI5 and she was going to kill me. So I led her out onto the marshes and strangled her. I was so horrified by what I done that I ran away. That was it."

"And they bought it?"

"Come on, Blake, we're talking DCI Leech, 'investigating' officer. It was December. He just wanted to wrap things up like a Chrimbo Prezzie and get back to the party. I wondered if the outfit had him put on the case deliberately."

"So you spent thirteen years in a secure psychiatric unit? That must have been hard," Blake said. "And you never knew who you were doing it for?"

"My wife was in on the deal, Blake. Couldn't bear it if she thought I was a real murderer. Anyway, once I was assessed, they saw I wasn't a threat. They moved me to an open prison. That wasn't so bad. The wife got regular payments from wherever while I was inside. I missed my little girl but she was safe and happy enough with her mum. Sometimes, being a dad, you just do what you have to do, don't you?"

Blake nodded. "Go on."

"Then when I came out, July 1995, this posh solicitor type comes rockin up to me. Gives me the keys to a house in Spital and a big fat cheque. I thought we were going to pause for a photograph or something, the way he shook my hand. And there I was set up for life, so you'd think. If anyone asked, I just said I won the lottery, didn't I?"

"The solicitor," Blake said. "What was his name."

"I haven't a clue. He was an old fella; didn't introduce himself. I bet he's dead now."

"Can your wife corroborate all this?"

Archer lay back on his pillow. Tears glinting in his eyes. "You know, sometimes I think I should've just let them get on with it."

"Sorry?" Blake said, frowning. "You've lost me."

"Millington and his pals. I should've just let them kneecap me or whatever it was they were planning. I should've told them to stuff their money." Archer stared into Blake's eyes. "Do you believe in judgement, Mr Blake?"

Blake shrugged. "You mean God? Fate? The Universe? I don't know."

“I do. I had a good life after prison. I had my Harley Davidson, my wife. My daughter got to go to that private school over in Parkgate. She got a good job and married a bank manager. Hard times, followed by good times. Then the judgement. My wife was on the back of the bike when that lorry ploughed into us at the traffic lights on the Chester High Road. It killed her but she shielded me, so I just ended up in a wheelchair. Around the same time, my daughter got breast cancer. It all happened so quickly. Like a sword came down and cut my family away. Maybe if I’d taken my punishment, none of that would have happened. I don’t know who he was but I covered for an evil man. I didn’t hesitate. I just said yes and let a stone-cold killer go free. It’s Karma, Mr Blake. What comes around, goes around. Sometimes, I wonder if whoever killed Drucilla Hunt suffered too. Maybe their life fell apart or maybe they got ill. In my darker moments, I worry that they’re still out there, living it up. That would be the worst.

CHAPTER 30

While the main team worked through any actions arising from the murders of Rebecca Thompson and Marcus Hunt, Blake had created a sub team of Kinnear, Chinn, Cryer, and Manikas to follow up the Drucilla case. This included the shoes that seemed to have started all the trouble.

The Stilettos and sandals had been retrieved from the charity shop in Heswall and had been passed onto forensics. The other shoes had taken a little while longer as the collection for recycling had gone on the Wednesday Rebecca was murdered. The recycling company took old clothing from many shops and the team who went there faced a sea of rags and footwear.

It had taken them the best part of a week to find one of the slippers with Josie Lock's name in it and a court shoe with 'Fiona James' written inside. The real kicker had been Forensics announcing that the shoes revealed next to nothing because they had been handled by so many people and moved to so many locations. All they could say were that they were 'quite old. Possibly 1980s' and that it was very likely that the names inside them had all been written by the same person with the same thick, permanent marker.

The team crowded round Tev, the Exhibits Officer's desk as he passed out the large plastic bags containing the shoes. Kath Cryer had clapped her hands like a little kid when the stilettos appeared in the office. "I got these," she said. Chinn didn't say anything. Instead she picked up the slipper and looked down at it like it was a live scorpion.

"Yeah, well don't try them on," Tev said. "Don't take them out of the bag. And don't take them out of the office. Okay?"

Sitting at her desk, now, Cryer stared at the name Carly Simmonds written in thick marker in the insole. She ran through what she knew about the case. It had been closed for nearly forty years, seemingly straight-forward.

David Collins, the man Drucilla had suspected of embezzling from her father's company, had been having an affair with her but then smashed her skull in with a hammer and committed suicide. A note arrived in the post from him, saying that he was ashamed.

She leafed through the notes and photographs, the dustiness of the paper tickling her nose. Where to start? That was the question. There were many reasons why Collins might have murdered Simmonds. She might have been threatening to tell his wife if he tried to end the relationship. He was funding the whole affair by fiddling the books at work. Perhaps the whole thing just got too much and he realised it was only a matter of time before he was caught out. But something was amiss, she felt it in her bones.

Vikki Chinn may not have put much store in gut-feelings or instinct but Cryer just knew when things weren't right sometimes. Not that you could submit that as evidence but it did point her in the right direction nine times out of ten. "So what doesn't feel right with you?" Kath said, holding up the stiletto in its bag. What did it say to her? Red, sexy. "Passion."

"What?" Kinnear said, looking up.

"Passion," Cryer replied. "These shoes say 'passion' to me. Somebody who likes the way they look and uses it. Whoever got involved with the wearer of these shoes would do so through passion, lust. I mean, men can't resist stilettos right?" She wiggled her eyebrows at Kinnear, held his gaze for just long enough to make him blush.

"Maybe some can't, Ma'am," he said, looking down at his file.

"Go on," Cryer insisted, waving the bag in front of Kinnear's face. "No red-blooded male could turn down a hottie in a pair of these, right?"

"I wouldn't know, Ma'am." He returned to his

notes.

"Anyway, if you were going to bump off your lover, it would be in the heat of the moment, right? A crime of passion."

Kinnear nodded "Possibly."

"You wouldn't skulk around on a canal tow-path waiting for her with a hammer, surely. He would have lost the plot in the hotel room and killed her there."

"I don't know, Ma'am," Kinnear said. "It's pretty thin. I mean he could have got himself worked up about it and planned to finish her off at the canal."

"It's a starting point, at least," Kath said and turned back to the shoe. "And who the hell posts a suicide letter?"

"Sorry, Ma'am?" Kinnear said again, trying to suppress the irritation in his voice as he dropped the notes he was trying to read.

She held up the letter. "He sent it by first class post. To the police, explaining why he'd killed Simmonds and himself."

Kinnear frowned. "Hmm, that is weird."

Cryer gave a sigh and jumped up. "I'm going to the canal." She bundled all the papers and photos into the file and tucked it under her arm. "To have a look at the murder scene."

"Take some bread, Ma'am," Kinnear called after her.

"What?"

"You may as well feed the ducks while you're there."

Kath Cryer sighed, glad to be out of the office and away from Kinnear. Something about him made her skin crawl. He had a kind of chubby face and often the stubble that sprouted from the pale skin made her shudder. It had nothing to do with him being gay. She wasn't homophobic but he should just keep it to himself. She wouldn't be surprised if he went running to Blake about her shoe comment. Ah well, let him. It was only a bit of fun. If he couldn't see that, well it was his problem.

Cryer focused on the case and tried to imagine the couple. Both young and stylishly dressed, attending parties and events like the Grand National. She got the impression from the rather scant case notes that Simmonds blurred the line between charging her clients for sex and expecting to be 'treated well.' That could be confusing for a young man.

Cryer imagined how her boyfriend, Theo would react if she told him he couldn't have it tonight because the restaurant he took her to wasn't classy enough. She smirked. Maybe she should try it. The look on his face would be hilarious. He'd probably sulk though, she thought, which left her frowning for a second. Yeah. He'd sulk for bloody hours.

It was possible that David Collins saw his relationship with Carly Simmonds as something more than just client and call-girl. Maybe he got jealous of her other clients.

Cryer parked in the racecourse and, clutching some of the scene of crime photographs, made her way down to the canal. Shoppers and a few locals bustled along the streets. Unlike the centre and the Rows, where shops stood in two storeys and sported blackened Tudor timber frames, this part of Chester was more modern.

On an October Tuesday morning, the towpath along the Shropshire Union canal was empty apart from a solitary dog walker. Kath Cryer stood with the map and the photographs, trying to get a fix on exactly where the body was found. A bridge crossed the canal behind her. Trees lined the towpath and, although losing their leaves, covered any real view from the road above. Behind them, the gable ends of buildings and the city walls made escape from the canal impossible.

Cryer frowned and looked up and down the towpath. There wasn't a place for an assailant to hide. Collins hadn't really said how he had killed her. It was assumed he'd lay in wait for her, but where? The towpath ended when it came to the bridge. She looked at the photograph of Carly's prone body lying on the ground, one arm dangling over the path's edge, her legs splayed and the dress ridden up revealing a glimpse of stocking top. No shoes. Her hair and face were matted with blood from the hammer wound in the back of her head. The place she lay offered no cover for a would-be assailant and it was obvious from the photographs that little had changed on this narrow towpath in forty years, probably more.

Carly Simmonds was struck from behind. If David Collins had appeared walking along the path, she would have stopped and have been facing him. So did Collins follow her down here and sneak up on her? That's possible. The whole place didn't seem to be Carly Simmonds' style. She wasn't a street worker; her work was conducted in the classiest wine bars, the quietest pubs and plushest hotel rooms of Chester and Liverpool. She didn't take punters down onto a canal towpath for a quickie.

"Then what brought you down here?" Cryer muttered at the photograph. Why would you make your way down to this dark towpath at night. Information? "Information," she said aloud and suddenly realised how alone and isolated she was. Not that she felt threatened; there was nobody about. Besides, she could handle herself; any bloke who had a go at her would get the shock of his life. But dwelling on the murder and looking at the pictures of Carly's battered body right where it took place, left her feeling spooked and vulnerable. Carly must have been lured down here. Had Collins told her to meet him? Or had someone else?

She went back to the car and pulled the file out of the boot, spreading it out on the back seat. The contents of Simmonds handbag were listed. It must have been a small bag; it contained a condom, a lipstick, a small bottle of perfume and a tampon. Cryer felt a stab of sympathy for the woman. To be reduced to lists of scant belongings, injuries, wounds and toxicology reports. To become a piece of paper in a file for someone to pore over decades later. Just because some man couldn't keep his shit together. "Get a grip, Kath," she muttered to herself. "There must be something here."

She picked up a blurred photograph paper-clipped to a sheet of paper. Collins and Simmonds sat in an open-topped Mercedes, beaming, all smiles and sunglasses like a pair of Hollywood movie stars. She turned it over and saw something scrawled on the back. 'September 1980 – suspects together, Southport - Drucilla Hunt and Mr Rees.'

Something about the writing made her uneasy. Kids spying on adults, informing on them. It just seemed wrong. But there was something else, one of those 'gut' things and Kath couldn't pin it down. A list on the paper sheet stuck to the photo stared her in the face. But one name stood out - 'Sister. Carol Simmonds...' Cryer looked at the address on the list. If Carly Simmonds had a living relative and still lived at that address, it was worth a try.

CHAPTER 31

Something about the conversation with Kath Cryer had thrown Andrew Kinnear. The way she had looked at him combined with her assertion that all men loved stilettos. It felt like a challenge or an accusation. Especially after her previous comments about paedophiles at the meeting on Friday. That gross old detective, Leech, had rattled him. He didn't hide his sexuality but he didn't shout it from the rooftops, either. It was nobody's business as far as he was concerned but every now and then, people made it their business. He could challenge open prejudice.

It was those little comments like the one Kath had just made that really got to him. And the looks exchanged between people. Or a raised eyebrow. They were traps to fall into. He could shrug them off, but they would sit there and fester, joining the hundreds of other, tiny slights that weighed him down. He could challenge it. Go to Blake and say, 'DI Cryer just looked at me and said that all men like stilettos.' How would that sound? Pathetic. Over-sensitive.

Kinnear ground his teeth and stared down at the Stephen Bradshaw file. He'd spent a fruitless morning trying to track Marcus Hunt's movements and come up with nothing. Hunt's car gave away nothing, his wallet had very little in it. In the end, he'd decided to have a look at the boy's file to see if anything there leapt out at him.

"Focus," he muttered to himself. Maybe he'd have a quiet word with Kath later. That might sort it. He turned a few pages without looking at them. Of course, she might take it the wrong way. "Focus, dammit." He picked up one of the sandals and looked at the thick, black letters inside. Leech had suspected that a serial killer was on the loose. The shoes could certainly be trophies. But to be so disparate; a prostitute in stilettos, a little kid and an old lady. Didn't serial killers have a typical victim? Didn't they follow patterns? The killer took shoes or footwear. Was that enough? But if there was a serial killer and Gary Archer didn't kill Drucilla, then why wasn't he used to cover up the other deaths?

Stephen Bradshaw had vanished from the front of his house and turned up dead a few days later, strangled and naked but not sexually abused in any way. Then soon after that, Cameron Lock was arrested with Stephen's clothes in his backpack. Case closed. The investigation had been haphazard. A number of local perverts were rounded up but they all had alibis. A wider search had been suggested but just at that point, Lock had been caught by Drucilla Hunt, arrested and the evidence found. All very convenient. Too convenient, bearing in mind that Leech was the investigating officer. Kinnear sat back.

“Okay,” he muttered to himself. “Reasons why Cameron Lock didn’t kill Stephen Bradshaw.” For a start, he wasn’t the sharpest tool in the box; he had learning difficulties which would make it hard for him to plan and execute an abduction without getting spotted or caught. “Plus, plus, plus,” Kinnear muttered, flicking through the pathology report. “No sex.”

If anyone had been listening, they would have thought Kinnear had lost it. But it was true. Lock committed sexual assaults or exposed himself. All the crimes were directed at girls. Not small boys. Why didn’t Cameron Lock abduct a girl? Surely, if he’d been responsible for taking Stephen, there would have been a sexual motive.

A movement behind him, made Kinnear turn. Manikas stood looming over his shoulder. “Jeez, Alex, you gave me a start.”

“Fiona James,” Manikas said, his eyes wide.

“What about her?”

“She was Stephen Bradshaw’s mother.”

CHAPTER 32

The house was a ruin. A few remaining roof tiles clung to the rotting roof beams. Steel shutters covered the windows and a sign warned of danger on each one of them. The garden and the hedge surrounding it were so overgrown that DS Chinn had trouble seeing beyond it at first. It was clear that nobody lived at 35 Crabtree Lane, Bromborough and hadn't for a very long time.

Vikki Chinn tried the gate and it scraped open. Brambles and bushes choked the path to the front door and Chinn began to wonder at the wisdom of coming out here. She'd seen Cryer go and decided that a breath of fresh air might clear her own head, too. The Incident Room had felt stuffy and she couldn't think freely with Kinnear puffing and sighing over his files. Looking at the information board was like staring at a complex puzzle that she had no chance of solving. But now, stood in this tangle of weeds and briar, she didn't feel any better.

Struggling her way round the back of the house, Chinn found herself in waist-high grass, standing at the spot where Josie Lock was killed. She opened the file and scanned the photographs. The old woman's long, white hair had splayed across the dark lawn. She lay with one arm stretched forward, the other back, one leg bent and the other straight. Almost as if she was pretending to swim. A huge rose of blood blossomed on her back and her nightie tangled around her legs. Chinn shuddered and the trees hissed in the cold October wind.

She turned and looked at the property. The back door had been kicked in; the steel shuttering only as strong as the rotten wooden frame that supported it. Still attached on one bottom corner, it hung inwards, inviting her. Vikki didn't have a flashlight but she poked her head through the door and wrinkled her nose at the stink of damp and stale urine. Clearly, the place was used as a drinking den, judging by the smell and the number of bottles and crushed cans lying around. Other stuff too, she thought, kicking at an empty syringe with the tip of her shoe. As her eyes became accustomed to the dark, Chinn could see that she was peering into what had once been the kitchen. The cooker and fridge had long gone but she could see a steel sink and some cupboards. Vinyl wallpaper hung in strips and the ceiling paint blistered. Beyond that a wall of darkness blocked any view into what would have been the hall.

Something moved behind Vikki and she whirled on her heel and, instinctively, raised a clenched fist. A stubble-face man with thin, lank hair gave a cry and staggered back. He wore a green shooting jacket with padded shoulders and held a walking stick in his hand.

"What're you playing at?" Vikki snapped, grabbing the stick from the man's grasp.

The man raised his hands to cover his face. "I'm sorry," he said. "I thought you were one of those flippin' kids who've been bunking off school and drinking down here. Causing trouble."

"I'm Detective Sergeant Chinn. Merseyside Police. I was looking around the property when you tried to assault me. Can I have your name please, sir?"

The man lowered his hands. And swallowed hard. Vikki could see him properly now; a middle-aged man, filling out his jacket, a scarf digging into his fat neck. "No! I mean. I'm sorry. I didn't mean to startle you. My name is Martin. Martin Johnson. I-I live across the road. I was only trying to frighten those little beggars off... I didn't mean..."

"I think in future, you'd be better off calling the police, Mr Johnson. If you hurt one of them, you could end up in serious trouble."

Johnson seemed to regain his composure at this advice. "I do ring the police, all the time. They never come. I've lived in this road man and boy. There was a time when you'd see a bobby walking around here but not any more…"

Chinn shrugged. "I can't help you there," she said. "Tell me about the house."

Johnson looked up at the roof. "This old place? When I was a kid, an old lady lived here and her son. But he went to prison and she was murdered right here in this garden."

Vikki didn't appreciate the relish with which Johnson said that. "You mean Cameron and Josie Lock?" she said.

"Yeah," Johnson said. "You know about it? Horrible business, really. I was a teenager at the time…"

"You must've known Cameron Lock then?"

Johnson shrugged. "A little bit. He went to a special school. Didn't really hang around with us. Weird kid. Used to strip off all the time. Looking back now, I think he might have been abused himself or something, the way he went on about sex but you don't think that when you're a kid. We just used to think it was funny."

"And what about his mother?"

"She was strange too. My mum always said to stay away from her. Never said why, though. She would stare at us through the hedge when we walked past. In fact, we always ran past the house unless it was for a dare. You'd see her walking up to the shops with her shopping trolley each morning. She looked more like Cameron's gran than his mum."

"And then someone killed her," Vikki said.

Johnson nodded. "They never found anyone did they? I thought that Drucilla Hunt would solve it..."

"You knew her?"

"Nah. But we were all big fans. She was a bit of a pin up of mine, to be honest. Teenage boy, you know how it is..."

"Right," Vikki said and looked back at the house, trying not to think about a teenage Mr Johnson's Drucilla fantasies.

"I saw her round here a few times though. Especially after the murder. That's why I thought she must have been investigating."

"Really? She came to the house after the murder?"

Johnson smiled. "Yeah. She was with that lad who always hung around her. Can't remember his name..."

"Gerald Rees?"

"That's him. They broke into the house. I watched them from my bedroom window. I remember it really well because I nearly went down and offered to help." Johnson's baggy face fell. "But I chickened out."

"So, shortly after the murder, you saw Drucilla Hunt and Gerald Rees break into Josie Lock's house? Didn't you think to call the police?"

Johnson's brow creased. "Why would I do that? They were on the side of the police, weren't they? They caught Cameron Lock. Anyway, it was just the Drucilla girl who went in. Rees kept lookout..." He blinked as if realising something.

Chinn shook her head. "Yes sir," she said. "Why would Rees need to keep lookout if they were doing something legitimate?"

"But they were around the house a lot and I just thought with her dad owning the properties, it was okay..."

"Victor Hunt owns the house?" Chinn said.

Johnson nodded. "Yes. All of the houses in this road belong to the Hunts. They've been our landlords for as long as I can remember."

CHAPTER 33

Although, she died in Chester, it turned out that Carly Simmonds grew up in Bebington on the Wirral. Francis Avenue was a small cul-de-sac behind the Oval sportsground. Kath had conflicting feelings about the Oval. Memories of swimming lessons that nearly drowned her vied with those of holding gymnastics trophies and medals at numerous competitions. That was a long time ago, now, though, and adult life, the job, years of desk work and driving around meant that she was constantly battling with weight.

Francis Avenue was a curious mixture of old Victorian villas with arched windows and pointed gables, interspersed with newly-built infill houses. The Simmonds house was one of the old ones; a tall, three storey semi with a narrow front door and a bay front window. The other half of the house, next door, had been rendered and whitewashed but Simmons' place remained dark brick. The front garden had been replaced with a concrete hard-standing for cars but none were parked there now.

Kath parked up and knocked on the shiny-black front door. Silence. Then a curtain in the front window twitched and she glimpsed a spray of blue-rinse hair and a cautious eye. A few moments later, the chain rattled on the door and it opened a crack. An old lady peered out, scanning Kath up and down. "Can I help you?" she said.

"I'm sorry to bother you, my name is DI Kath Cryer Merseyside Police. I'm looking for Carol Simmonds," Kath said, showing her warrant card.

The woman paused for a little while. "What's it about?"

"Nothing to worry about. I just wanted to ask her a few questions about her sister Carly. I'm just reviewing the case and want to get some facts straight in my head."

"Reviewing the case?" The old woman said and closed the door. Kath could hear the rattling of the chain and then the door swung open again. "I'm Mrs Simmonds, Carly and Carol's mother. You'd better come in."

Kath followed Mrs Simmonds as she shuffled her way back to the front room of the house, using a Zimmer frame. The old woman settled herself into an armchair that was surrounded by small tables piled with magazines, knitting and an extraordinary number of television controllers.

The woman was very old. Possibly in her nineties. Thin veins snaked under her paper-white skin and deep wrinkles lined her face. But those eyes were sharp and keen and her hair, although thin, was immaculately coiffured. She looked up at Kath. "Now, love," she said, breathlessly. "What do you want to know?"

"Thank you Mrs Simmonds," Kath said, settling on the sofa next to the old lady. "I know it might be difficult, going back over these things..."

Mrs Simmonds waved a hand and her gold rings flashed. "Call me Vera, Kath," she said. "And don't you worry about asking any hard questions. Carly lived life to the full. She was a bright flame in our lives and sadly snatched away but it was many years ago."

"Thank you Mrs... Vera," Kath said, pulling out her notebook. "So, you said Carly lived life to the full. What did you mean by that?"

Vera Simmonds gave Kath an arched look. "She liked to party," she said. "Carly was always off galivanting around Liverpool or hob-knobbing with the Cheshire Set. There wasn't a weekend that she wasn't driving over to Wilmslow for some reception, or even down to London. She loved the big shows...went to the first night of Evita and met Andrew Lloyd Webber at the after-show party. Oh, the stories she came back and told us! She was so full of life..."

"She was a beautiful woman. Did she have

many admirers?" Kath said.

Vera waggled her penciled-on eyebrows. "Of course she did but she wasn't a tart. The police said she was a 'call girl' and suggested that she took money from men. There was none of that. She made a living selling perfume and she was a great saleswoman. The men she dated were perfect gentlemen…"

"Apart from David Collins."

"No. He was a kind man. Very gentle and unassuming. I never understood that," Vera said. "How could a man that nice hurt anyone?"

Kath frowned. "You don't think he killed Carly?"

"I don't know, do I?" Vera said and shrugged. "It just seemed odd to me. Of course, we didn't know he was married and had two little girls, did we? But on the face of it he seemed just a perfectly normal, friendly young man."

"Did you see Carly on the night she died?"

Vera gave a sad smile. "Yes. She was buzzing around this house, getting ready. Worrying about her hair and her make-up. She looked like a film star. I was so proud of her."

"Where was she going?"

"To meet David Collins," Vera said. "They were going away for the weekend. To Ireland, I think. They had ferry tickets booked."

"And was she seeing anyone else at this time?"

Vera looked cross for a moment. "No," she said. "I told the police at the time. There was nobody else but they kept talking about 'clients' and how Collins was jealous. My daughter didn't have 'clients' and she didn't two-time anyone."

Kath chewed the end of her pen for a moment. "So, you're saying that the police came to the investigation with their minds made up about Carly."

"I think they did," Vera said. She rolled her eyes. "It was always the case. Still is, isn't it? A young woman goes out and gets attacked and it's her own fault. Her skirt was too short, her heels were too high, she'd been drinking, she was asking for it. Because my Carly wore a mini dress and high heels, they decided she was a... a... prostitute. And then they worked from there."

Kath nodded. Carly's mother mightn't be able to think badly of her daughter, but Cryer felt guilty that she hadn't questioned the assumption herself from the start. "Did Carly ever say anything about Collins having problems with work?"

Again, Vera shook her head. "Nope. All this stuff about him fiddling the books came out later. It does explain how he lived such a lavish lifestyle and I felt really sorry for his children..."

"Not his wife?"

"No. She was a monster by all accounts. We only heard later, of course, but his wife was cruel. Always nagging him and belittling him. Overly strict with the children. It all came out at the inquest. If you ask me, she pushed him away."

Or maybe Mrs Collins was upset that he was spending all the housekeeping money on pretty little Carly Simmonds and her jet set lifestyle, Kath thought but she just nodded and made more notes. "And Carly had never said anything about Collins hurting her or being controlling?"

"No," Vera replied. "You said that you were reviewing the case. Can you tell me why?"

"Just routine, really, Vera," Kath lied. "Every now and then, we pick an old case and check it was investigated thoroughly. Do you have any pictures of Carly from back then?"

Vera's eyes twinkled. "Of course I do," she said and pointed a bony finger towards an old cupboard at the side of the chimney breast. "Open that door, there. It's a bit stiff..." Kath did as she was asked and found herself crouching by the open cupboard. "Now," Vera continued, "there's a box of wine glasses, pull them out. And just behind them there's a scrapbook. Careful how you handle it, it's quite fragile." Kath eased the scrapbook out of the cupboard, resisting the temptation to blow the dust off it. She brought it up and placed it on Vera's knee.

"Here we are," Vera said, opening the book. The first couple of pages were family events, weddings, her and her late husband's Golden Wedding, school photos. Carly and Carol looked like typical little girls, ponytails, round faces, gappy teeth. Carly a couple of years older. But as they moved through the book, Kath watched Carly blossom into a bubbly-haired beauty and Carol fade into mousy obscurity beside her.

At fifteen, Carly made her Guide uniform look like a raunchy fashion statement whereas Carol still looked about seven. Soon, Carly dominated the book. Pictures of her on an advertisement for Browns of Chester where she worked, a photo of her with the Duke of Westminster. And then pages of pictures cut out of Cheshire Life showing Carly at the elbow of various well-to-do gentlemen, holding a glass of bubbly.

"Oh, she was always appearing in Cheshire Life," Vera said. But Kath stared down at one picture of an older man. His hand snaked around Carly's waist, grinning like a lottery winner at the camera.

"That's Victor Hunt, isn't it?"

"Oh yes, dear," Vera chirped. "They were an item for quite a while. Now he was a true gentleman. Are you alright, dear? You've gone a bit pale."

Wednesday October 30th

CHAPTER 34

It didn't seem possible but Victor Hunt looked even more frail than the last time Blake had seen him. It was understandable, though, considering the incident with Ken Thompson and the fact that counsellors had broken the news to him of his son's murder the previous day. Staring vacantly at the wall of the private room he'd been moved to, Hunt didn't even acknowledge Blake as he sat down on the chair next to the bed. DS Chinn stood, her hands clasped in front of her.

"Mr Hunt," Blake said. "I'm sorry for this but we need to ask you a few questions. About your son. And other matters, too."

"Of course you do," Hunt said, not looking at Blake.

"Do you know of anyone who would want to harm Marcus?"

Hunt shook his head slowly. "Only one person and she's long dead. Drucilla. She hated him with a passion. She would have happily killed him. I thought he was safe but she has a long reach, it seems."

"With respect, Mr Hunt," Blake said. "I don't think we can blame Drucilla for your son's death.

It must have been someone with us, now. Have you any idea who it might be? Someone who wanted to get to you, perhaps?"

"That's very possible, Detective Blake," Hunt said. "But I have no idea who it could be. I'm very tired. I can feel my energy slipping away. It'll all be over soon and that'll be an end of it."

"It's come to light that Gary Archer didn't kill Drucilla, sir," Blake said, quietly. "Again, would you know anything about who paid him to make a false confession?"

Hunt swung his head round and fixed his stare on Blake. "Why would anyone admit to doing something so horrible? Even for money?"

"I don't know, sir," Blake said. "He said it was the only way he could see out of the predicament he put himself in. Plus he wanted to provide for his wife and daughter."

"A noble sentiment," Hunt snorted. "Tell me Mr Blake, you must see all kinds of people in your line of work. Do you think we're born innocent? Free of sin or blame?"

Blake shrugged. "I suppose I do."

"So, for you, it's all nurture? Nobody is born wicked? It's experience that shapes the innocent?"

"I would say so, sir."

Hunt gave a grunt and looked away again.

"You told Kenneth Thompson that you had a daughter. Would you forgive her anything, Detective? I mean anything?"

"I'm not sure, sir. She's no longer with us."

Hunt seemed oblivious; lost in his own grief and torment. "But there comes a time when children are responsible for their actions. Do parents have to forgive everything?"

"I don't think a parent ever stops loving their child, sir," Blake said. Giving Vikki a sidelong glance.

"I suppose that, given your circumstances," Hunt said, "it's a hypothetical question for you."

"Quite, sir," Blake said, wondering if Hunt had meant to be so brutal. "Can I ask, sir, what was the nature of your relationship with Carly Simmonds?"

Hunt froze for a second and then relaxed. "We were lovers. We saw each other for a couple of years and we were very happy. I nearly proposed to her but she found another."

"That would be David Collins?"

"Yes," Hunt said. "She might have been better off if she stayed with me but somehow, I doubt it."

"Did you speak to the police about your relationship with Miss Simmonds when they were investigating her murder?"

"I spoke to an Inspector Leech, I believe," Hunt said. "I told him my whereabouts on the night of the murder and he was satisfied. Then, if I recall, Collins killed himself and left a note confessing to the crime."

"You had no feelings for Carly once you'd separated?" Blake asked.

"Of course I did, Blake. I'm not inhuman. But I acknowledged that she needed a different kind of man. She made an unfortunate choice, it would seem."

"And how did Drucilla get mixed up in all of this?"

Hunt narrowed his eyes. "How do you mean? She wasn't anything to do with Carly. She was investigating Collins and his extravagant lifestyle. I knew nothing about it until she brought me papers from my office and showed me how he was fiddling the books. If he hadn't killed himself, I would have dealt with it myself; sacked the man and got the debt collectors to retrieve what they could. I wouldn't have involved the police."

"But you did notify the police," Blake said. "Didn't you?"

"No. Drucilla notified them. She dragged us into the papers with her glory hunting and, to be frank, I could have done without it. We had words about that but she went ahead and carried on hanging around with that idiot Gerald Rees."

“And of course, then she solved the Stephen Bradshaw case. Getting Cameron Lock convicted,” Blake said.

“We weren’t aware that you owned the Lock’s house, sir,” DS Chinn said. “That must have been embarrassing; having a killer as a tenant.”

“Death follows me like a shadow,” Hunt said. “It’s not embarrassing. It’s tragic. I’m getting weary, now, detectives. I want to grieve for my son in peace.”

“We have a witness that says he saw Drucilla entering the house after Josie Lock’s death...”

“That wouldn’t surprise me,” Hunt said, massaging his temples. “She was probably trying to solve that case too. My daughter craved attention, Mr Blake. Any kind of attention, good or bad. That was my fault. Don’t get me wrong, I loved her and she could be loving back but there was a wildness in her that couldn’t be tamed. Now, if you’ll forgive me, I’ll have to insist that you leave. I am very tired. It has been the worst kind of day.”

Blake could see his own frustration mirrored in Vikki's face as they strode across the Hospice carpark. “He’s holding something back,” she said. “He knows something and he won’t tell us.”

“He’s involved with Simmonds, he’s involved with the Lock case,” Blake murmured as they drove back to the station. “Always in the background."

"Suppose he killed Simmonds out of jealousy," Vikki said, "and just wanted to get rid of Josie Lock as a tenant?"

"I could see him killing out of jealousy. But he only had to evict Josie Lock. I imagine the Locks weren't popular in the area. And anyway. Once she was dead he would have rented the house out again. But he left it to rot, which is strange in itself."

Back at the Incident Room, Manikas and Kinnear were waiting eagerly for Blake and Chinn. "What's up with you two?" Blake said. "You look like you're going to wet yourselves."

"We did some digging, sir," Kinnear said. "And it turns out that Fiona James, the owner of the court shoes, committed suicide after her son's murder."

"Her son was Stephen Bradshaw," Manikas added.

"Right," Blake said, a frown creasing his forehead.

Manikas, opened up a file. "So we found some old news cuttings about the suicide. Apparently, she threw herself off a footbridge onto the A41 in front of a lorry."

"Okay, that's sad but..."

Kinnear held up the paper. "Look at the headline, sir: ‘Tragic Mum Walks Barefoot to her Death.’ Fiona James wasn’t wearing shoes when she died.”

CHAPTER 35

The fact that Fiona James had walked barefoot from her home to a nearby footbridge in the middle of the night may not necessarily have been that much of a revelation on its own. But as Blake read the paper clipping, his blood ran cold. "An eye witness, Drucilla Hunt, had been driving past and stopped her car but was too late to intervene. 'It was so tragic,' she said. 'Had I been there a few seconds earlier, I could have stopped her. I feel responsible.' My God," Blake muttered to himself.

"Read on," Manikas said.

"'In a bizarre twist, Hunt recognised Miss James as a member of her father's domestic staff. Fiona James worked as a cleaner at the home of Victor Hunt for several years. 'The family is very upset by the sad news,' Drucilla added. 'She was a much loved and valued member of the household team. Fiona will always be in our thoughts.' Friends report that Fiona James had been depressed for some time after the murder of her son Stephen Bradshaw...' Didn't anyone think it was even slightly fishy that Drucilla Hunt just happened to be driving past in the middle of the night and saw someone she knew?"

"What was it her father said? She craved any kind of attention?" Chinn said. "Do you think she knew James was going to kill herself and followed the poor woman?"

"I think you're being charitable there, Vikki," Blake said. "I'm beginning to think Drucilla Hunt was capable of a whole lot more." He turned to Kinnear and Manikas. "Well done, you two. Do a bit of digging. Find anyone who knew Fiona James. Let's get a full picture of her links to the Hunt family."

"We're onto it, sir," Kinnear said. "We've found the name of Stephen Bradshaw's father. Thought he might be worth talking to."

"Great. Vikki, can you go back to the charity shop and see if there's any way we can figure out where those boxes came from? I know we've asked but a second look might just jog someone's memory. I'm going to talk to Gerald Rees again."

"Right, sir," Vikki Chinn said. She gave him an enquiring glance.

Blake raised his eyebrows and then looked over at the growing mountain of paperwork on his desk. "That's me for the rest of the day, Chinn. If I don't tackle that lot, I'll need crampons to get the top files."

Walking through Bromborough from the car-park to the charity shop, it struck Chinn that the vast majority of people she passed wouldn't have a clue what went on in their local community. The weirdness and downright nastiness that she was confronted with everyday depressed her sometimes. The thought that such darkness could lurk under a veneer of normality would drive her mad if she didn't acknowledge that there must be acts that contradicted this pattern. For every crime or callous cruelty she encountered, there were small acts of kindness and love shown between family, friends and neighbours every day.

The charity shop was a good example of that; people giving up their time to support the hospice. That's how Chinn liked to frame the world, anyway. She knew a few people on the force who viewed whole swathes of the population as scum but she couldn't do that. The revelations of this case shook her faith in humanity, though, it had to be said.

At the hospice shop, Jamie stood at his post, larger than life and twice as cheerful. "Shall I wrap that for you, love, or do want to wear it now?" he said to an old woman carrying a flowery dress from the clothes section. "You goin' to seduce your fancy man, tonight?"

The old lady gave a shrieking laugh and draped the dress over the counter. "Give over, Jamie," she said, giggling like a schoolgirl. "It's for the British Legion on Friday."

"What? All of them? Ooh, you saucy minx!" he said, giving her a theatrical wink. "Well, I think you'll be the belle of the ball. Or is it bingo on Friday?"

The old woman left chuckling and Jamie turned to Chinn, who held up her warrant card. His face fell slightly. "How can I help?"

"Could I have a look round, Jamie?" Chinn said. "I'm trying to see if there's a way we can work out where those boxes came from. I just want to get my head round how this place works. You know, in case there's something we've missed."

Jamie pulled a face. "Be my guest," he said. "Natalie isn't around but I'm sure she wouldn't mind. Any queries, just ask."

"Natalie Murphy? Is she normally off?"

"Never," Jamie said. "But she's hardly been back since last week when all this kicked off. Her mum didn't do very well after that choking fit apparently."

"I see," Chinn said. "Can I?" She pointed to the back of the shop and the sorting room.

A couple of volunteers were busy pulling old clothes out of plastic bags and assessing them for shop-worthiness or recycling. Chinn gave them a nod and flashed her warrant card. "Morning Ladies," she said. "Can I ask you a few questions?"

The women were as forthcoming as they could be, but knew nothing. One had been on holiday last week and the other had only just started. Chinn looked around at the piles of jumbled clothes in cages, the furniture and the bric-a-brac. The place closed in on her. She'd never seen so much stuff all jumbled together. It was a testament to how much junk was thrown away every day and how many things we buy that we really don't need.

A doorway led further back into the building where an office crammed full with plastic chairs and coffee-making facilities, paper and folders, looked out across the sorting room. Behind the office, a corridor led to a flight of steps. Vikki made her way up and found herself standing in a long room, stacked to the ceiling with second-hand goods. If she'd felt overwhelmed by the amount of junk downstairs, this room made her feel positively small.

On one side of the room cage after cage full of clothing stood, just waiting to be sorted. On the opposite side of the room, row upon row of clothes hung on hangers and next to them stood empty filing cabinets, a rocking horse, bags of golf clubs, stacks of board games, bedheads, chairs and tables, even a couple of old tills. The centre of the room was filled with a column of crates stacked on top of each other full of crockery, paper, toys, books, magazines and ornaments. A few mannequins poked out of the crates and stared at her with blank eyes. Chinn shivered. The tube lights flickered up here and it smelt musty and damp. It felt like she'd wandered into some kind of underworld.

Somewhere further back in the room, something rustled and moved slightly. Chinn crept along the rows, holding her breath. As she approached the end of column of crates, a man appeared and almost walked into her. Chinn gave a yelp and the man jumped back.

"Blimey, love, you frightened the life out of me," the man said, steadying himself on the crates. He was short, with a shock of white hair and a pot-belly that his simon shirt and baggy corduroy trousers accentuated.

"I'm sorry," Vikki said, laughing. "That's the second time this week someone has crept up on me. DS Chinn." She held up her warrant card. "I'm just looking around."

"Is it about the shoes?" the man said.

"I suppose everyone's heard about them."

"Jamie is hardly what you'd call discreet. If you want a message to get out, just pass it on to Jamie, he'll broadcast it to the world. I'm Sean, by the way. Sean Miller. I do all the PAT testing on the electrical goods up here."

"What days do you work?"

"Most days, really. It gets me out of the house and there's an endless supply of things that needs safety checking and testing."

"Were you here when the shoes were delivered?"

"Yeah. It was the Monday evening before that poor kid was killed. The shop was shut and I was up here when the buzzer rang and, as there was nobody else here, I went down and opened the back door."

"And someone had left the boxes?"

"No. It was the house clearance lads, Barry and Nick," Sean said. "I told Natalie all this. Asked her if I should go to the police but she said she would pass it on."

Vikki frowned. "So, the house clearance men brought the boxes?"

Sean nodded. "That's right. The lads were full of it. A big old house. It was quite a haul. The owner sold the furniture and anything really valuable but he gave what was left to the hospice. It was mainly clothing and such but a lot anyway. The lads brought that here. I remember the boxes coming in because they looked a bit unusual."

"The big house. Can you remember where it was?"

“Oh yeah, it was an odd name too,” Sean grinned. “Priest House in Raby.”

CHAPTER 36

Peter Bradshaw, father of Stephen, the murdered boy, proved harder to track down than Kinnear had hoped. His last known address proved to be a homeless hostel in Birkenhead but he'd moved on from there a couple of weeks ago. The manager of the hostel told them that Bradshaw had a sister in West Derby, over in Liverpool; he even gave them an address. Kinnear sat in the driving seat of the car and drummed the steering wheel impatiently. "I thought we were onto something."

Manikas frowned at the rain trickling down the windscreen. "Don't worry. We can check out his sister's over in Liverpool."

"I know," Kinnear said, smiling. "Just these people with their lives, moving around with no regard for us."

"Yeah," Manikas said, grinning back. "Who do they think they are? Don't they realise Merseyside's two greatest detectives need to talk to them?"

"Come on, let's go over the water."

Kinnear drove down through the terraces of Birkenhead towards the river and the Mersey

Tunnel entrance. “Abandon hope all ye who enter here,” he said as the mouth of the tunnel enveloped them.

“I never got that rivalry between Liverpool and the Wirral,” Manikas said. “Seems a bit weird to me.”

“Don’t think it’s rivalry, really,” Kinnear said. “Liverpool couldn’t give a toss about the Wirral. It’s people on the Wirral who get their knickers in a twist about scousers…”

"I take it you've had Blakey's 'Wirral talk' then," Manikas said. He put on a pompous voice. "This is the Wirral, Kinnear, strange, weird..."

Kinnear laughed. "Yeah, once or twice. You're entering the Twilight Zone..."

“People always think the Wirral is dead posh but if you stood in most streets in Birkenhead or Wallasey,” Manikas said, “you could be in Liverpool and vice versa. There’s no real difference.”

“Not until you get over to Caldy. Footballers live in Caldy. Different world, there, mate. All sandstone and iron gates.”

Manikas grinned. “And then there’s Neston…”

“Nobody talks about Neston,” Kinnear said shaking his head melodramatically.

Pete Bradshaw’s sister’s house backed up Manikas’ argument. She lived in a small mid-terrace in West Derby almost identical to the houses they'd passed driving into Birkenhead. It was clean and whitewashed, the front garden concreted over and the wall knocked out to accommodate a car.

A short, trim, middle-aged woman with her dye-blonde hair scraped back in a ponytail answered the door. She wore marigold gloves and held her hands in front of her like a surgeon about to operate. "Hi," she said.

"DC Kinnear, madam, this is DC Manikas. Merseyside Police…"

"Is this about our Peter?" The woman said. "I'm his sister, Kirsty. What's he done this time?"

"Nothing, madam," Kinnear said. "He's not in any trouble. We just want to ask him a few questions. About Fiona James."

Kirsty's face hardened. "I haven't seen Peter for weeks. He's not doing very well, I'm afraid. And bringing up all of that business again won't help him. He never got over it."

"Have you any idea where we might find him?"

She thought for a moment. "He hangs around the city centre. Usually round the Adelphi or Lime Street Station. Pissed off his head or Spiced up to the eyeballs. You won't get much sense off him."

"Thanks," Manikas said and turned to leave but paused. "Can I ask? Did he have much to do with his son, Stephen and Fiona?"

"He did at first but then something changed just before Stephen went missing. He stopped seeing them as much. He took all the pictures of them down in his bedsit as well. He'd always had problems with drugs and drink and I think losing the kiddie and Fiona finished him off, to be honest. But it had started long before that."

Back in the car, Kinnear exchanged a meaningful look with Manikas. "So what changed things, before Stephen died?"

"I can have a good guess but I'd love to hear it from Peter Bradshaw's mouth before I commit myself," Manikas said.

A fine drizzle had set in over the city, making the paving stones around Lime Street slick and shiny. They parked behind the station and walked down towards the Adelphi Hotel.

"I never saw the sense in it myself," Kinnear said. "Moving all the shops down towards the river. It just pulled all the shoppers away from this end of town. It's all just fried chicken joints and vape shops here, now. Lewis' is empty and in the middle of it all is the Adelphi. Did you know Charles Dickens used to stay there?"

"Liked the footie, did he?" Manikas said, with a grin.

It didn't take long to find Peter Bradshaw. A

woman wearing three coats and fifteen scarves tried to scrounge some cash off Kinnear and got a fiver for leading them to the man himself. Peter Bradshaw was emaciated. He looked thirty years older than his sister. He leaned against the steps on Bold Street, his eyelids heavy and his cheek bones jutting through a long grey beard. He reminded Kinnear of a picture of Rip Van Winkle from a kid's book. His toothless sunken mouth meant that his features seemed to fold in on themselves. He wore an old green army jacket and stained jeans. Kinnear squatted down and shook the old man. "Peter Bradshaw?"

Bradshaw startled awake and scurried back away from them. "Fuck off!" he yelled swinging his head around to see who he was yelling at.

"Easy, fella," Kinnear said. "Listen, we only want to talk to you. Can we buy you a hot drink. Maybe some food?"

The mention of food brought Bradshaw up short. "Burger King," he said, narrowing his eyes. "You bizzies?"

"Yeah. You're not in any trouble, Peter," Manikas said. "Just a quick word."

The attendant at the Burger King eyed Bradshaw with disapproval as he stood next to Manikas and Kinnear. They must have looked a peculiar sight. The two policemen in dark suits and Bradshaw in layers of crusty jumpers topped off with a stained green jacket. Kinnear could smell the stale odour from the man. They sat down and watched as Bradshaw wolfed the food down and swigged great mouthfuls of coffee laced with about ten sachets of sugar.

"So, we wanted to talk to you about Fiona, Pete," Kinnear said. Bradshaw froze, his cup still at his lips. Then he slammed the cup down, making a number of customers glance across at them.

"Bitch," he hissed.

Kinnear raised his eyebrows. "Really? I thought you'd have a bit more respect for the mother of your child."

Bradshaw stared at him from under his bushy eyebrows, revealing years of pain and hurt still smouldering. "Not mine," he said.

"What?"

"Wasn't my child," he said. "I thought it was but no. Then he was taken, wasn't he? Taken away." Bradshaw gazed into his coffee.

"So you're saying that Stephen Bradshaw wasn't your son?" Manikas said.

"I thought he was but he wasn't," Bradshaw muttered, scratching his beard and smearing coffee and mayo into his moustache. "She told me. Said she was going to make him pay."

Kinnear leaned forward, oblivious to the

smell. "Make who pay? What do you mean?"

"She was going to get money. What's the word?" Bradshaw clicked his grubby fingers. "Blackmail. Yeah that. Blackmail. She said he'd pay for Stephen like he should. They were going to have a better life. But then he was taken. Taken away. Taken away."

"Who was she going to blackmail, Peter?" Manikas said. "Who was Stephen's father if it wasn't you?"

Bradshaw blinked at them both. "Posh fella. Victor Hunt."

Maybe it was the break from routine or the thought that they might be helping with a serious crime investigation but Barry and Nick, the clearance lads for the shop, were more than happy to escort DS Chinn to Priest House to show her where the boxes had come from. They'd driven behind her car in the hospice van, grinning like lunatics and chatting so animatedly that at one point, Chinn thought they hadn't noticed she'd stopped at some lights and were going to ram into her. They arrived at the house without incident and the two men bundled out of the van.

"Do we need to suit up?" Barry said, looking at the blue and white police tape that fluttered across the door and window. “You know, those white suits and masks they have to wear at crime scenes…”

“Oh yeah and those rubber gloves,” Nick added, extending his hand and miming slipping a latex glove on. He even made the snapping sound.

“No,” Chinn said. “It’ll be fine. I think CSI have finished with the place. Best not to touch anything, though, okay?” Barry and Nick nodded enthusiastically and followed as she let them in.

Priest House lay dark and cold. Chinn could just see the edge of the blood stain on the bare floorboards in the front room. She turned, facing the men so they had their backs to it. “So, where were the boxes?”

Barry pointed to a cupboard under the stairs on her left. She pulled it and was rewarded with an echoing creak that told her that the door opened onto a much larger space than just a cupboard. She flicked the light on and saw a flight of stone steps leading down into a cellar.

“Marcus Hunt had sold and sent all the big furniture to the auction rooms to sell. But there was still a lot of bits and pieces he didn’t want; you know, modern stuff, some clothes and the like. So we spent a few days clearing the place. Thought we’d finished but then, on Monday, just as we were doing a last check, Nick found the cellar," Barry said, raising his voice above the clatter of their shoes on the stone steps. "We couldn't find the key at first but then, we realised it was on another set that we'd found upstairs. So we opened it up. The orders were to clear the place, after all."

They stood in the middle of a square room. The whitewashed walls had been painted over some time in the past with images from the seventies; Rolling Stones tongues and rainbows jostled with wizards in pointed hats, dragons, demons and stars.

"There was a big oak wardrobe in the corner, locked but with the key in it. That's where we found the boxes and all the clothes and things." Nick shuffled a little on the spot. "To be honest, some of the things were a bit odd. Handcuffs, ropes and syringes. It all looked a bit weird. We chucked them out."

"The place hadn't been opened for years. It was like it had been sealed up and left. A time capsule sort of affair."

But Vikki had stopped listening. She was mesmerised by one wall in particular. It was dominated, floor to ceiling, by a single word written in thick, blood-red capitals 'DRUCILLA.'

CHAPTER 37

After hours of combing through interview accounts, assessing evidence and writing reports, Blake wondered what on earth had led him to make the call. His head thumped and he still ached from the close encounter with Adam Sampson's back gate. The garage had rung to say that they had a part for the Manta on order and should have it back to him for tomorrow. Blake smiled. If he wasn't going to give up on Serafina, he wasn't going to give up on the car. Sometime in the day, he'd even found time to phone Laura to see if there was any chance of an appointment on his way home.

Serafina's truce had lasted no time at all. That morning, Blake had been awakened by a screeching and wailing and when he went downstairs, he found a huge section of hall wallpaper scratched to tatters. When he'd prepared Serafina's food, she'd bitten his hand; not a great idea as the old adage goes. But part of him wanted to see Laura again, too. Having someone in the house had made him realise just how lonely he was.

Laura Vexley picked up straight away. "Will, how's it going?"

"Not great, I'm afraid," Blake admitted. "She's using the litter trays but she scratched the hall wallpaper to bits this morning."

"Well, it is a bit old-fashioned, Will," Laura said. From her voice, Blake thought he could sense a smile.

"So you're telling me Serafina is making statements about the house décor, now? Maybe I should contact an interior designer instead of a cat shrink."

"I can come round tonight with some wallpaper samples and see what she has in mind for the decorator?"

Blake grinned. "That would be great, Laura. And I must pay you for your last session. The litter trays worked, so you've given me good advice."

"Don't you worry about that. We'll settle up when Serafina is happy. I'll be round about eight, yeah?" She hung up, leaving Blake staring at the phone with a vacant smile on his face. The headache seemed to have faded and he was left wondering quite what had been arranged.

Laura Vexley turned up holding a bottle of wine and wearing an electric blue jumpsuit that looked ready for the dance floor rather than

Blake's living room.

"Hi, come in," Blake said. "You look great. Going on somewhere?"

"No," she said. "I just thought you might like a glass of wine after such a busy day, that's all."

Blake frowned. "How d'you know I've had a busy day?"

"You're a policeman; all your days are busy, aren't they? Besides, I could tell by your voice on the phone." She waggled the bottle. "You want some?"

Blake took the bottle and led Laura into the kitchen. "Thanks. It hardly seems very business-like. Plying your clients with wine and not telling them how much you charge," Blake said, pulling the cork from the bottle and finding some glasses. "Do you normally do this?"

"Not really," she admitted. "Most of my clients don't need my help as much as you do."

"What's that meant to mean?" Blake said, raising his eyebrows at her.

"Whatever you want it to," she said, raising her glass. "Here's to happy cats."

Blake raised his glass. "To happy cats," he said and sipped the wine. "So how long have you been an animal psychologist?"

"I did a Psychology and Counselling degree a

couple of years back," Laura said, folding her arms and leaning against the sink. "But I've always been interested in animals. I decided to have a go at the animal psychology quite recently, really."

"How recently?" Blake said, narrowing his eyes at her over the rim of his glass.

She grinned at him. "I can see why you're a policeman. A few days ago? After I met you, actually. You're one of my first clients..."

"How many other clients have you got?"

"Just you," she said, breezily. "But you have to start somewhere, don't you?"

Blake put his wine glass down. "Let me just get this straight. When I came to the RSPCA Centre the other day, you weren't a practising animal psychologist, were you?"

"That's a bit of a bald statement. I'd been flirting with the idea..."

"So you dived in the back, wrote down your name and number and gave it to me. Did you make up all that Paws for Thought: Behaviour Saviour stuff on the spot?"

She took a gulp of her wine and grinned again. "No, I'd been throwing ideas around for a while and then you turned up and I thought, 'why not?' The psychology is as much the owner as the pet, you know. And you, Detective, intrigue me."

"I see," Blake said. He was surprised he didn't feel angry about Laura's admission. Maybe it was because her advice was sound so far or maybe it was something else. "So what's your assessment of me, then?"

She smiled again. "I haven't made up my mind yet. Anyway, I'll ask the questions, if it's all the same to you, Mr. Policeman. How long did your mum have Serafina before she left?"

Blake picked up his wine and took another sip. "I don't really know. Five years, maybe? She didn't have her when I first moved in..."

"So, your mother was fine when you moved back in with her?"

"Yes," Blake said. "Well, no. These things don't happen overnight, do they? If you must know, I'd split up from my wife and had nowhere to go."

"When you first invited me in, you said it was your mother's house. Don't you see it as your home too?"

Blake took a long swig of his wine. "I don't suppose I do," he said. "And my brother would have something to say about it if I got too comfy. I crash out here. Eat. That's about it."

"Where's Serafina now?"

"I don't know. Living room I think." They went through and found the cat asleep on his mother's chair once again.

"Maybe she feels secure when there are voices in the house. People having conversations, doing things. It all feels normal to her."

"I'll have to get you to come round more often," Blake said. "Or take in lodgers."

"Don't take in lodgers," Laura said, leaning over and stroking Serafina's ear. The cat purred loudly and tilted her head to get the most out of the contact. "You see, the odd stroke now and then works wonders. If you spend your time ignoring her then she'll become stressed."

"I don't ignore her," Blake said. "I feed her. I say hello. I wasn't ignoring her when I was up the tree at the front at whatever ridiculous hour the other day..."

"That's something else you can do for me," Laura said, her green eyes teasing him. "Next time you're out on an important case, have a look in any trees you pass. See if you can find any cat skeletons."

"Cat skeletons?"

"Yeah. You know. If cats genuinely got stuck in trees all the time, some would die up there, right? But they don't because most cats eventually get themselves down. Give her a chance to sort her own problems out."

Blake nodded. "Fair enough." He paused and looked at her. "You did a psychology degree, right? Like a human one..."

"Yes," Laura said, laughing. "I told you. Why?"

"What do you know about revenge? I don't mean cutting up another driver because they annoyed you on the road. I mean long-term, grudge-bearing, over years, possibly decades. Does that happen?"

Laura thought for a moment. "I think it does. Some narcissistic individuals might harbour a sense of injustice about something and have fantasies of revenge for a long time. Certain people who have experienced social rejection and isolation because of some event may turn to ideas of revenge. I suppose if those ideas were reiterated and reinforced over the years then the person might eventually act on them."

"How do you mean, reiterated?"

Laura shrugged. "Some of the cases we studied were feuding families. You must have seen films about the frontiersmen in the US. Whole families fighting over an old grudge. Well, that occurs all over the world. It tends to be confined to criminal cultures where there is a resistance to policing. Criminal gangs can succumb to violent feuds. So if a member of that group is brought up hearing all the reasons to hate another group of people, they might become overzealous."

"Do you think it could happen in a family

group? Round here?"

"I don't think we've got the Hatfields and the McCoys battling it on Bidston Hill, have we?"

Blake laughed. "No but on a smaller scale. If a child was fed a particular story about an injustice against their father or another family member. Some kind of grudge could be fed, couldn't it?"

"It could, I suppose," Laura said. "Look, I'm no expert and it'd have to be some kind of dysfunctional family but some kind of blood feud could be encouraged. They're generally 'eye-for-an-eye' kind of things, I think. Families taking tit-for-tat revenge on each other." She paused. "I don't know. To be honest, I feel more comfortable talking about cats."

"Me too," Blake said, "but you may have helped me more than you think."

Laura held his gaze and smiled. "Good. Now the other day, we were talking about fun…"

The shotgun barrel felt cold in her hands but she liked that. The best things are done cold. Anger gave you that surge of strength to finish the job. When Marcus Hunt had died, she was cold and calculating until the first blow. That had been her strength. She'd picked up his shotgun and brought it with her. It would be useful.

She'd be cold like the shotgun barrel. She cracked it open and frowned. It would all end tomorrow. One way or another. She wouldn't let the dying man slip away without paying him a visit. But he was last on her list.

The idiot had to get his comeuppance first. And someone, no, something else. The sense of betrayal had grown these last few weeks but it had been there from the first moment she saw the dying man in the hospice. All those years of giving, of sacrifice, just so they could pay some bimbo nurse to plump his pillows and flutter her eyelashes at the old goat. No. That's not good enough. She snapped the shotgun shut.

Thursday October 31st (Hallowe'en)

CHAPTER 38

He didn't have to be the world's greatest stand-up or raconteur to deliver information to the team in the Major Incident Room but Blake was firmly of the opinion that Detective Constable Ian Ollerthwaite shouldn't be allowed to talk in public to any group, however small. In fact as the briefing went on, he became convinced that Ollerthwaite shouldn't be allowed to talk to anyone at all. Ever again.

Ollerthwaite was a member of the wider team and dealt almost exclusively with any aspects of fraudulent accounting. Blake could feel his eyes grow heavy as the thick-set constable droned on about Victor Hunt's business interests.

It was vital information and should have kept him riveted but something about Ollerthwaite's delivery was vocal ketamine. Blake glanced around, gratified to see Kath Cryer stifling a yawn and Manikas rubbing his eyeballs into the back of his head.

Memories from the previous night filled his head; he thought back to Laura and how she'd wrapped herself around him. How he'd frozen, unable to return her warm kiss. She said she understood; that it was too soon but she didn't know. Didn't know that he didn't deserve affection. It had been almost thirteen years since Ellie had died and he'd split up from Nicole. Everything had vanished in that year, Searchlight, his daughter, his wife, his future.

Since then, he'd immersed himself in work. He'd buried his feelings of guilt and grief. And just when he was beginning to find his feet, his father died and his mother began her slow decline into dementia. Why risk even a moment of happiness when it can be snatched away from you so suddenly and brutally? He couldn't explain all that. And so she'd left. Blake snapped himself back to the briefing.

"So, in conclusion, it appears that most of Victor Hunt's business rivals have either retired," Ollerthwaite counted the options on his chubby fingers. "Died or moved abroad. Some have done both..."

Kinnear put his hand up. "What, Ian? Died and moved abroad."

Ollerthwaite's droopy moustache twitched back and forth as he ruminated on Kinnear's question but he didn't crack a smile. "No, retired and gone abroad. I see my error there. I'll amend that in the written report. Thank you, Andrew, that's a very helpful observation."

"So, we can rule out any financial or business rivalry as a motive in this investigation?" Blake said.

Ollerthwaite nodded slowly. "I believe so, sir. Hunt retired from business a long time ago and has benefitted from investments and passive income. Even when he was more active, members of the business community who are still with us have only good things to say about him. He was a shrewd businessman but surprisingly popular. A deeper investigation into his finances might reveal something but..."

"We'd have to be certain what we were looking for and have a justifiable cause to go rooting. Which we haven't," Blake said, winding Ollerthwaite down. "Two of Hunt's children have been killed. It can't be coincidence."

"Anyone who might have a grudge against Hunt from around the time of the original murders is either dead or too old to have committed the current crimes," Vikki said.

"Children," Blake replied. "What about the victim's children?"

"Guv?" Kath Cryer said.

"I was thinking about revenge last night. Who in this group of people might have been left destitute or shamed as a child by the murders?" Blake said, turning to look at the cluttered picture board. "What if they blamed Drucilla and, by association, Victor Hunt for some reason?"

"Why would they blame Drucilla, sir?" Cryer said.

Blake rubbed his temples. "We're pretty certain she planted evidence on some of the people she had arrested. She certainly gained a certain amount of fame from the cases. Imagine if someone's life spun out of control because of one of the murders. They're likely to blame Drucilla and, maybe the whole Hunt family for the disaster, right? Gerald Rees said that Rebecca was the spitting image of Drucilla. Maybe it triggered some terrible reaction." He slumped against the desk. "I don't know. Maybe I'm clutching at straws."

Kinnear shifted in his seat. "Fiona James and her son are dead and I can't imagine Peter Bradshaw getting it together enough to catch a bus back to the Wirral let alone plan and commit murder."

"The Locks had no other relatives as far as we know," Vikki said. "The house is a ruin. Hunt never rented it out again. There's nobody there who might want revenge."

"Carly Simmonds had a sister, Carol," Kath Cryer said, slowly. "Always in her shadow. Carly had a thing going with Hunt before she moved onto David Collins. Collins was embezzling from Hunt. Could she have blamed Hunt somehow?"

"Did you meet her?" Blake said.

"No, I interviewed her mother. Carol was out."

"Go and find her. Talk to her. Kinnear, you go with Kath."

Kinnear looked as though Blake had slapped him in the face. "Who me, guv?"

"There's nobody else called Kinnear on the team. It's possible we're dealing with a violent psychopath; I don't want anyone out on their own."

Cryer rolled her eyes. "Don't worry Kinnear, I won't bite you."

Manikas raised a hand. "Guv, didn't Collins have a couple of kids, too? He was publicly shamed by Drucilla. If anyone might hold a grudge against the Hunts, it could be someone from the Collins family."

"That's true, Manikas, you and Vikki see if you can find where they are now," Blake said, turning back to the photo board. "Maybe we're getting somewhere."

An awkward silence filled the car as DI Cryer and Kinnear drove down the M53 towards the Simmonds' house. Kinnear hated it. He felt as though an invisible barrier had fallen between them. He looked out of the window and watched the green embankment flash by. Every now and then, a housing estate or school building would reveal itself as the slopes and fenceline dipped. He took a breath. Wasn't he going to have a word with her, rather than take it to Blake? But now his words felt trapped in his throat. If he spoke now, he'd end up shouting.

Suddenly, Kath broke the silence. "So, what's your problem, big boy?" she said, staring ahead as she drove.

"Sorry, Ma'am?" Kinnear said, raising his eyebrows. "What d'you mean?"

"Well, it seems like whenever I make any kind of comment, you grind your teeth and go as red as a nun in a pole-dancing club."

"It's nothing, Ma'am."

"No, really. You can be straight with me," Cryer said.

Kinnear searched her face for a smirk or any sign that she was trying to be funny. "Well, it was just that some of those comments you made felt like they're directed at me. Because of who I am."

Kath raised her eyebrows. "Really? Why? cos you're gay?"

Kinnear hated himself for it but years of hiding still made it hard to just acknowledge this and let the conversation flow. "Yeah," he said, trying to sound casual.

"Well, you're going to have to man up, aren't you Kinnear?"

Kinnear felt as if he waser who called falling down a lift shaft. "Man up? What d'you mean by that?"

He noticed Cryer give him a sidelong glance. "I worked bloody hard to get where I am, Kinnear. And I didn't spend my life worrying over comments about my tits or whether I had PMT or who I shagged to get promotion. I just got on with it. I expect you to do the same. I'm not the most touchy-feely of people but I'm good at catching criminals. You will be too if you stop getting all twitchy about every other word someone says. Just for the record, I don't really care if you're gay, straight, bi or whatever so long as you do a good job. Okay?"

Kinnear felt numb. "With all due respect, ma'am, I thought we'd got beyond that...

"Beyond what?"

A spark of anger flared in Kinnear's gut. "All this 'banter' and 'leg pulling.' Just because you've had to put up with crap like that all your life, doesn't give you the right to shovel some my way. You should know better. I don't care if you're the best DI in the world. Taunt me about my sexuality one more time and I'll take it to DCI Blake. Ma'am."

Cryer glanced at Kinnear and pursed her lips.

"Suit yourself," she muttered, locking steely eyes on the road ahead.

Kinnear stared out of the window at the passing cars and houses. He didn't feel any better. And he knew he'd made an enemy, but he was glad he'd stood his ground. They drove on in frosty silence until they came to the address and pulled the car over outside Carol Simmonds' house.

A mousy, middle-aged woman was climbing into a Ford Ka and paused as they walked towards her.

"Carol Simmonds?" Kath said, flashing her warrant card. The woman nodded. "We'd like to ask you a few questions. Is that alright?"

"I'm on my way to work," Carol said.

Kath gave a tight smile. "I honestly don't think this'll take long."

Carol led them back into the house and into the back room which had a dining table and some elegant oak chairs sitting around it. Kath glimpsed Carol's mother dozing in her armchair as they passed the lounge. "If you can keep your voice down, don't want to wake Mum. Were you the officer who called the other day?"

Kath nodded. "Yes, we're investigating a crime that happened recently. We think it might be linked to the murder of your sister in some way.

Could you tell me where you were on the evening of October 23rd?"

"That was a Tuesday wasn't it? Yeah, I was hand bell ringing at St Oswald's Church just down the road. I go every Tuesday. It starts about six, so I have some tea at work and then go straight on."

"And there are people who can verify this?" Kinnear said.

Carol looked pale. "Course there are, about twelve others and we went to the pub quiz at the Acorn afterwards. What's this all about?"

Kath gave a tight smile. "Don't worry Carol. We're just eliminating you from our enquiries, as they say. I can't really explain more than that. Could you just do me one more favour and roll your sleeves up?"

Carol Simmonds blinked and licked her lips. "Do I have to?"

Kath Cryer shrugged. "You really don't but it would just help us a great deal if you felt able to."

"Oh, alright then," Carol muttered. She pulled off her coat to reveal a Sainsbury's tunic and shirt. Rolling her sleeves up, she revealed her skin crisscrossed with tiny scars; evidence of anxiety and unhappiness. None of the cuts were fresh. "I don't do it anymore. But when Carly went, I couldn't stop. It was my only way of coping. I felt guilty because I was angry with her. I think I was angry with everyone."

"Carol, I'm so sorry," Kath said. "If we'd known, we'd never have asked. It's just that the person we're looking for has scratched arms. Fresh scratches from someone they attacked. As I say if..."

Carol held up her hand. "It's alright, officer," she said. "You've got your job to do. I hope you catch whoever it is. Can't see what it's got to do with Carly but I suppose that's none of my business. It never goes away, you know."

"Sorry?" Kinnear said.

"Whatever you do, it doesn't bring anyone back. And even if someone's in jail, it isn't the end of it. We have to soldier on."

Kath nodded. "I know. Carol. I'm sorry."

"You just have to put it behind you but some can't. Like that Collins woman..."

"Collins woman?"

"Yeah," Carol said. "She came round here a month or so ago. Trying to rake it all up. Making up wild stories about the Hunts and how they killed her dad and it wasn't suicide. I sent her packing, I can tell you. Naomi, she said her name was. Naomi Collins."

Kath sat herself down on a dining room chair. "Carol. Do you mind telling us all about that? It could be useful."

CHAPTER 39

Nobody really expected to find the Collins family in the original family home but for them to have vanished without trace came as something of a surprise. Blake ran his fingers through his hair and sat on the edge of his desk. "Nobody knows where they went?"

Kinnear leafed through some papers. "Licence check and electoral roll drew a blank. We're running some other searches. I thought a door-to-door might get an early result but nothing. One neighbour thought they might have gone down south, another thought she'd heard a rumour that they'd emigrated to Canada..."

"Thought she heard a rumour?" Blake muttered.

"The rest didn't know who they were."

"It was forty years ago, I suppose, Kinnear. Well. I suppose we cross them off the list of people pissed off by the Hunts enough to want revenge."

"Northwich," Vikki Chinn said as she walked into Blake's poor excuse for an office.

"Pardon?" Kinnear said.

"I couldn't find any trace of Naomi or Mrs

Collins at all. But there were two Collins girls, Naomi and Samantha," Vikki said. "Samantha Collins changed the address on her driving licence four years ago. She was living in Northwich, then. I took the liberty of phoning her. She was hesitant at first, saying she didn't have anything to do with her mother or sister. She hasn't since she was sixteen. But she was happy to talk to us."

Kinnear looked at Blake. "Think it's worth a journey out, sir?"

"Yeah, I do. If Naomi Collins has been trying to spread stories about Hunt, her sister might know about it. Or at least know where she lives."

Samantha Collins filled the doorway when she answered Blake's knock. Her tiny house in Barnton, a quiet estate built around a village on the outskirts of Northwich, seemed way too small to accommodate this giantess. She had a spray of dyed black hair and tattoos sleeved her arms. The heavy eyeliner and long, black dress completed the goth look. Blake introduced himself and Chinn, showing his warrant card.

"You'd better come in," Samantha said, stepping back from the door.

Inside the house was clean and orderly. The décor was strangely eighties, with red skirtings and striped wallpaper. Pictures of cats filled the walls. Samantha settled herself in a black, leather armchair and waved a hand to the matching sofa.

"Thank you for your time, Miss Collins," Blake said.

"We're just trying to get a bit of background on an old case..."

"Drucilla Hunt?"

Blake raised his eyebrows. "Yes. How did you know?"

Samantha Collins gave a feline smile. "I read the paper. I heard about that poor girl and that there was interest in the Hunt case."

Vikki Chinn frowned. "I don't think it had made the Nationals. Do you get a local Wirral paper?"

"I do," Samantha said, her face hardened a little. "Just keeping an eye out."

"An eye out for what, Miss Collins?" Blake asked.

Samantha Collins turned her gaze on him and looked him up and down. "Developments," she said. "I left Bromborough when I was sixteen, Mr Blake. As soon as I could get away from my so-called mother and that bitch of a sister, I ran and I didn't look back..."

"You weren't happy at home. Was that because of your father..."

"I was unhappy long before my father killed himself. Ours wasn't what you'd call a perfect family. My mother was very free with her hands and my big sister took her lead from mother. They gave me a dog's life and if my mother was picking on me, she was leaving Naomi alone. When she did pick on Naomi, then my sister passed the shit down the line to me right away."

"I'm sorry," Blake said. "So, when your father died, I imagine things got worse?"

Samantha Collins snorted. "Dad was out most of the time. Or working. When we did see him, we were excited. It was a rare event. But he should have been there for us more. He wasn't. He was off galivanting with his fancy women."

"Your father was seeing other women as well as Carly Simmonds?"

"Sometimes, he'd take us out with him. It was like being in a film and these women were so glamorous. Looking back, now, I can see why he did it. It showed off his caring side, the father figure. A man who cares but is tormented by his bitch of a wife. Yeah, there were many women. Simmonds wasn't all that special."

"Then why do you think he killed her?" Vikki said.

A smudge of crimson tinged Samantha's cheek. "He didn't. Why would he? He was a good-looking man, detective. There were plenty more pebbles on the beach."

"Then who did?"

Samantha Collins paused, mustering her thoughts, getting the words she was about to say in the right order. "At first, I thought it might be my mother. She watched my father get ready to go out that night. He was packing a bag. Then, when he left, she did too. Telling us to be good. Naomi spent the whole evening tormenting and hurting me, but I couldn't forget the look in Mother's eyes. I was only seven but I could see it. Murderous."

"So you're saying she killed Carly Simmonds?"

"No, Mr Blake. I think she would have if she knew where Simmonds was or could have found her but a neighbour brought her home. She'd been drinking all evening. I don't know who killed Carly Simmonds but I know Drucilla Hunt killed my father."

"Really?" Blake said. "By exposing the fact he was fiddling her father's accounts?"

Samantha shook her head. "No. She got him blind drunk. Drugged him with sleeping pills and left him in his car with the motor running and a hosepipe stuck through the window."

"You're saying that Drucilla actually killed your father?"

"Sounds incredible, doesn't it? But we had years to look into it, my mother and my sister and I. We were obsessed with the idea. We found witnesses in the Jockey who swore they'd seen my father and Drucilla drinking together on the night he died. She'd promised to have a word with her father, beg for mercy. One of the lads at the Jockey over in Neston had supplied her with sleeping tablets. He could barely walk out of the pub."

"Drucilla Hunt did all that on her own?" Chinn said. "Seems hard to believe."

"She wasn't alone was she? She had that idiot boy, Gerald Rees, with her."

"Why didn't your mother go to the police with all this information?" Blake said, realising the answer as he spoke.

"Our word against the Hunt family's? How ridiculous would it sound? And would any of those witnesses from the Jockey come forward? No. Their silence was bought with money and fear. My mother became obsessed with revenge. She was psychotic and her rage was turned on us. She hated her husband but blamed the Hunts for his death. Somehow, my sister managed to push all the blame and focus mother's rage on me. Maybe it was because I looked the most like my dad. I nearly died twice from her beatings. I started staying out, sleeping on friends' sofas or bedroom floors when I was twelve. I went back to the house on my sixteenth birthday and Naomi held me as mother came at me with a carving knife. I managed to fight my way free and never went back."

"And Social Services were never involved? Surely the neighbours would have noticed all this going on," Blake said.

"Early on, a social worker called round but by the time I was a teenager, nobody was interested. The neighbours were just plain scared. I worked all over the country and ended up singing on cruise liners. I've been back in the country a few years now but I keep my eyes peeled for any news from the Wirral..."

"You think your mother and sister are still there?"

"They won't have moved far..."

"We couldn't trace them at all. No driving licence or council tax in their name."

Samantha shook her head. "Neither of them drive. My mother reverted to her maiden name. Naomi took it on, too. She even took my mother's middle name. It might be worth searching for a Natalie Murphy."

CHAPTER 40

It makes sense, now, sir," Vikki Chinn said as they drove back from Northwich. Blake was glad to have the Manta back but his resolve to keep it had been slightly dented by the repair bill which, even though it was in numbers, could have spelt 'sell a kidney.'

"Natalie Murphy or Collins or whatever her name really is," Vikki said, enthusiastically, "told us that the boxes hadn't come in with the Hunt house clearance. Why do that unless you wanted to confuse the issue and slow down any investigation?"

"It didn't slow us down that much," Blake said. "But I agree, it does look like she's been interfering. She told the man doing the PAT testing at the charity shop that he didn't need to see us about where the boxes came from. She said she'd pass the information on and then didn't…"

"Despite having plenty of opportunity to tell us when Cryer and I interviewed her," Vikki said. "I bet you she's at the bottom of all this."

Blake frowned. "Killing all of Hunt's children, regardless just for a twisted sense of revenge? That's an awful lot of hatred to keep smouldering for so long. Maybe it was just a perfect storm of events; Rees turning up at the shop, the shoes appearing too. She'd know that Hunt was in the hospice because Marcus had donated stuff from the house to the shop. All that might tip her over the edge." Darkness crept across the landscape as they drove. Despite trying to appear dubious about the revelations about Natalie Murphy, he couldn't shake a sense of disquiet. "If she's right and Drucilla was responsible for Collins' death, it's just possible that she killed the other victims too."

"She 'caught' Cameron Lock, and she was seen at Josie Lock's house around the time of her death," DS Chinn said. "Fiona James allegedly killed herself but Drucilla was there. But if she killed them…"

"Who killed her? I have my suspicions, Vikki. Let's just focus on Natalie Murphy. If she thinks Gerald Rees had a hand in her father's murder, then he could be in danger. And I want him alive to answer questions."

"Should we warn him?"

"I'll call Kinnear and get Murphy's address. We could call in on Mrs Murphy on the way back." Blake said, pulling his mobile out. "Kinnear can go and check on Rees, too."

The Murphy house stood on a small cul-de-sac

that ran off the A41 in Bromborough. Here and there small groups of children in fancy dress carried bags and torches. Every single one was escorted by an adult. As they drove through the village, they saw gangs of teenagers roaming the streets, some dressed as Clocky with white coats spattered in blood and alarm clocks on chains. Blake winced at some of the hideous zombie masks worn by the children. As they pulled up outside the house, volley after volley of fireworks exploded overhead. Blake clambered out of the Manta as screams and yells filled the air.

"Jeez, Hallowe'en is usually mad but this is like the end of times."

"I think the Clocky thing has got out of hand, sir," Vikki said.

The garden gate was rotten and hung from its hinges. Everything around Natalie Murphy's house was overgrown and the building itself looked in desperate need of a lick of paint. Blake rapped his knuckles on the peeling green front door and waited.

Silence.

Vikki leaned back, trying to see in through the front room window but heavy curtains hung at the sides, blocking any view from the door. Blake knocked again.

"They must be out," Chinn said.

Blake frowned. "Wasn't Mrs Murphy an invalid? I thought Natalie had to stay at home and care for her."

"True," Vikki replied. "So, she should be in at this time."

Blake's third knock was more insistent. "Mrs Murphy? Are you in? It's DCI Blake and DS Chinn. We'd like to ask you some questions."

"Nothing," Vikki said after a pause.

Blake edged past her and pushed his way through the straggling bushes that grew in front of the window. He pressed his forehead on the glass, shielding his eyes from the streetlight so he could see inside.

An old woman lay on the living room floor, a cup of something spilt and soaking into the carpet beside her. "Call an ambulance, Chinn," Blake said. "Looks like Mrs Murphy has had a fall." Bracing himself, Blake shoulder-charged the front door. The rotten frame gave a satisfying splintering crack but didn't completely give way. A second rush forced the door wide and sent Blake stumbling into the hall.

The first thing that hit him was the smell; a cloying sweet smell as if the bins hadn't been emptied for weeks. It was ridiculously warm in the house, too. His hand grazed a radiator in the hall as he hurried to the front room and he snatched his hand away, hissing in shock at the heat. A thick layer of dust coated every surface and cobwebs billowed in the corners of the room as he knelt down to the prone old lady. She stared, glassy-eyed across the room, an old, pink dressing gown wrapped around her shoulders. Her stained nightie told Blake that she hadn't been changed for some time. A livid bruise blossomed on the grey skin where her forehead had hit the ground.

"Ambulance on its way, sir," Chinn said, looking over Blake's shoulder. "Is she…?"

"Gone," Blake said, rising to his feet. He dragged an old throw that covered a threadbare sofa and wrapped it around Mrs Murphy. "I'm no pathologist but she's been dead a while." He turned and listened to the silent house. The idea that Natalie Murphy might still be in the house somewhere, hiding, brought an involuntary shiver. He loosened his tie, feeling the sweat drip down his back.

A large dining table squatted in the middle of the back room of the house, surrounded by bookshelves and an old record player from the eighties. Back in the day, it would have been state of the art, all wood veneer and silver knobs. A sound system, radio, double tape deck and a turntable all in one. In fact, Blake noticed, the whole house seemed frozen in time. If you discounted the dust, this would have been a very fashionable property, forty years ago, with its Laura Ashley wallpaper and dado rails. It reminded him of his own home. A mausoleum.

The small kitchen smelt dank and rotten. An overflowing pedal bin and two bin bags sat by a fridge freezer and a sink full of pans and dishes. As if someone was too busy to clear up. It wasn't years of neglect; Blake had seen kitchens where nobody ever took responsibility for cleanliness, and this had none of that ingrained squalor. But it looked as though nothing had been cleaned for many days, possibly weeks. He went back into the hall and headed up the stairs, pausing to look up and listen for any sign of life. The landing above stared back at him, silent and impassive. A light on the chairlift winked continuously at him.

It was slightly cooler up here but the smell of the bins had crept after Blake, following him as he checked the front bedroom. A double bed that looked like it hadn't been slept in for months lay in the middle of the room. Again, the décor was forty-years-ago chic; fitted wardrobes with mirrored doors made the room look twice the size and a miniature chandelier hung from the ceiling. Blake stepped out, opened the back-bedroom door and his scalp prickled. "Vikki," he called down, whilst slipping a pair of latex gloves from his pocket. "You'd better come and have a look at this."

CHAPTER 41

The lights blazed at Gerald Rees' house as Kinnear and Cryer pulled up outside. As soon as Blake had given them a brief run-down of the Collins' interview over the phone, they had hurried over to Rees' place as instructed.

"That doesn't look good," Cryer muttered. Kinnear said nothing, their heated exchange from earlier in the day still scalding him. But he had to agree. Normally, a house with all the lights on invoked a sense of comfort and welcome but now, as they got out of the car, it just looked threatening.

"Not good," Kinnear said at last, staring at the front door that hung wide open. Kinnear hurried up the path, not waiting for Cryer.

Inside, chairs lay turned over. In the hall mirror, Kinnear could see multiple versions of himself in the spiderweb cracks where a shoulder or maybe a head had crashed into it. A light spray of blood reddened his reflection. Papers lay scattered on the floor, a cup of tea overturned had pooled its contents onto the dining room table and soaked into a copy of the Wirral Globe.

"There's been a struggle," Cryer observed.

A thump and a muffled curse came from the living room at back of the house. Kinnear stepped into the hall. "Police! Mr Rees are you all right?"

A woman stepped out from the rear room and Kinnear just had time to glimpse the shotgun in her grasp before Cryer barged into his shoulder, knocking him to the ground. The hall erupted in an explosion of fire as Kinnear fell to the ground. Stars blossomed before his eyes and a sharp pain stabbed down his neck.

Cryer stumbled backwards over him, pushed by the impact of the shot. He heard her head crack on the front door. Something hot scorched a path across his cheek. His ears rang with the noise of the shot in such a confined space and he tried to get up but Cryer's legs were tangled in his. The back door of the house slammed and a cold draft blew the acrid, metallic smell of gun smoke further up the hall.

Disentangling himself, Kinnear made for the back of the house, then looked back to Cryer. She lay deathly still, her arms outspread like she'd been crucified, her head propped up against the front door. The front of her blouse looked shredded and bloodied. He couldn't leave her and give chase. Gently, Kinnear lifted her away from the front door and checked for a pulse.

Blue lights from the road flashed through

the windows and the thunder of boots on the ground followed them soon after. Three uniformed officers burst through the door.

"Police, stand where you are!" One of them shouted, then pulled up short. "Bloody hell, Andy? What's going on?"

Kinnear recognised the uniformed officer from another case. "Scott?" he said, flashing his warrant card for the benefit of the others who he didn't recognise. "Call an ambulance. Shotgun wounds. She's still breathing. But I... couldn't stop it... she jumped in front of me..." The world spun around Kinnear as the shock took hold.

"Whoa, steady, Andy, come on, sit down," Scott said, placing a firm hand on his shoulder.

Kinnear sat on the bottom step of the stairs. "Just got a call from Blakey. Asked us to come down and check on Gerald Rees. Part of the Becky Thompson investigation. Then this mad woman leapt out on us with a shotgun."

"Where is she now?"

Kinnear jumped up and turned to the two officers he didn't know. "Check out the back. Be careful. She's probably long gone but you never know." He looked down at Cryer, who lay in the recovery position. She gave a little groan and Kinnear's heart leapt.

"Ma'am, Kath, Can you hear me?"

Cryer's eyes opened a fraction. "You look like shit," she whispered. Her grin turned into a grimace and she doubled up in pain. "Chest feels like it's on fire..."

"Don't worry Ma'am, you'll be fine," Kinnear whispered, partly to convince himself. "Why did you jump in front of me?"

She gave a strained smile. "I saw it happening, made a call... you'd do the same... we're a team, right?" She closed her eyes.

"Where's that bloody ambulance," Kinnear hissed. Cryer looked bad, there seemed to be a lot of blood.

Some pellets had nicked the side of her neck but her body had taken the main brunt of the blast. He caught a glimpse of his own face in the fractured mirror and noticed a fine cut across his cheek. Blood smudged his face. A stray pellet must have grazed it.

The other officers came back in. "Nothing there. Neighbours say they saw Gerald Rees, the man who lives here being forced into a blue Toyota Yaris at gunpoint by a woman in a hoody. They drove away."

"What about the woman? Any more detail?"

The PC shrugged. "Not much help. Slight, small build. It was dark."

"Okay," Kinnear said. "Get Rees' Reg number.

Notify any cars that might be in the area and warn them, there's a gun. I'll contact DCI Blake. Get back onto control and hurry that ambulance!"

The bedroom could have belonged to a couple of unruly teenagers once; a bunk bed sat in the corner, the top mattress bare but the bottom had a bundle of sheets and a duvet, curled up into a nest. A sea of discarded underwear and clothing lapped against a white dressing table. But there the similarity ended because, instead of posters of popstars, the walls were covered with pictures of Victor and Marcus Hunt, Drucilla, Gerald Rees, along with newspaper clippings of the Becky Thompson case.

Marcus and Drucilla's photos had lurid red crosses daubed across them. But there were older photographs up there too and documents typed on yellowing paper. To one side of the photos, at the edge of the wall, a picture of the hospice shop had been pinned up and 'Burn St Judas. BURN!!!' scrawled across it and underlined several times. Blake inched through the abandoned clothing, trying not to disturb things; this was a crime scene.

As he drew closer to the documents on the wall, his foot bumped against something under the clothing. He squatted down and gently drew back the old sweatshirt that lay over the object. It was a shoe box, plain and brown with a number six written in the corner of the lid. With a single, gloved finger, he pulled back the lid, surprised that it slid open so easily.

Vikki Chinn appeared at the threshold, recognising what Blake had found straight away. "Is it another pair of shoes?" she asked.

"No," Blake said, leafing through gently. "Looks like more papers and photographs." He stood up for a second and took a picture of the box's location in the room, then picked it up. "Let's take this downstairs."

"What about Mrs Murphy?"

"Have any uniform arrived yet?"

"Yes, just but..."

"There's not much we can do and we're better employed here."

Chinn hurried off to sort out the ambulance team. Blake knew he should have left the evidence for CSI to process but what he had glimpsed inside had answered all his questions. He took the box to the dining room and placed it on the large table like a priest lowering a holy relic on an altar. He eased open the lid again and began to take out each sheet, searching it for information. Vikki returned and settled beside him, watching as he unearthed the past.

Fading polaroid photos of a child on a tricycle lay between sheets with numbers, dates and times on them. “It’s a timeline,” Chinn said. “An observational timeline. Look there, ‘11am FJ opens door to check.’ And that one: ‘fifteen minutes max time alone.’ FJ. That must be Fiona James, right? Stephen Bradshaw’s mum.”

There was more. A photograph of Carly Simmonds taken from Cheshire Life. She was dressed to the nines, smiling whilst nestling in the arms of a beaming Victor Hunt. Her face had been crossed out with two thick, black lines from a permanent marker. Beneath that was a grainy, blurred polaroid photo of Simmonds’ body lying by the canal side. More observation notes of Simmonds, Stephen Bradshaw and Cameron Lock followed. The sheaf of notes on each victim was divided by a large photograph of their face crossed out with a black ‘X.’

“The photographs act as a cover,” Blake murmured. “Each one is like a book that maps out how the murder was committed. Bloody hell.” He turned over the next sheet and saw the name Josie Lock scribbled in block capitals at the top of the page. There was a map of the house and in the garden, a large ‘x’ dominated the diagram. “They even planned where to kill her.”

Vikki looked up at Blake. “The two pictures

of Marcus and Victor Hunt. They're from some time ago. Marcus is a little boy on it."

"Natalie Murphy didn't compile this," Blake said. "She would have been a child herself when this was all kicking off. She must have found this box with the other ones that came in and taken it home when Gerald found Drucilla's shoes."

"All this information could have tipped her over the edge, like you said."

"If everyone featured in this box is a potential murder victim, then we have to assume Marcus and Victor were on the hit list," Blake said. "It seems Natalie picked up where the previous killer left off."

Vikki lifted the lid. "Could her mother have been the killer all those years ago? Maybe she knew about Stephen Bradshaw's link to Hunt. Natalie would be carrying on her work..."

"If Mrs Murphy was the killer back then, why would she kill Josie Lock? They had no link to Hunt apart from being tenants of his. Plus, I can't imagine Mrs Murphy engaging the services of Drucilla, right after she'd just exposed her husband as a fraud and an adulterer. Not to mention the allegation that Drucilla actually murdered her husband and made it look like suicide! No, Natalie Murphy is continuing somebody's work but it isn't her mother's."

"Drucilla, like you said before?"

“But she was one of the victims,” Blake said dropping the papers back on the table. “She didn’t strangle herself.”

“She’s the only one missing from this box, sir,” Vikki Chinn said. “There isn’t even a crossed-out photograph. The picture of her upstairs is a photocopy of an old Newspaper report. There’s nothing here outlining Drucilla’s movements. She’s got an intimate connection with every other death”

“You’re right,” Blake admitted. “But someone else killed her. Maybe to stop her from killing again or…” Blake looked down and fell silent.

At the bottom of the box was one last photograph. Sixth-former and love-struck teenager, Gerald Rees in jacket and tie grinned up at them from what was clearly a school photograph. “He was the next victim?” Chinn said.

Blake pursed his lips. “If he wasn’t then, he certainly is now.”

The phone buzzed, startling Blake and Chinn. “Cryer’s down, sir,” Kinnear said. “A woman with a shotgun jumped us. Kidnapped Rees. Neighbours saw him being hustled off in his car. I’ve alerted all units. We don’t know where he is but somebody’s just reported a break-in at the hospice shop in Bromborough…”

CHAPTER 42

Flames had already started dancing in the upper windows of the St Joseph's Hospice charity shop when Blake arrived. A small gang of teenagers in cloaks and face-paint laughed and pointed at the burning building. More fireworks went off around them. A girl screamed and someone shouted something about Clocky wanting his shoes back.

After the call from Kinnear, Blake had turned and hurried downstairs to his car, almost chased by Chinn. "Sir, where are you going?"

"Charity shop," Blake had called back. "That's where Natalie first got reacquainted with Rees. She's furious with the hospice for looking after Hunt too. Remember the picture? St Judas? What better way to punish them than to burn their source of income down?"

"With Rees in it?" Vikki said, slamming the passenger door behind her as they sped off.

"Two birds with one stone. I hope I'm wrong. I really do," Blake had replied but as he slammed on the brakes outside the shop, he could see the fire. "Call the firefighters and an ambulance." He climbed out of the car and started towards the shop but Vikki ran around and grabbed his arm.

"Sir, you can't run into a burning building," she said. "Rees might not even be in there. You'd be risking your life for nothing."

He hesitated but then a silhouette rose up in one of the second-floor windows and head-butted the glass. It was Rees. Blake could just make out something binding his arms. The man would die if he didn't do something. "Fuck it," he said, breaking free from Vikki and sprinting to the front of the shop.

A forlorn, stone planter, relic of a distant Britain-in-Bloom competition, sat forgotten at the side of the shop. Mustering all his strength, Blake heaved the planter above his head and brought it down on the glass of the front door. It splintered, crazing into a thousand white lines. Grunting, he hefted it up again and threw it.

This time, the glass gave way and the door shattered into glittering fragments all over the shop floor. Cautiously, Blake stepped into the shop. The smell of smoke was strong and the lights had already shorted, meaning he was walking into darkness. Slowly, he edged his way to the back of the shop, trying to remember the layout from his last visit.

Something hit his legs just below the knee and he realised too late that he'd walked into a coffee table. A sharp pain blossomed on his left side as he fell, clipping the table and falling heavily on the hard floor. Cursing, he clambered to his feet, groping his way further back. Coat hangers rattled as his shoulder brushed a rack of clothes, he kicked over a vacuum cleaner that got in his way and tripped headlong over what looked like a golf bag that lay across the aisle. Finally, he got to the back room.

A faint, orange light illuminated the room and Blake realised with a sinking stomach that it was the fire upstairs that provided the light. Squeezing round cages of clothes and bins full of cardboard, he began to question the wisdom of coming in; this fire would spread quickly. The smell of smoke grew stronger and he could taste it in the air.

Keeping low, he hurried around to the back office and the stairs behind it. Smoke pooled around the ceiling here, thick and black. He clambered up the stairwell, his throat raw and his breath laboured. Two flights of steps brought him to a door that stood wide open. The heat blasted from inside and Blake blinked in the orange glare.

Bales of cloth, old dresses and suits, books and card, blazed all around the room, plastic toys melted and popped and TV monitors from old computers exploded. A thick veil of smoke was slowly descending from above as it filled the room. In the centre of all this, Gerald Rees whirled around on an old computer chair, throwing himself from side to side in a pathetic attempt to break the bonds that tied him to it.

Coughing and spluttering, Blake rushed forward to unfasten the old belts and ropes that had been used to bind him. Rees grunted at Blake through the pair of stockings that had been stuffed in his mouth.

"Hold still," Blake croaked. "I'll get you free."

Gerald Rees shook his head and wriggled harder, his eyes widening as the pitch of his grunts rose to a terrified, animal squealing. Blake frowned and turned just in time to glimpse Natalie Murphy's snarling face and hear the whoosh of something heavy cut through the air. It sounded like a golf club, he thought, briefly, then stars exploded before his vision and a blinding pain lanced through his head.

Dazed, Blake staggered from the blow. He watched as Natalie Murphy vanished out of the door. He lurched drunkenly after her and fell to the floor. The smoke thickened. It was on his tongue; reaching into his throat and choking him. Intense heat seared his skin and the bright flames blinded him. All around him the fire roared in his ears.

Gerald Rees screamed, his hair aflame, clothes flickering with blue fire. Through sheer animal fear, he had managed to drag one arm free, the belts had torn his flesh but he obviously hadn't cared. Now he beat at his head trying to kill the flames. Shaking himself, Blake dived forward, pulling at the man's bonds. One came free, then another. He tried not to breath as the smoke and heat tore at his throat. Another belt came loose and a scarf that had partially burnt through snapped. Unconscious, Gerald Rees fell forward, pinning Blake.

With a grunt, Blake pushed Rees over. In front of them, the inferno blazed. Not many things at the far end of the big room retained their original shape or form now, some furniture was still recognisable, but most things were a blazing, molten mass. Plastics had melted onto the tiled floor and formed burning pools that slithered towards them. Grabbing Rees beneath the armpit like a swimmer rescuing a drowning man, Blake began to slide backwards on across the floor towards the exit, dragging Rees with him.

The fire chased them, seizing on a rack of wedding dresses by the door and rearing up next to them. Rees groaned but showed no sign of regaining consciousness. With a final effort, Blake scrambled out of the door, kicking it shut, then rolled down the first flight of stairs with Rees, oblivious to the pain inflicted by the hard steps. He found himself pressed up against the back door of the building and reached up to find an opening bar.

The door swung open as he pulled it down, sending him flying backwards with Rees on top of him. The cold air bathed him and swept into his lungs. Strong hands gripped his arms and suddenly he was weightless as he flew from the blazing building. Blake closed his eyes and let darkness take him.

Two nurses and a volunteer huddled over a phone in the corridor outside Victor Hunt's private room, talking animatedly but keeping their voices hushed so as not to disturb anyone. Hunt was a man who knew the value of being alert. It had served him very well during his army days and even when he went into business, he'd found it wise to constantly review his surrounding for any imminent threats. Although painkillers and sedatives coursed through his veins these days dulling the ever-present pain, he never let his guard down. He could hear them saying something about a fire at the charity shop in Bromborough. Someone on social media had said there were people in there. There were police cars and ambulances, a fire engine, the lot. He knew it was time. She was coming. But he was ready.

CHAPTER 43

The sway and rattle of the ambulance drilled through Will Blake's head. A plastic mask blasted cool oxygen through him but he could still smell and taste the smoke. His throat felt like it had been sandpapered and his lungs burned every time he breathed in. Every muscle in his body ached and sharp pain stabbed at his ribs. He tried to sit up but the paramedic eased on his shoulder, forcing him back onto the trolley.

"Steady, mate, you've had a rough time," the paramedic said. "Just take it easy. You saved that guy's life. You've earned a rest."

Blake tried to say something but the paramedic just frowned and shook his head. Blake pulled the mask off. "I have to go to the hospice," he croaked.

The paramedic gave a confused laugh. "No, you'll be fine. You don't need a hospice just yet, mate." He tried to put the mask back to Blake's face but Blake slapped him away.

"No. You don't understand," Blake said, the effort of talking making him breathless. "The man I saved was tied up. The building set alight to kill him. The woman who did it is on her way to the hospice to kill another man there. I have to stop her."

The paramedic looked alarmed and confused. He must have known Blake was a police officer but his duty was to get Blake to hospital. "Should I get the driver to radio control? They could send some officers to the hospice."

"Yes, do that but tell your mate to drive there too..."

"I dunno. You're in a bad state..."

"Just do it," Blake snapped. "Or I'll have you charged with obstruction." The chances of that happening were nil but the paramedic didn't know.

"Alright, keep calm," the paramedic said, his eyes widening. He knocked on the window that linked the driver's cab and the back of the van. "Oy, Kieran. Change of plan. We're going to St Joseph's."

"What? The Hospice? What for?" The driver said.

"Never mind that, just do it. Police business," the paramedic said. He eyed Blake. "Get the lights on too, put yer foot down."

The siren wailed and the whole ambulance rattled as they rumbled along the road. Blake gripped the sides of the trolley he lay on, feeling his innards swirl around as they hurtled around corners, braked suddenly and swerved around something. "Is it far?" he asked, his voice coming out as a low rasp.

"The hospice is on the way to the hospital anyway, detective," the paramedic said, gripping the sides of his seat. "Should be any minute now." He'd barely finished his words when the ambulance came to a sudden halt. Blake closed his eyes and swallowed his stomach back down. He eased himself up off the trolley, wincing with every electric stab of pain.

"Thanks," he said as the paramedic opened the rear doors. For a moment Blake hovered on the back of the van, staring down. The ground seemed like a million miles away. Would his body survive the fall?

"I can get you a ramp," the paramedic said, without a trace of humour.

Blake shook his head and half-fell, half jumped down, yelling in pain as he landed, though he couldn't have pinpointed where the pain was; it was just everywhere. Giving the ambulance a feeble wave, he shuffled down the ramp towards the main entrance of the hospice.

It wasn't until the woman on duty at reception stared at him with wide eyes that Blake considered what a sight he must seem. He turned to look at his reflection in the glass door.

His neck ached so he moved his whole upper

body. A scarecrow of a man stared back in dazed bewilderment at him. His hair sprouted in all directions like an exploded straw bale. Ash blackened his face, darker where blood had streamed down his cheek from the wound just on his hairline. His eyes looked ridiculously white and his lips red like some bad-taste minstrel act. And the right arm of his suit had completely vanished. He stank of smoke, too.

"I'm sorry," he said and his voice sounded strange and strangulated. He rummaged in his pockets, eventually locating his warrant card. "I'm DCI Blake. I need to see Victor Hunt as a matter of urgency."

Then he realised that the woman looked terrified. "She's in there… right now I… she's got a g-gun…"

"Have you called the police?"

The woman nodded. "Y-yes."

"Good. Now, get out of here," Blake muttered gripping the door to Hunt's room and pushing it open.

Natalie Murphy sat on the far side of Hunt's bed, staring at Blake as if he'd burst out of a grave. Apart from the shotgun in her hand, she looked like she'd just arrived from a day at the shop, ready to do a spot of visiting. Hunt sat up in bed, a glass of scotch in one hand and four tablets in the other. "Good God, Blake. What happened to you?"

"She did," Blake said. "Put the gun down, Natalie. More officers are on their way. There's nowhere to run."

"I'm not running," Natalie Murphy said. "I've almost finished, here. Then you can take me away." She looked at Hunt. "Go on, then."

Hunt looked down at the tablets and then back up at Blake. "She's right, Blake. I'm better off dead..."

"You all are," Murphy hissed jabbing the gun at him. "It's in your blood. You're bad to the bone. You, Marcus, Rebecca Thompson," she paused. "Drucilla."

"Yes," Hunt said, nodding. "Bad blood, that's what it is Blake. All my kids have turned out to be wicked..."

"Stephen Bradshaw?" Blake said, leaning heavily on the door jamb. "He was only six. How could he be anything but innocent?"

"Yes, he was one of mine. Given time, he would have shown his true colours," Hunt said, taking a sip of whisky. "I see that now. We're born killers. Drucilla..."

"She killed my father," Murphy said, the shotgun trembling in her grip.

"Well, yes and no," Hunt said, smiling at her as if she was a small child who hadn't quite worked out the way of the world yet. "She did kill Carly Simmonds, though!"

Natalie Murphy narrowed her eyes. "What do you mean?"

"It's true, believe me. I'm about to die. I've no need to make things up. Consider this my confession," Hunt said. "Drucilla had hated Carly Simmonds since she first walked into our house all those years ago. She was young and beautiful, no replacement for Drucilla's mother. The polar opposite, in fact. Jealousy was Drucilla's main weakness. Anyone who took my attention away from her became a focus for her hatred. But I think she killed David Collins just to tie a neat bow under the whole thing and avoid a proper investigation."

"Bastard," Natalie Murphy hissed, her eyes glittering with rage.

"Jealousy. Is that why she killed Stephen Bradshaw? Another male Hunt to crowd up the nest? How did Marcus survive so long?" Blake said. He knew his voice was slurring. Simply standing up was becoming a challenge, too.

"Boarding school," Hunt said, a wry smile cracking his face. "And when he was at home, I watched him like a hawk. Do you want a chair or something?"

Blake shook his head. "But why kill Fiona James?"

Hunt's smile slipped. "Pure jealousy, again," he said. "Fiona had been the object of my affections. She saw that as a betrayal of her mother, I suppose."

"Cameron Lock? Josie?" Blake said, the room swam in and out of focus.

Hunt thought for a moment. "Maybe she envied the kindness I showed them. The Locks lived on my largesse, barely paying any rent. I felt sorry for them, even though they were problematic tenants to say the least. Technically, she didn't kill Cameron Lock..."

Blake gripped the door frame. "She sent him to his death. He didn't last ten minutes behind bars."

"I think by then, she'd just got a taste for killing, too, and thought she could get away with it forever." He looked at Natalie. "Do you know that feeling?"

"If you knew about all this, then why didn't you stop her?" Natalie Murphy snapped, ignoring the jibe.

"He did," Blake said. "Didn't you, Victor?"

Hunt raised his eyebrows and his face darkened. "Once I became aware, I did stop it, yes," he said. "How did you know, Blake?"

"The shoes kept in Drucilla's den," Blake said. "The booklets with notes and photographs.

They were trophies but there wasn't one for Drucilla, just Cameron Lock's shoes. We realised there must have been more than one killer. Besides, you confessed to me. Didn't you? You said you were the worst father possible. I didn't realise what you meant then."

Hunt looked into his whisky glass. "Bravo. I'd known her nature since she was a small child; so many friendships ended suddenly, pets killed or injured and no remorse shown. Nannies who quit without notice. But it wasn't until the Lock case when she really courted the attention of the media and the authorities that I became alarmed."

"Frightened of the adverse publicity, Victor?" Blake said. He'd slid down the door frame and realised he was sitting on the floor.

"You don't have to believe me but I was upset to hear about people close to me dying. One day, she went out to meet that idiot boy for some reason and I took the chance to go down into her cellar and have a rummage around. You can imagine how I felt when I found the boxes."

"When you realised how tainted your bloodline was, you mean?" Natalie Murphy spat. "How crazy you all were..."

"That too, Naomi, that too," Hunt said, almost dismissing her. Blake frowned, wondering why the old man had used Natalie's old name. "Then she came home. She was in a furious rage. Apparently, Gerald had gone on holiday to Scarborough with his parents. He was meant to stay at home. After all the horrors he'd helped her with, he didn't have the backbone to stand up to his parents."

"And that saved his life," Blake said. "If he'd stayed at home, his parents would have returned from Scarborough to find him dead."

Hunt nodded. "She caught me looking at Carly's shoes and flew at me, all teeth and nails." He looked up at Blake. "And I strangled her. What would you do if you found out the daughter you cherished was a monster? I loved my daughter, Blake, but I put her down. Right there in the house."

A silence filled the room. Even Natalie's breathing calmed as they all contemplated Hunt's simple admission. Finally, Blake broke the silence. "But why did you take the shoes from her?"

Hunt sighed. "Taking the shoes diverted any attention away from Cameron Lock and therefore Drucilla and, of course, from me. I had to keep all the evidence of Drucilla's crimes. I couldn't throw it away. It's a burden I carry as a father. Whenever I questioned my actions on that terrible day, I could look at her cold, clinical notes and remind myself that my daughter was a cold-blooded killer."

"And you paid off Gary Archer to confess to killing your daughter," Blake said. "So it was all neatly gift wrapped for Leech."

"Indeed," Hunt said. "You don't rise up in the world as I have without making some shady acquaintances. I dumped her body on the marshes and made a few calls to people I knew could sort the problem. They arranged the cover up. I paid for it."

Outside, the sound of sirens broke the silence. Natalie shifted in her seat, realising that the balance of power and attention was slipping over to Hunt. "That's enough, old man," she said. "You've said your piece. Now take your punishment."

Blake tensed himself, wondering if he could possibly get up off the floor in time to knock the tablets from Hunt's hand. Urgent voices and bodies filled the corridor outside. Victor Hunt lifted the handful of tablets to his mouth and took a sip from the glass. Then he paused and looked at Natalie. "Before I die. There's one more thing you need to know," he said. "And you're not going to like it."

CHAPTER 44

Natalie Murphy's screams sent a jolt of adrenalin through Blake's body. He didn't even have time to register the shock of what Hunt had just said. All he saw was the gun barrel levelling on Hunt. Blake's body was on fire with pain but somehow he was weightless, soaring over Hunt's bed and grabbing for Murphy's wrist. The gun roared, blowing a hole in the ceiling. Blake landed heavily on the bed, sliding over it onto the floor on the other side and dragging Natalie with him.

"Let me go!" She howled, beating down on Blake's head and shoulders. "Let me go! He has to die!"

Blake looked up into the staring dead eyes of Victor Hunt who lay on his side, one arm dangling out of the bed. "I think he's gone."

More commotion filled the room as police officers piled in, dragging Blake and Natalie to their feet. Blake said nothing but kept a close eye on the shotgun that lay just under the bed. Vikki cuffed Natalie Murphy and issued a caution and uniformed officers led her off.

"You got her, sir," she said.

Blake swayed a little and steadied himself on

the end of the bed. "We all got her, Vikki. I think." He looked at Victor Hunt. The old man's eyes were vacant, but he was smiling. The tablets that Murphy had tried to force down him were still in his hand. "He knew he was dying. He timed this to perfection." Can you do that? Blake wondered. Can you hold death off by sheer force of will? If anyone could, it would be Victor Hunt. The only thing the wicked old man probably regretted was the scotch spilled on the bed covers. Damn waste.

"Timed what sir?" Chinn said.

"I'll explain later," Blake said, reliving Hunt's last few moments of life.

Hunt had paused to take another sip of whisky and then smacked his lips. "You started your crusade against my family many years ago, didn't you, Naomi?" he had said, staring into the golden liquid.

"Don't call me that," Natalie Murphy snapped.

He ignored her. "And I have to say, your logic is hard to argue with. It's deep within us. Even Rebecca Thompson was turning out bad, wasn't she?"

Natalie nodded sullenly. "She had to die. She looked so like Drucilla it wasn't funny. She gave me such a shock when I first saw her in the shop. I'd tracked her for some time. Watched her buy her drugs and torment those boys much like Drucilla tormented poor idiot Gerald. It was only a matter of time before she really hurt someone. So I followed her, saw my chance and choked the badness out of her. Just like you killed your own daughter."

"And in all those years that you kindled that hatred, Naomi, did you never once look in the mirror?" Hunt winced in pain.

"What do you mean?" Natalie said, glancing at Hunt.

"I mean, did you never look long and hard at yourself and wonder where all this spite and anger came from? All this... envy?"

"No," Natalie snapped, shaking her head. But it wasn't a reply. "Shut up."

Hunt sighed and nodded. "Now you understand. Your mother and I were very close once. David used to bring her to my parties. They were 'those' kind of parties, Naomi, you know, car keys on the table. No strings attached. I turned a blind eye to Collins' embezzlement of the company funds because he was supporting you. Of course, I couldn't ignore it once Drucilla made it public but..."

"Stop it."

"It's true. Do you really think your mother loved David Collins so much that she would dream of revenge for his murder? Or do you think it's more likely that her hatred for me and my family was borne out of something deeper and more visceral?" Hunt coughed and screwed his eyes tight shut for a moment. His breathing became ragged. He panted out the next sentence. "It was me she loved. She wanted to take her place in Priest House. She wanted to be Mrs Hunt."

"Shut up!" Natalie moaned, burying her head in her hands. "Shut up. Shut up. Shut up."

"You see what I meant now, when I said that Drucilla did and didn't kill your father? You're my flesh and blood. And I must say, you're a chip off the old block…" Hunt said, his voice had become a low whisper. He gave a gasp, his face contorted in pain. "If you are to rid the world of all the bad blood, then the next thing you must do is… kill yourself…" Hunt's body relaxed as the life flowed out of him.

That was when Natalie Murphy screamed.

CHAPTER 45

Blake spent three days in hospital. Unable to think of another person to do the job safely, he'd phoned Laura Vexley and asked if she could look in on Serafina. Laura had come by to pick up Blake's house keys.

She looked pale and worried when she first saw him. "What happened to you?"

"Victor Hunt's family tree fell on me," he said. "Look, about the other night. I'm sorry..."

Laura put a long finger on his lips and then kissed his forehead once. "Don't say anything. We can talk later. Okay?"

Blake nodded and handed her the keys. "Just don't be going through my smalls draw..."

"You know your own tricks best, Mr Policeman," Laura said. "I might just do that, now."

Laura stayed and made small-talk for a while but more needed to be said. Just not here. When she left, Blake went in search of DI Cryer and found her in a private room just around the corner. She looked washed out but otherwise fine.

"As fine as you can look in a gown that shows your arse to the world, sir," she said, making them both laugh and wince.Blake looked up at the flowers. “I thought they weren’t allowed,” he said.

Kath Cryer winked. “Not what you know...” she said. “They’re from Andrew Kinnear. Bloomin’ soppy get.”

“You took a bullet for him, Kath,” Blake said. “I’m not surprised he’s grateful. We all are.”

“I had my stab-proof vest on, sir,” Kath said, airily. “Wasn’t sure if Kinnear had his. I’d clocked the gun. Reckoned she didn’t know how to use it properly so took the chance.”

“Still, there’s a lot of variables there...”

"And one constant, boss. Kinnear's one of us."

Blake could only smile and nod.

“Anyway, it's just a couple of broken ribs and a slight concussion, sir. Kinnear thought I was dead but my neck wound bled like God knows what. They got the stray pellets out of there. All fixed up.”

“I still say it was brave, Kath.”

“We watch each other's backs though, don't we, sir?And Kinnear’s a good copper.”

Blake found himself back in hospital shortly after. He was meant to be taking sick leave, to recover from smoke inhalation, broken ribs, and the various cuts and contusions that covered his body. After a couple of days sitting around the house, however, the need to talk to Gerald Rees had become an itch Blake could no longer ignore. It needed a good, long scratch.

Rees had looked better, Blake thought, but at least he was alive. Rees sat up in his hospital bed, bandages wrapped around his scalp and half of his face. His arms were similarly covered and, like Blake, he had some glorious purple and blue blotches all over his skin.

Blake placed the cardboard box he had been carrying on a nearby chair and sat down next to it at the side of Rees' bed. "How are you, Mr Rees?" Blake said, still marvelling at how husky his voice sounded.

"Not bad," Rees said. "I've a plentiful supply of painkillers. I don't know what I'll look like when the bandages come off but the burns weren't too bad and I was no oil painting before all of this. I'd like to thank you, Mr Blake, for saving my life. I owe you a debt of gratitude. If there's anything I can do..."

"You can start by telling the truth," Blake said.

Rees scowled for a moment, looking like a petulant little boy, even through the bandages. Then his face cleared. "Okay. Ask me anything."

"Drucilla killed so many people. You must have known."

"I swear. I didn't suspect a thing. I watched people for her, did a lot of donkey work; following suspects and the like but I never harmed anyone..."

"You must have suspected, though, you aren't blind. You helped bundle a drugged David Collins into the back of his car!"

Gerald Rees looked down at the bed covers. "Yes and then Drucilla drove him away. I didn't suspect anything sinister. Oh, she'd turn up with 'evidence' that Leech had given her. I knew that a lot of our 'detective work' was a fraud, Blake, I'm not an idiot. But I never thought she was actually killing people. Not until..." Rees fell silent.

"Until when?"

"It was after we heard the news about Cameron Lock dying in prison. Drucilla was giddy with excitement at the news. She even hugged me. She said something about Lock being 'one of hers' but I wasn't sure what that meant. If I'm being totally honest with you, Blake, I was still reeling from the hug and didn't think much about what she said. Then she began to plan to break-into Josie Lock's house. She said something about there being other kids who had gone missing and how we might find more evidence there. It all sounded a bit made up to me but I went along with it."

"But you didn't think she was planning to kill

Josie Lock?"

"No. As it was, I couldn't do the observations of Josie Lock, too much homework and school had complained about my missing deadlines. Drucilla was mad with me and did them herself. Anyway, After the Josie Lock murder, Drucilla seemed even more determined to break in. I had to keep watch. She said she was looking for clues but all she came out with were Cameron Lock's baseball boots. She was so pleased because they fitted her perfectly."

"And that was the first time you were suspicious?" Blake said, trying to hide the incredulity in his voice.

"She paraded around in those boots. When we were talking to Leech she'd often look down at her feet and then smirk at me as if she was sharing a private joke. I didn't get it, at first. But then the penny dropped. She was gloating. I realised that Lock had been framed. All of Drucilla's allure vanished. It was as if a mask had slipped and everything innocent and pure now went rotten and wicked. I saw her for what she truly was and it frightened me."

"So you went to the police?"

"You know I didn't, Blake," Gerald said. "What would DCI Leech have said? He'd virtually been her accomplice as much as I, hadn't he? No. I went to her father."

"You told Victor Hunt that you thought his daughter was a murderer? I bet that went down well."

"He told me to leave and to stay away from Drucilla. But he wasn't angry. It was more like a warning. It was as if he was afraid for me."

"Hunt told me that he had worked out what Drucilla was up to himself..."

"Typical of him to airbrush me out of the story. He'd never give credit to someone like me," Rees said, that petulant tone surfacing briefly. "My parents were going on holiday the following week. Drucilla wanted me to stay at home. She'd dropped all kinds of hints about the delights that might be mine if I didn't go to Scarborough with Mum and Dad."

Blake raised his eyebrows. "A teenage boy turning down the chance of a wild night with Drucilla Hunt? I find that hard to believe."

"She frightened me by this time. I was nervous in her company and too scared to say no. I hoped that by going on holiday, she'd see that I wanted to get out..."

Blake plonked the box onto Rees' bed and opened the lid. "Lucky for you, then that Victor killed her," he said, pulling out a photo. "We found your picture in the sixth box."

Even though his skin was reddened with

burns, Rees paled and lay back against the plumped-up pillows that surrounded him. "I was next on her list?"

Blake nodded. "Why did you take those shoes from Rebecca Thompson's feet?"

Gerald Rees shrugged. "There was no malice in it, Blake," he said. "I suppose I hoped that, if I took them, then nobody would link the murder to past events or to me. I just wanted Drucilla to go away, back to the past. But Drucilla Hunt doesn't leave you alone. Not even when she's been dead for nearly forty years."

"This is an ongoing case, Gerald," Blake said. "If you're sincere about owing me your life, you'll cooperate fully with any officer investigating it. We know who killed Rebecca Thompson. DNA evidence from under Natalie Murphy's fingernails matches and she's confessed to that and the murder of Marcus Hunt. But we only have anecdotal evidence of the past crimes. I expect you to help in whatever way you can."

Gerald nodded. "Believe me. I will."

Blake picked up the box and left.

DCI Will Blake sat in his mother's armchair with Serafina purring on his lap. The sun streamed in through the backroom window, warming him as he absent-mindedly stroked his fingers through the soft fur. Laura flicked through a pet supplies catalogue on the sofa next to him. "So, how has she been?"

Blake shrugged. "Fine. I haven't really been anywhere much so she's getting used to having me round, I suppose."

"Hmm. You'll have to be careful when you start back at work. She could relapse into those behaviours. Have you decided about the house?"

Blake nodded. "I need to square things with Jeffrey and Rosie but I don't think there'll be a problem. Once we have mum declared deceased, we can start probate and sell the house. I need to move on. Get my own place."

"And how will Serafina cope with that?" Laura said, raising one eyebrow.

Blake smiled back at her. "I don't know. I think we'll both need expert attention."

"Well, 'To create a little flower is the labour of ages.'"

"What's that meant to mean?"

"It's William Blake," she said. "You ought to know."

ABOUT THE AUTHOR

Jon Mayhew lives on the Wirral with his family and has done all his life. A teacher for many years, he enjoys traditional music and plays regularly in ceilidh bands and sessions. Jon is also an award-winning children's author, his dark children's books are published by Bloomsbury.

Find J.E. Mayhew on Facebook

J.E.Mayhew's Blog is at www.jemayhew.blogspot.com

ACKNOWLEDGEMENTS

There are many people to thank. You for a start, for reading this book.

My wife, Lin for reading the various iterations of this tale and for listening patiently to my ideas and then picking holes in them.

Thanks to Barry Hutchison, AKA JD Kirk for help and guidance over the years. You're a true gent and generous to a fault.

Rod Yates for giving me the low down on local policing. If there are any inaccuracies, they are there because of me not wanting to let facts get in the way of a good story!

Kate Bendelow, author of The Real CSI for reading the manuscript and giving me some factual pointers.

And to my local Wirral readers: Clare Hulme, Jan Jones, Amy Rebecca Thomas, Laura Colwell, Suzanne Thomas, Frauke Hoffman and Beverley Giles-Stewart whose comments have, I hope, made this an even better book!

Thanks to Meg Cowley for her endless patience and incredible cover-design skills.

And everyone in the Collective – you know who you are… Cheers!

MORE FROM DCI BLAKE

Wondering what happened on the night that Blake's mother vanished? Join the JE Mayhew mailing list on Bookfunnel and get a free DCI Will Blake prequel.

https://dl.bookfunnel.com/gs5oc6n68k

BOOKS BY THIS AUTHOR

Fearful Symmetry

Hilbre Grove is a quiet cul-de-sac like many others on the Wirral. But when a couple return from their holidays to find a mutilated, decomposing body in their bungalow, The Scissor Man's reign of terror begins. With another woman missing, DCI Will Blake is determined to stop the psychopath from killing again.

And this case is personal. As bodies pile up it becomes clear that the killer is fascinated by Blake's past appearances on Searchlight, a true-crime TV programme. To hunt down The Scissor Man, Blake must face up to his painful past, and put his career on the line. But every home has its own dark secrets, nowhere is safe and time is running out for Blake and all he holds dear.

Fearful Symmetry is the second exciting Merseyside Murder Mystery thriller in the DCI Will Blake crime series.

Made in the USA
Columbia, SC
01 March 2021